Our Demons

Cameron Dawkins

DEDICATION

To my hero, my father.

CONTENTS

ACKNOWLEDGMENTS

My Editor, Sara Oakden,
Photographer, Ben Costigan
Mat Runacre

GIVING TO THE SHARPENED EDGE

What was she doing? Why was she hurting her? Her dry, coarse palms gripped a woman by the throat.

The span of her hands was bigger than their usual size. Her fingers had more girth and their reach was like nothing she had felt before. They held more power than she could have normally realised, and they were using this new-found strength to great effect.

Such a tight, angry grip. The young woman couldn't speak, she gasped for air, trying with every sinew in her shaking body, but the pressure on her airways was vice-like.

She began to fall, her body trying to slide its way down the abrasive tree bark, but the hand held her upright with ease.

The veins in her neck bloated and pushed back against the constriction.

Why was she doing this to this poor, helpless woman? She was killing her but she didn't understand why, she didn't even know her.

The lower lids of the victim's eyes were hidden below a flood of tears, the unadulterated fear in them pushed her pupils to their boundaries.

The woman in control looked down at her hands, one

busy restraining her victim, the other pulling back, priming itself. She couldn't stop herself if she tried, and she was trying. Wasn't she? A glimmer of cold, metallic menace flashed through the air.

The young girl's body twitched and writhed as she realised the pain about to come, for the first time she truly knew how much trouble her fragile body was in.

The attacker wrapped her fingers tightly around the hilt of the large weapon, pushing against a small amount of resistance as she stabbed repeatedly. The skin held for a microsecond before giving to the sharpened edge. It pushed and tore its way through flesh, scraping relentlessly at her ribs. Each blow penetrating with slicing ease, faster and smoother than the last. Bones splintered as the metal swiftly penetrated in and out.

The victim's throat burned in pain as she screeched, desperately trying with everything she had in her to survive.

Warm blood hit both of them in the face, but only one of them felt excited. The ruby droplets momentarily blocked the attacker's vision, giving gravitas to the occasion. She was wearing the other now, the young woman's life-force decorated her skin and clothes.

She needn't wipe the blood from her eyes, the body was now forsaken, laying on the floor she didn't need to see it. Scarlet forearms continued to stab, leaning over the body, until they felt the first signs of fatigue over the warmth of the body-temperature fluids.

The now-murderer smiled as she looked down at the figure at her feet. She was almost satisfied, but not quite. Her knees rested on the back of the lifeless corpse and her hands clasped around the handle of the blade, as she used the strength of her entire body to bring it down, point first, into the back of the victim's neck.

The body gave one last convulsion as the knife lodged itself deep into her spinal cord.

She was the victor but she didn't understand why.

She didn't know who she was, she didn't feel attached to this reality, and it was a dream that felt real, it was reality that felt like a dream, or rather a nightmare, and then she's home.

Her hands were her own again, they looked the correct size as she held them up to her face in the rich, grey hue of the evening. The rest of the room pushed its way into focus in the illumination of the open fridge.

There's no blood, only spilt milk on the floor where two cats stood lapping at it. She examined herself for a moment. She couldn't believe that she hadn't just murdered that poor girl, that innocent victim taken from the world so cruelly. She couldn't stand it any longer and her eyes gave in to the mounting pressure, tears rolling down her cheeks, following the age lines and contours to her chin, where they dripped gently to her nightdress.

The dripping of the kitchen tap matched her crying and helped to bring her back to herself, turning the cold tap as tight as she could.

She tried to look outside but the window reflection of her own face was intrusive, like it was a strangers, and gave little comfort.

Only moments before she had been a murderer and it wasn't a dream, it was reality, just not hers.

Her mobile phone was in its usual space on top of the microwave, plugged into the wall on charge even though the battery hadn't been low.

Swaying softly, she picked it up and dialled nine, nine, nine without conscious thought. A warm voice spoke back to her on the other end, it was slow and comforting but that's as much as she could understand, her brain not yet able to digest communication. She spoke words back, at least she thought she might have said something, she might have just been silent, or could even have discussed a novel's worth. Time and most of what normally felt tangible remained out of reach. The phone was back on top of the appliance. Had she put it there? Had she made a phone call at all? Standing still in the centre of the kitchen for a while, the veil of confusion slowly pulled itself back and revealed nothing more than her house, a broken milk bottle and two happy cats.

She picked up the ginger and white cat and placed him on the kitchen side, and reached for a plastic tub from the window sill. Knowing his treats were imminent, the cat began to purr loudly, rubbing his head against his owner's hands. The warmth of his fur shocked her; it was a sudden reminder of the blood from moments before.

After wincing for a moment, she probed her fingers into the tub and produced a snack for the animal. The second cat, recognising this opportunity, jumped up also. The woman fed them absentmindedly as she peered past her own reflection and out upon her garden. She could see her bare apple tree with its burnt, golden leaves strewn across the lawn, just like the ground on which the helpless girl had been.

She stroked the ginger cat gently behind one ear. 'The demons are coming again, Jasper.'

SMELL OF BLOOD

Jack O'Connor walked his way up the steep bank in Leigh Woods, a quiet piece of woodland about a mile or two from the heart of Bristol. A cool autumn fog rose from the ground as the blue dawn warmed up the earth, leaving dew drops on anything willing to wear them. Even though it was cold the sun shone brightly, aggravating the eyes.

'It's a nice place for a picnic,' he thought to himself as he stepped over an exposed tree root. He had been there a couple of times before, once with his gran when she was in a wheelchair, where the second stroke had left her.

It had been the middle of summer then, and the paths were easy for him to guide her along to the picnic tables, where they had eaten pâté sandwiches.

Jack had given his to a dog that a walker had been following some way behind. He never had the heart to tell the old dear that he hated pâté and would have much preferred some cheap corned beef instead.

This time in the woods was much different; for a start, he was considerably older and found navigating the steep inclines far more difficult that he ought to.

Dozens of police officers filled the normally tranquil setting, a few in pure white boiler suits. A couple were taking photographs at a spot in the centre of the commotion, which had been lit with tall, standing site-lamps. They brightened the leafy floor better than even the brilliant morning sunlight, allowing every detail to be seen clearly.

One officer, not in a forensic boiler suit, had just finished taping off the area as the detective arrived.

'Sir.' He gave Jack a small nod and lifted the blue and white tape for him to pass under.

The detective looked around and found someone in a boiler suit holding a clipboard. Jack had discovered early on in his detective career that the person holding the clipboard was the one in charge. This was crucial as once people put on the white forensic get up they all looked the same. Knowing who the best person to speak with was would have otherwise been a guess.

'What have we got?' he asked them, looking intently at the face of the body before it disappeared beneath the black plastic of the body bag as it was zipped up.

The white-clad figure pulled off her mask and lowered her hood off of the back of her head.

'Hi, Jack.' A woman with long brown hair tied up loosely took a deep breath, enjoying the clean, uncensored air.

Jack knew her well, now that he could see her face. It was Aubrie Sellers, the best forensic pathologist on the force – and one of the youngest.

She was the head of her department, a position a lot of other officers always assumed she reached due to her father being a senior politician.

But Jack knew otherwise. He was smart enough to realise that any politician worth half the weight of their seat in the House of Commons would rather have anything other than a police officer in his own house. And a lot of them had plenty of the anything else.

She got a lot of stick down the station, mostly from men, but she seemed to shrug off the peacocking bastards; and those who she couldn't shrug off, Jack would normally have a quiet word with.

She was good at her job, bloody good at it. Her moral compass was always straight and she always played by the rules. Jack respected that, as it was more than he could say for himself, but he'd be damned if he was going to let any of her colleagues belittle her for being a better person than them.

Her hazel eyes met his. 'Young woman, mid-twenties, multiple stab wounds, some signs of strangulation, but it was the blood loss that killed her. Also, it looks as though the killer punctured both lungs and caught the superior vena cava, causing masses of internal bleeding. In short, a bloody mess. He went to town on her and made sure she was good and dead. Friends and family have been notified, she had ID on her, and the woman who found her has given her statement, but she's quite shaken up. She's over there in the ambulance.

There's some evidence around the body, such as a footprint, possibly two, a handprint in blood on the tree there.' She pointed at an area about three feet up the large oak tree behind where the body was now being prepared to be moved. 'It looks as though the killer leant a bloody hand against it to help himself up, and that's about it, to be honest.'

Jack took a deep breath and looked at the scenery. 'No weapon then?'

'No, the killer must have taken it with him. I'm going to go back with the body; there's some pretty clean indentations on her neck, should give us some decent finger prints to go with the ones on the tree.'

'Can't believe they didn't wear gloves,' Jack said, sounding surprised. He knew he should have sounded relieved that there were signs of ineptitude, but he knew all too well that getting your hopes up in this game clouded judgement.

The woman unzipped her long white boiler suit and stepped out of it, slipping the blue shoe covers from her heels at the same time. 'Well, there's a couple of nail marks that broke the skin, so definitely no gloves, but that's about it at the moment. I'll meet you at the station in a couple of hours, I should have a lot more for you then, murder weapon, etcetera, there was enough bloody stab wounds. I'll be able to tell you the type of blade, the length and spec of it.' She dropped the professional persona for a moment, 'You doing ok though, yeah, Jack?'

He didn't reply but instead warmly squeezed her elbow. She walked away to the top of the hill, helped load the gurney and then jumped in the back of the unmarked black ambulance with the body.

Jack surveyed the area again. The smell of blood was so strong he had to cover his mouth. The iron tang overwhelmed his senses for a second, he wanted to breathe fresh air but right now there was no escaping from the thick, dank musk.

He watched the photographer take pictures of the last pieces of evidence. He could see why the body was able to be moved relatively quickly – it was the only real piece of evidence worth examining closely. Sure, the footprint and handprint were going to be crucial, but they were pretty self-explanatory, and if they didn't point a big blood-covered arrow at the killer, then the body should definitely betray the murderer their identity.

He turned his head upward to see a press helicopter. 'Shit, that was quick.'

Jack walked over to the nearest officer. To his disappointment, it was one of his team – one of his team that he wished he could stick on the bench and forget about.

Taking over a team from his predecessor meant that, unfortunately for him, he wasn't given the opportunity to pick all of its members. A few of the old crew were there on friendships made down the pub rather than merit. In truth, he had wanted this particular member to move departments about a year ago, but, due to some pay disputes, he had stayed put.

'Officer Peters, close the gates to the carpark immediately. If the press get in I will be holding you personally responsible, understood?'

The large man's bulk turned around, startled – so startled that he almost dropped his pasty.

'And he's eating, at a bloody crime scene, is there no end to this man's gluttony?' Jack raged internally.

'A pasty, really? It's eight o'clock in the morning.'

The bulky man looked ashamed as he expelled pastry flakes from his moustache with his sleeve. 'Sorry, sarge, I was hungry, I got here at five thirty. Didn't have a chance to eat before I got the call.'

Jack hated the man's facial hair and he knew the only reason he nurtured such a ridiculous atrocity was because he grew up in the seventies. Jack also knew that this meant watching awful cop shows that harboured too much hair and not enough substance.

The man had based his whole life around them, just not his waistline, apparently.

'But the body's been moved, nothing but a few red puddles for them to see now,' the policeman said to his sergeant after a weary look up the hill towards the entrance of the woods.

'You lazy shit,' Jack thought to himself. *'You can't even be bothered to walk six hundred yards.'* He managed to keep his mouth somewhat more civil than his mind.

'Just do it, and then phone through to the station to get the rest of the team assembled in a room for ten o'clock. No excuses.'

The large man opened his mouth to protest, but Jack didn't give him the opportunity. Instead he walked off back to the carpark. Approaching his car, he caught a glimpse of himself in the reflection on the window. He rarely used a mirror these days, and as such his own image always jarred him. It looked like a face he knew but couldn't quite place.

He got in and inspected his stubble and dry skin in the car's vanity mirror. The bulb had gone, or the fuse had blown, he couldn't care enough to actually find out. He slammed the sun visor back up and turned the engine over. Taking a deep breath, he rested his head on the window, giving himself a second to think.

His mind hurt. He didn't know if he could deal with this today, today of all days. He needed something to ease the pain, something strong, something non-prescription.

ROCK BOTTOM

The bouncers of the underground club nodded Detective O'Connor through, they both knew him professionally and socially of late. He had worked enough late-night, drunken manslaughter cases now to know most of the door staff in Bristol.

There were a few clubs open at that time of the morning in Bristol, but this one had a certain quality that Jack liked. That quality being free drinks, bar staff that didn't ask any questions and no CCTV.

Dull, thudding drum and bass music played through the speakers. Just a cd now, the DJ set had ended a couple of hours before.

Jack walked down the grubby stairs; dark graffiti murals on both sides made the space feel narrow and embracing. Some unrelated tags had been written in vulgarly coloured glow-in-the-dark paint.

Stepping over one of the remaining customers, who was lying dead-still, half-propped against a pillar, clearly too drunk to remove himself from the property, Jack made his way to the main bar.

He was glad to see a face he knew waiting there to serve him.

'Ah, Detective Superintendent O'Connor, good to see

you, me old mate. Drink?'

It was the manager, Steven. It was obvious that he was the manager – being double the age of all the other bar staff made him stand out a mile – he was the kind of guy that could only be described as a good bloke.

'Yeah, something strong, it's going to be one of those days.'

The barman got down a glass from the top shelf, reserved only for moments like this. Ninety-nine per cent of their stock was served in plastic cups, the kind that, if they were full right to the brim, were impossible to pick up without squeezing and spilling. He pushed the glass up against the upturned bottle of Jack Daniel's and gave Jack a healthy portion.

'I would offer you ice, but, well, you know how it is in this place.'

Jack waved a hand dismissively to indicate it really wasn't an issue as he threw the drink at the back of throat.

'Jesus, that bad?' the barman asked, refilling the glass and placing it back in front of him. 'It's not even nine o'clock and you've already got a murder on your hands, have you?'

The barman's intuition didn't shock the detective. The man behind the bar was well aware of his line of work, and he also knew just how gruesome it could get. Last year alone this particular club had been at the centre of three incidents of stabbing, one of which had later transpired to be a fatal one. The young lad had managed to hang on for three days but died later in hospital. Jack had investigated this particular case personally, and did his best to keep Steven the bar manager out of the press. It did well to accumulate small favours here and there across the city.

'Yeah, a nice bloody one today. That's the real reason I'm here.' It wasn't, but the barman needn't find out that Jack actually enjoyed being in what was, essentially, a dive.

The manager of the club laughed. 'And there's me thinking it was for our wine list. I got you, Jack, I'll keep my ear to the ground. It's not like it used to be, though, no gangsters in here anymore. We get the dealers and the odd gun or two turn up, but nothing like the old firm. Especially if it was a contract killing, it's all done from abroad now, eastern Europeans, you know, untraceable. But, like I said, I'll keep my ear to the ground and if something rumbles, I'll let you know.'

The boy that Jack had stepped over at the bottom of the stairs interrupted them. He made a large hacking sound preceded by a deluge of vomit that was impressively turquoise in colour.

'See what I mean? Place ain't what it used to be,' Steven said, waving a hand to the girl working the bar on the other side of the room. She had been restocking the fridge when she heard her boss shout across, 'Clean up on aisle nine.'

Her face screwed in disgust, she muttered something under her breath that Jack bet he could have guessed as she disappeared for a second before re-emerging with a mop and bucket, and began filling it with water.

'No, I wasn't exactly thinking contract killing. I was edging more towards gang initiation. I know a couple of crews where they do things like gang rape, armed robbery, that sort of thing. Just wondered if this could be the new thing.'

The barman dropped his head. You would have thought that their worlds would have been poles apart, but both men had seen things that they wished they hadn't.

'Could very well be, I suppose,' Steven replied. 'We get the odd gang member in here, trying his luck to see if we would let their dealers be onsite. Funny, the more you turn them away, the more keen they seem to be.'

'Any trouble with them?' Jack had negotiated with people in drug rings before, and it was a tough pastime.

Steven shook his head. 'Not really. I pay through the nose for protection and, so far, it's seemed to hold up. It's all young kiddies these days anyway, they don't have enough about them to give us any real trouble. Unless you're right about this gang initiation thing. That would be stepping it up a level.'

Jack slid the glass back across the bar. 'Yeah, well, it's just a thought. You've got my number anyway.'

Jack went to walk away.

'There is one thing, Jack, you might be interested in.'

Steven pulled out a small, transparent packet from his pocket and pushed it across the bar.

The detective picked it up and looked closer. He recognised that the bag was full of what kids referred to as 'tabs' – small pieces of sugar paper coated in all manner of drugs. Jack used to be able to guess what they were made of back in the day, but on today's streets, the punters really were spoilt for choice.

'You know this isn't my department, or my cup of tea, don't you?'

The barman gestured for Jack to keep them. 'No, I know that, but you might be interested in the fact that it's being sold at rock-bottom prices all across the city.'

That teased the detective's interest a little, like a cat drawn to a sharp light out of the corner of its eye.

'How much is rock bottom these days?' he asked.

The barman laughed. 'I mean rock bloody bottom. That bag you're holding there was twenty quid.'

'What?' Jack held the packet it up to get a better look. 'There's about two hundred quid's worth in there, at least, surely? That's about a pound a tab. What is it, dodgy gear?'

Steven shook his head. 'No, it's legit, well, you know what I mean. Anyway, I thought you might want to look into it – after all this murder stuff is done and dusted, of course.'

The detective thanked the barman, walked over to the rather sorry looking young lad on the floor, heaved him up under an elbow and helped him to become somewhat steady on his feet.

Jack realised he was a kid, just drinking age, if that,

even if he was wearing a Nirvana t-shirt. His wild, strawberry blonde hair displayed his sick triumphantly as the detective pushed and pulled him to the top of the stairs. It was like battling with a sleepwalker on a boat stuck in rough seas. He hailed a taxi for the drunk and pushed him down into it. The young lad landed on the floor of the car and, instead of trying to manoeuvre the dead weight on to a seat, Jack picked up his feet and folded in his legs.

'Take him to A and E,' he said, giving the driver a ten pound note. The boy vomited a small puddle of soup-like substance down his cheek and onto the car floor.

The driver gave the officer a blank non-committal look, pretending as if Jack was speaking the wrong language.

'Fine, here, take this.' Jack handed him another twenty pounds.

'Yes, boss,' the driver said, suddenly springing into life, speeding off in the direction of the BRI hospital.

Jack knew that the club wasn't the most likely of places for a murderer to appear but he needed alcohol to blunt the sharp edges of the world today; that, combined with the prescription medication, should just about do it.

He took a slow drive back to the station. The radio in his beat-up car managed to pick up Radio Four for most of the journey; he learnt something new about genes that he promptly forgot and found some breath mints to cover up the smell of whisky. The city was in full flow now, its main arteries filling with long lines of workers in their vehicles, trying to get to offices on time. Push bikes with people dressed in work clothes weaved their way in and out of the standstill traffic, receiving the odd beep from a car driver who was actually just resentful for being stuck with no means of escape.

Jack knew the back streets well enough to take them. hoping this journey might be longer than the conventional way, but it was much nicer than remaining between sets of traffic lights for minutes at a time, and the glaring red of the brake lights from other road users would have driven him to self-destruction.

The station was humming with the energy of every officer they could afford to get in diligently busying themselves, paperwork was being stacked and phones on each and every desk had someone speaking on them.

'Well, this one stayed quiet for all of five minutes,' thought Jack as he made his way through the throng to one of the incident rooms. He guessed it would be the largest of them as to befit the chaos this case was already making. It, too, was full of officers, predominantly plain-clothed, like Jack was, but a few beat officers were there to lend a hand as well. He let the vast amount of noise and sporadic movement, wash over him.

The dead girl's pictures from the scene had been put up, along with other signs of evidence and her university graduation photo. Her name was written on the shiny white surface in blue with a list of next of kin below. Whoever had been given the markers had gone to town, underlining the victim's name three times in red. A man's name was directly below that of the girl, a female uniformed officer reached up and wrote Switzerland next to it, and then in brackets *(arriving home later tonight).*

Jack hated this, it was the exact thing he was trying to avoid by taking the long way back to the station. He wanted all of his jigsaw pieces to hand before trying to fit them together; that was his talent: seeing the bigger picture once he had all the straight-lined and corner pieces ready for him. He sat on the desk quietly, waiting for everyone to do their jobs; if he allowed the chaos to sweep him along with it, it would swallow him up and spit him out the other side without so much as an apology and most likely with a p45 in hand.

He trusted everyone in that room to do their jobs – well, everyone except Officer Peters because he was, once again, eating, this time a chocolate bar.

Over the next thirty minutes, the business in the room concluded and one by one everyone had done their little part in the investigation and either found a seat or perched themselves on a desk. The one under Peters' bulk creaked as it took the strain. Each officer looked to their leader, the one who had been calm and quiet throughout, all hoping that together they had the vital clue. Jack picked up a piece of paper from the table and stood up to speak when a gentle knock at the door interrupted him.

Aubrie stepped just inside the room, folders in hand, and lcant against the doorframe.

Jack gave her a warm smile, his breath deepened with relief at her presence as he knew that if she was there she had something of worth to divulge, she was never a time-waster.

'Victim's name is Emma Jennings,' he read. 'Aged twenty-eight. She was out jogging in Leigh Woods, a mile from her home where she lives with her boyfriend, and this morning she was found brutally murdered. So,' Jack paused, it wasn't for effect but it had one. 'So, what do we have?' Jack asked his team, all looking too sheepish to answer, he knew this meant that they were somewhere between not a lot and bugger all. He picked on his least-favourite member first.

'Peters, you first.'

He had been avoiding his senior officer's glare the hardest, and therefore gave Jack the suspicion that it would be prudent to get him over and done with and out of the way first.

He flustered at the sound of his own name. 'Err, well, we, err …'

'Cameras, sir,' Officer Kapoor, Peters' closest friend, rescued him by interrupting. 'We obviously have a fair few around the suspension bridge heading north of the location, none heading south until you get to the motorway and we are trying to find out if there are any in Long Ashton village. There isn't a lot of chance of spotting anything suspicious but we may be able to get a list of the vehicles that used the roads in the surrounding areas, it was early in the morning so shouldn't be too many. The immediate area is pretty much a dead zone for CCTV, but I'm figuring that, because of the location, our killer either lived within walking distance or had to drive.'

Jack's anger for him bailing out his friend was short-lived and by the time Officer Kapoor had finished he pretty much had all but forgotten. He expected that this was probably the Officer's plan and why he had spoken for such length with very little content.

'Good, fair to say that's a reasonable assumption. You two get onto the camera front, then. I think the bridge is an unlikely escape route for a killer, unless he had the exact amount of change to hand to cross it – he would have to be a pretty cool customer to think that far ahead. Check all the vehicles anyway, any that speed or drive erratically should be prioritised. Ok, what's next?'

One of the officers O'Connor had chosen to be in his team, Officer Ricky Edmonds, spoke next, 'We don't have any witnesses whatsoever, no one that saw anyone walking that morning, so instead I managed to hang around the gates and get the names and addresses of those who were coming to walk their dogs and who walk them there fairly often. Also got the name and address of a couple with no dog, but who were both wearing long jackets and not a lot else. I think they may have been on their way for a bit of bird watching, if you get what I mean.'

A few in the room chuckled at this.

'Watching or being watched?' Officer Kapoor replied, causing a few more in the room to laugh, like school children might try to get away with in front of a supply teacher.

Jack's impassiveness soon spread to the other officers, who quickly recognised that their superior was not in the mood.

'Ok, good work, carry out the interviews ASAP, our

murderer may have been there with our victim before or may have been there alone, scoping out the site. What about friends and family, anyone standing out as a suspect?' Jack asked the question but with no feeling behind it, it didn't feel like a crime of passion, it didn't even feel like a crime of hate. This one was tricky – so far it didn't feel like much of anything else he had encountered before.

The small, plain-clothed officer holding an iPad cleared her throat and read from it, 'Parents Janet and Andy Jennings were at a charity function all night and then returned home at around three in the morning. Both have pretty much had a breakdown in our family room. Boyfriend is abroad having meetings. He's an investment banker attending a conference in Switzerland and will be home tonight at some point for questioning. All in all, a grief-stricken family, sarge.'

Jack knew this already, had guessed as much, he moved on quickly. 'Photographs from the scene, are they back yet?'

'I picked them up on my way through,' Aubrie replied.

Jack raised his eyebrows to her, in this small facial gesture he had said, 'Please tell me some good news because so far I've got nothing.'

She opened her cardboard folder and removed a small stack of photographs. Aubrie went and stood in front of the board and used the circular magnets to hold them all up in place.

'I'll start with the evidence found around the body.' She blew some hair from her face and stood sidelong on to the adorned photographs. 'Right, well, we have two clean footprints, measuring a size nine – safe to assume they're male prints. The indentation is deep, if I had to guess I would say we are looking at a suspect of some considerable weight, close to twenty stone, maybe. They're fairly unique prints, definitely a boot, work boot possibly. The handprint on the tree had some very clean prints and, guess what, no match. The blood splatters are irrelevant, she was stabbed so many times that it's impossible to identify the initial blow, or what hand the killer may have used, and that's it for any external evidence.'

She turned back to the board again to put up some more images.

The room went deathly quiet; these new depictions were of the deceased, and they left nothing to the imagination. Jack wasn't sure if Aubrie had done it deliberately, but they seemed to be in order of graphic violence. The last one showing the back of their victim's neck, the flesh peeled away to reveal the spine.

'As you said, our victim was twenty-eight years of age, in very healthy condition, an athlete of sorts. She was stabbed at least fifteen times, mostly to the torso.' She pointed at the main bulk of the pictures. 'A closer look confirmed my first suspicions – that both lungs were punctured along with substantial damage to the main arteries and veins to the heart, liver and bladder. The cause of death is either blood loss or internal bleeding. I'll be opening the body up later and I should be able to identify which killed her first. Either way it was definitely the stab wounds and not the strangulation.' Aubrie indicted the photo on the top right. 'The strangulation appears to have been to subdue our victim, rendering her oxygen-deprived, but not chocking her completely. Our suspect had large, strong hands, the span would suggest a height of over six foot. Again, we were able to take clean prints and they matched the one on the tree. Not many defensive wounds on the victim's arms, so I would think the killer caught her by surprise, hiding behind the large tree next to where she was killed, maybe, but there is no trace evidence there. The stab wounds are a little different to usual, so maybe we will have more joy looking at this from the murder weapon angle. There are two types of wounds, one with a single, clean, penetrative, deep entrance, the skin is cleanly split with no tearing. This would suggest a sharp, curved blade, approximately eight inches in length.' She ran her finger across a picture, showing the neat scarlet line on the young woman. 'This one, however ...' She pulled one of the pictures down and held it against her stomach, facing the room. It suddenly became more real as the image, being almost that of life size, now looked as though it had been inflicted on Aubrie. 'This one is trickier. The skin is badly torn, can you see there?'

A couple of the beat officers that were joining them clearly hadn't been on many cases like this, they looked uncomfortable at how real everything was becoming.

'This is all indicative of a serrated blade. Very long, but also rather wider than you would expect of this type of knife. Along with these puncture marks next to it ...' She pointed to two red dots on the flesh, they were small and roughly two centimetres apart. 'Well, I'm thinking a carving knife, the kind with the forked tip. Only I have never seen one with dimensions as large as these. So, at the moment I can say that there were definitely two blades, and one large killer. I will look into it some more, a knife this size and shape should be rather rare.'

Jack felt a bit perplexed, one killer, two knives – this was becoming unusual, to say the least.

'Could there have been two killers, one for each knife?' he asked Aubrie.

She returned with a very weak smile. 'I can't say for sure that there weren't two killers, but, right now, there is only evidence of one. I'll calculate the stab wounds some more, see if there is any difference in depth of thrust, angle of penetration, etcetera, but, at the moment, one killer, Jack.'

The room was subdued, it was all too clear that a young woman had painfully lost her life and they had no hard clues as to who done it. The pictures on the board painted a bloody mosaic of fear and lust.

Jack needed to be alone with the evidence, he needed to think, think in the only way that he could. He sent everyone off to do their jobs, only Aubrie braved hanging around after.

'Do your thing, Jack, you'll catch him, you always do.'

She placed a comforting hand on his back. She knew how much these murders affected him, she knew he empathised with the victims to the point of implosion, and she also knew that is what made him different, made him a great   detective.

BORDERLINE PERSONALITY DISORDER

Seven years earlier, Jack sat in an unnecessarily cold room, not in air temperature but definitely in decor. Its beige walls offered nothing to inspire the imagination, there was just a single, impossibly low coffee table where his plastic cup of water sat, and three chairs. Two very deliberately facing the other, the one where he sat.

The seats were in keeping with the rest of the room, there were no discernible features on them at all. The clock ticked louder than any other he had heard, or at least he thought it had in the five minutes he had been left in there alone.

It was four weeks after Jack O'Connor had a nervous breakdown and had been hospitalised overnight, the details of which were not accessible to his mind. He figured he must have blacked out, but the doctors called it a psychotic episode or psychotic disconnection, depending on how intelligent they wanted to sound.

Two middle-aged women re-entered the room, both with practiced, concerned yet professional looks on their faces. Jack was thirty but felt like an embarrassed teenager, which apparently had also been one of the indicators of his mental health. He had been to this office twice previously, seeing a different woman from the caring two in front of him, she had dismissed him both times, telling him that 'anxiety is what's wrong, it's your lifestyle, it's stressful, and that is all'.

Anxiety hadn't been the cause of his black out. His partner had told him afterwards that he had screamed and curled up in a ball, saying he wanted to die – words that he had never said before, not even in his nightmares. Thankfully, the mental health team had thought it prudent not to continue with the same coupling of minds, not after his partner had insisted on getting the name of the woman who had previously reviewed Jack, and told them that her editor at the paper would run any column she wanted because he owed her a favour. His partner's name carried more than enough weight in circles that knew her, and in the ones that didn't automatically, they soon learnt to shudder at her gaze, and, failing all else, a quick google search would reveal more than enough.

'Jack, you have a mental health condition,' one of the women told him, opening a file holding the questionnaire she had asked him to fill in.

He had done about ten of these god damn forms now, scoring very high, higher than any other test he had ever taken, at eighty nine percent, if it had been any other situation he would have been proud.

'It isn't bi-polar as you suspected, however—' she tried to continue, but Jack couldn't hold back.

'But the mood swings, the depression, it all fits. I took the bi-polar type two test three times online.'

'They are a guideline, they only indicate that you have bi-polar-type-two-like symptoms. No, what you have is very similar – sometimes considered to be a more severe condition. Due to its nature it's incredibly hard to diagnose. You have borderline personality disorder. This is why you have been prescribed antidepressants at certain stages throughout your life. Because at those times when you have visited the doctors, depression would be the only symptom that you would have been presenting, when in fact there is so much more under the surface.'

The other lady in the room, clearly a little worried that Jack was going to either have an outburst of rage or tears, nodded in agreement and looked as sympathetic as she possibly could.

'Someone should tell her it's highly annoying,' Jack thought to himself as he left the mental health consultation room, with its interior dreary enough to give you a break down on its own. He sat in his car and looked at the leaflet they had given him. So, apparently two sides of A4 paper was enough to ensure that he didn't hang himself. It was now just a case of getting in to see his doctor and talking through medication options.

'God I hope it's strong stuff,' his thoughts fogged a little and his work slowly focused. A murderer was on the loose and all this crap with his brain meant he was missing out on the action. Luckily, for once the complete incompetence of the National Health Service meant that no one at his work had found out about the break down – a few days of compassionate leave and no one was any the wiser. Luckily for him, his partner, Jessica, had some very old relatives, one of whom had the foresight to pop her clogs a few days before. Jessica hadn't been close to her but his superiors weren't to know that, all they needed to be informed of was that the death of a relative meant he would need to be home looking after his daughter while his grieving wife did whatever it was that grieving people did. In reality, they had barely got an invite to the funeral, and when they did attend they took their little girl, Felicity, with them. Jessica had tried quite unsuccessfully to introduce Jack to her extended family and that of the deceased. After two wrong names and three incorrect relation statuses she gave up and Jack decided to drive, allowing   Jessica   to   hit   the   free   wake   wine.

EMPATHY

Today's investigation needed Jack to be fully focused. When he was doing what the other officers called 'his thing', his mind would often think back to those happier times, the sickeningly embarrassing ones were his favourite, the ones where afterwards the only thing you could do was laugh about them. Not now, though. Things were complicated and things were lost, gone but never forgotten, just like the murdered girl looking back at him from the university photo.

Jack rubbed at his unkempt hair and thumped the palm of his hand against his head, desperately trying to kick his brain into gear, like people used to do with old radios and televisions.

He repeated the dictionary definition of empathy to himself with his eyes closed.

'Empathy, the ability to understand and share the feelings of others, the ability to understand and share the feelings of others.' He turned it into a mantra.

Empathy was one of the only good symptoms to have come from his borderline personality disorder, now that he had managed to control and harness it. A lot of the officers referred to it as his secret power, but Jack knew it was just another human trait that anyone could achieve if they were taught how, and had a brain that functioned in different kaleidoscope images, like his own.

He opened his eyes and stared at the pictures up on the wall. The bloody one of the body, the one of the footprint, the one of the tree with the handprint next and his eyes made to move on, but they stopped, fixated on the image of the tree. All this bloodshed, all the horrid malice, and yet this picture had got him. He took it down from the board and held it up in front of his face.

'I'm excited,' he thought to himself as he let the image in to his mind. *'This is where I lie in wait, I can see her coming, she didn't spot me, and this tree will shelter me from view. My heart, it's thumping and I can taste adrenaline in my mouth, she's so close. And then I launch myself out, startling her, but now I'm nervous.'*

'Quick, grab at her throat, you fool,' Jack spoke to himself quietly, so gently that it was close to a whisper. The photo had taken over him now, the dark background of the woods, a backdrop for the illuminated tree in the foreground. He felt himself hiding in the shadows from his prey, a gentle breeze played with his fingertips as they twitched eagerly, readying themselves for going on the attack.

'That's it, weaken her, we need her weak, we need to be able to overpower this little thing.'

Jack's empty hand reached up into thin air and squeezed in on itself so tightly that his nails dug into the flesh of his own palm.

Jack dropped the picture to the floor carelessly, and plucked another from its magnet on the board. This depicted the body of the dead girl, from the neck bruising down to her punctured and split navel.

'Now that you cannot fight back I can have some fun.' His fist loosened slightly but not by much as his imagination forced the hilt of a knife into it. His arm swung back before taking the ultimate plunge, his smile sharpened at the edges and lengthened across his face with the mime of the killing blows.

'This is fun, this is what I wanted. Stabbing her just how I dreamed of doing with no one to stop me.'

'Sarge, you ok?'

The spell was broken, Jack was back beneath the brilliant white lights of the office and back to himself. He turned to see Officer Smith, iPad in hand.

'Yeah, yes, sorry, I was just—'

'I've got something for you, it's probably nothing but I thought I would show to you just in case.' He knew that she had interrupted him to save him the effort of making something up and no doubt embarrassing himself.

She handed him a piece of paper, it had a name and address at the top and a printout of a conversation below.

'It was a call that came in about the same time as the murder. That's what the woman said, there.' She pointed to the last few lines.

Jack looked at it quite surprised. 'Ok, a little strange … could be a coincidence, I suppose. Thanks, I'll check it out.'

Officer Laurel Smith left him to his thoughts as he read the manuscript of the phone call again. He shoved the paper into his jacket pocket, it was probably just a coincidence and he had some real police work to do for the time being.

DEMON OF MY OWN

The weather was mild for a late autumn day, blue sky stretched to the horizon, all of the usual clouds banished, making way for brilliant sunshine.

Tending to her plants in a warm, dry, airless greenhouse made her work hot and heavy going. She knew it was neither the right time of year nor the best gardening technique to be doing it now, but it was therapeutic, and that was what mattered right then. Her gloves fumbled at a brown stem, shaking while she attempted to get her secateurs on it, her eyes making it harder work than it ought to be as tears gathered and produced a cloudy film over the world she was seeing. She blinked and the salty droplets ran down her cheeks, settling on her top lip as it trembled.

'Poor little thing, she didn't deserve that, no one deserves that, and he didn't even care. Didn't care at all, didn't care one little bit. Poor little girl, so much life ahead of her, so pretty, so, so young. She didn't deserve that, horrible man, horrible demons, horrible, just horrible.'

The woman spoke quietly, not realising, not thinking, just trying to stay busy to clear her head. Even a few remaining butterflies that had survived the cold climate by hiding in there weren't enough to lift her broken heart. As she raked the soil around the base of a dead tomato plant something sharp snagged her skin through her thick gardening gloves. Pinching and pulling at the material on each fingertip, she removed it to find a small piece of glass sticking out of the fleshy part of her thumb. The shard came away easily from the skin and allowed a few scarlet droplets of blood to run smoothly down to her wrist.

'It looks as though I have a demon of my own.' She held her hand up in front of her face to watch the injury closely. 'It doesn't want me to forget last night,' she said, transfixed on the scarlet balls trickling their way down her skin.

AUBRIE'S NECK

It was cold in the mortuary. But, then again, it always was, the air conditioning being on all year round to prevent what Jack liked to think of as 'thawing accidents'. He actually quite enjoyed the atmosphere there, if he were honest. The slow, methodical process created a calm environment, something that was a constant polar opposite to the 'real world' police station.

When you were dealing with things as small as DNA, perhaps it was best to go slowly so you didn't miss anything. The detective knocked on a glass door.

Dr Aubrie Sellers pulled down her mask and smiled to him, she activated the door lock with her elbow.

'Hey Jack, I could have come to you, you know. I've got a couple more bits for you,' she told him, replacing the cloth over her mouth. 'I just want to double check her hair a minute for foreign bodies.'

He watched as she pulled a freestanding magnifying glass around to the head end of the polished-steel autopsy table. The young girl now wore a large red letter Y on her chest that started from both shoulders and went all the way down to her navel, the horrific remnant of the initial insertion of the scalpel. It looked just as graphic as the scattered stab wounds now that they had been cleaned up.

And the stitching was clearly the handiwork of someone practicing practicality over aesthetics.

Jack didn't say anything – there was nothing to say – so he stood back and let the doctor work unimpeded.

'No, nothing. Well, nothing that wouldn't have come from the ground anyway. We have dirt, seeds, some creepy crawlies, but other than that she's clean. Either our killer was good or he was lucky. Can you finish up, George? Shave the head also and put the hair through a microscope, there has to be something.'

She pulled off her gloves with a neat slap of rubber and the other person in the room started to take interest in the dead girl.

'No link to a killer at all?' Jack asked as they walked up and out of the sterile laboratory and down the hall to her office.

Aubrie took off her lab coat and threw it down on the desk. 'Nope, not a single fibre or hair, drop of blood, or semen sample. Some sweat on her neck we think transferred from his hand with the initial grab, but it's mixed with so much blood a DNA sample is going to be nearly impossible to get.'

Jack leapt at the tiny morsel of hope she left for him, '*Nearly* impossible? That's not the same as completely impossible, now.'

Aubrie sighed. 'No, it's not completely impossible, but look at this way – it's not impossible to win the lottery, either. And even if we did,' she raised her hands to make air quotes, '*hit the jackpot*, there's no guarantee that we would have a match on the database, his prints certainly weren't, so unless you have a suspect to compare it to …'

'Yeah, yeah, ok, we still wouldn't have a lead. Fine, ok, I'll just have to do it the old-fashioned way.' Jack straightened up and raised his eyes to the ceiling, looking for some possible divine intervention.

'He must have been wearing something plastic, or leather maybe – I mean to be that close to her, all over, in fact, and leave nothing. I've got a little more on the body, if you want?'

Jack reluctantly forced himself to be a part of the conversation again.

'Yeah, sure, we don't have much else to go on so far, now, do we? No suspects, no weapon, no match on the prints.' His tone was harsher than the words had meant to be. Even in his own head he could hear the condescending implication, like a teacher to a student.

Aubrie's smile was nearly well practiced enough to hide the injury his words had just inflicted, but Jack spotted it. He knew he had offended her and there was a time where he would have apologised profusely. But not now. It's ok for people to be affronted, it keeps them working hard, stops them from thinking their job is done. It was these times that would have played on his mind before, the snippets of life would get deep into his psyche and make him question who he was. Now, though, he doesn't care who he is, he doesn't matter anymore, and neither does whatever anyone thought of him. All that matters is the murder.

'Always the optimist, aren't we, Detective O'Connor?' Aubrie said, playing it cool.

'That's Detective Superintendent to you, Dr Sellers,' Jack said. It was just playful enough to rein the conversation back in.

'Sorry, where are my manners, Superintendent? Well, if you weren't impressed before, you're not going to like this either. Your murder weapons: I don't have a match on any knives. The one that I thought was a bread knife or carving knife with the two points? Well, the serration pattern is too large. The teeth are about thirty millimetres apart, we estimate – the skin was torn badly, you have to remember – but I think that's pretty accurate. And the sharp-edged knife is long, curved like a sabre but with an incredibly thick base. Nothing in our database at all with these exact measurements, here.' She opened her laptop and a picture appeared on the digital whiteboard behind her.

Jack would remember this piece of technology during the next budget review and ask why his department didn't warrant such a thing. On second thoughts, his officers would no doubt just amuse themselves with it, or end up breaking it.

'I've mocked-up some drawings with scale sizes beneath.'

'How did you do it so quickly?' The detective was amazed at her efficiency. So far he had shouted at a room full of fellow officers and drunk drove his way to work that day – hardly productive. Maybe he had been a little hard on her.

'I input the measurements and select types of weapons as I inspect the wounds and the computer does the rest. Jesus, Jack, it's called an app, wake up to the twenty first century one day, will you? There, look, two knives, completely different but used at the same time on one body.'

'But only one killer?' Jack added.

Aubrie shrugged her shoulders. 'Nothing to suggest otherwise. One set of footprints in damp, muddy ground, one set of fingerprints on the tree and the girl's neck. Unless the other killer can float, I don't know what to tell you.'

Jack looked closely at the board, the representation of the knives looked so real, but something in his head just couldn't sit quite flush with the facts.

'Neither of these knives look like they would sit in a sheath, do they?' he asked Aubrie honestly.

'Don't look like the type of hunting knives. The serrated one definitely not. Most sheath knives that we see in the UK are folding ones these days, also. What's your point?'

Jack gave himself a second to think, still staring deliberately at the white board.

'Well, it's just, it's pretty difficult strangling someone, I should imagine, quite a struggle, I mean, probably just about doable with a knife in one hand, could even use it to stun your victim.' He picked up a pen from the desk and held it up like a dagger. 'If this was a knife and I put this right in front of your eyes, well, you would be scared, wouldn't you? Stop running, maybe.' Jack reached his free hand up and placed it gently on Aubrie's neck. He instantly felt her chest rise and fall heavily.

'See, even my touch on a friend has a visible reaction,' he thought to himself.

'Strangle you until you're weak and then.' He swung his hand towards her stomach and stopped a few inches before stabbing the pen into her.

Aubrie winced slightly.

Jack lowered his hand away from her throat. 'That makes sense, but how can I do that if both my hands are full? These knives are too big to fit into a pocket and you said both knives were used at the same time, not one after another.'

The doctor straightened herself up. 'That's how it would appear. However, most of the serrated stab wounds come from an upward motion and the other blade a downward one, but not all. Also, the consistency of the depth of the blade would suggest either both knives were used in one hand, probably the killer's stronger arm, or that he was ambidextrous.'

Jack threw the pen down on top of her coat. 'Great. So, we are looking for a killer who is around six foot, weighing around twenty stone and has, what was it, size nine feet?'

Aubrie could only nod, she had nothing to add.

'Size nine? For a male of six feet, at least? That's unusually small, isn't it?'

'It is, but not unheard of,' she replied.

Jack deflated inside and knew it was apparent on the outside too.

'It's ok, Jack, I'll keep looking with my team and we'll

find something, we always do. Why don't you go home, have a shower and food, give all us lackeys a chance to do our jobs and by this evening we'll have pieced it all together.   Yeah?'

VIOLENT HALT

He knew why she was being kind. It was the anniversary, the day of each year that plunged him into darkness. It was five years to the day that his wife and daughter had been cruelly taken from him, the night when his world collapsed, the night when they were murdered. The day that seemed to be lasting forever, the pain never subsiding, always pounding inside his head, giving a horrid sensation to everything else that still existed. He forgot every other date in his calendar, even his mother's birthday – which he lived to regret last year – but this day was such a black hole in his life that it pulled him towards it, every year threatening to collapse him to oblivion.

Jack's mind was racing, he didn't want kind words, he wanted screaming, shouting, fighting – anything that would override the agony of emptiness. He walked to his car with the hum of city life playing in his skull, trying to nullify all of his perceptions. His existence became the intolerable hate he had come to understand.

He was driving out of the city. He didn't even remember starting the car, but now he was on the A37 hitting eighty miles an hour and overtaking quarry trucks through Gurney Slade as if they were creatures deliberately blocking his path. He punched his rusty Ford Capri into fifth gear and floored it, his heart began to accelerate along with the roar of the engine and rise of the thin, red needle. Not even glancing at the speedometer, the sides of his vision began to blur and he only just saw the white van pull out of a mostly hidden turning. Relinquishing the accelerator, he stamped both feet as hard as he could down on the brake pedal, knees locking up, the nineteen seventies technology letting him down, it always did.

'Fucking drum brakes,' he said, as the wheels jolted into a single, stiff position, the car fishtailing towards the back end of the white van. He braced himself against the steering wheel as his vehicle closed in on the rear loading doors of the other.

The van driver must have spotted him and, in reaction, floored the accelerator pedal, trying desperately to put distance between him and the speeding car. The Capri came to a violent halt of its own accord, and somehow not at the expense of the other road user. Jack looked down and realised that he had instinctively pulled the hand brake up, causing the car to avoid hitting the van by a matter of inches.

He released a long, hard breath that he must have been holding, getting himself ready for an impact that fortunately never came. He was impressed by himself, he hadn't realised that his sense of self-preservation had still been switched to the on position. He saw the van's window open, followed by a protruding hand giving him the finger.

Jack was annoyed at himself, he should have been shaken up or, at the very least, feeling grateful. His heart took only moments to reset to resting rate, anger gritted his teeth and turned the keys off and on, restarting the car so he could drive it to a nearby lay-by where truckers parked.

He always had medication in the car, at least some diazepam to take the edge off, but where was it?

He checked in the door compartments, leant over to the glove box, but all he found was empty blister packets; some of the small, round compartments looked full until he examined the foil side. He groped inside his jacket pocket and emptied it, pulling out bits of chocolate bar wrappers, some change, the small packet of drugs the barman had given him – which he couldn't deny were tempting – a piece of paper and, finally, some medication. Not even bothering to read what it was, he expelled two from their packaging and swallowed them dry.

The windscreen started to steam up in front of his eyes, giving him cause to wind the window down and breathe some fresh air. The car, now thirty-seven years old, soon became stuffy and would often have a smell twice its age – much like himself, Jack had figured.

A combination of a gentle breeze and the medication calmed his erratic thoughts so much so that he was able to take notice of something. It was the piece of paper he had removed from his inside pocket in his manic thirst for medicinal help. It was the address and manuscript from the strange late-night phone call that the young Officer Smith had presented to him.

'Twelve Torview, Glastonbury,' he read the address aloud. 'Glastonbury,' he repeated, as he only now recognised just how far from the city he had driven.

'Haven't been there since I was kid, it's only a couple of miles away, would justify me being here, I suppose,' he convinced himself as he flexed his neck and turned the key once again. The old engine sprung to life as best it could.

YOU DIDN'T DESERVE THEM

He was right – the small cottage had only been a short drive, one that he had taken far slower than the previous part of the journey. There was a time when he would have straightened his tie and ensured his breath was minty – or at least not smelling of gin – before going to interview someone. In fact, due to his borderline personality disorder, he would have often been too concerned, so eager to please that the actual interview could even become jeopardised. This was one of the symptoms he and his therapist had tackled – the constant need to have others like him. He had always despised himself for it but couldn't bring himself to change but, surprisingly, his therapist had praised him for it.

'It's an excellent coping strategy you have honed to protect yourself, and, I must say, Jack, you do it incredibly well. Everyone I have spoken to in connection with you is in agreement that there is hardly a bad word to say about you.'

Jack had noticed the word 'hardly' in the middle of the sentence, it had given him anxiety for a week. Now, however, since five years ago to the day, Jack had not given a second thought to what people thought of him. His appearance would crop into the foreground of his thoughts once in a blue moon, but he had clippers for his hair, a razorblade for his beard and flannel for his face, beyond that he didn't see why any other grooming tools were necessary. Since the murder, he let his mouth do the speaking, not caring if his brain had formulated the way in which to put it. No more sparing people's feelings or manipulating people into liking him, just the raw truth. One of his superiors had said he 'was like a new man' and that he 'always shot from the hip'. Jack hadn't been sure if that was, in fact, a compliment, but he knew it was meant as one so he took it gratefully.

His new attitude may have ruffled more than a pillow's-worth of feathers, but he really didn't care and, all in all, he was happier that way – or not anxious that way, at least. His career had gone into overdrive since the destruction of his family, and he had suspected that it was sympathy to begin with, but that was five years previous now, and his last promotion had only been three months ago. No, it was the 'I don't give a fuck' attitude that he had recognised in successful business managers and tycoons all his life that now got him travelling up the greasy pole faster than ever. A pole he could either take or leave, greased or otherwise.

He walked up a tiny path to the small, red-brick cottage that was hidden away, set back just far enough for the garden trees to obscure it from the rest of the world. He noted how the garden was unkempt, full of burnt-coloured autumn leaves, mirrored by the flaking red paint on the door. The number two was hanging loosely on its last remaining screw, he lifted it into place just to reassure himself he was indeed at number twelve. The doorbell was interesting, it was a long handle protruding from the top of the doorframe, and rang softly like an old-fashioned shop bell, but had a more musical note to it. He pulled on the iron bar twice but no one answered.

'I had better make sure everything is ok,' he said, loudly enough for anyone nearby to hear, giving him legal grounds for checking around the rear of the property. The path down the side of the house was overgrown and limited in space, but he finally reached the back garden. It was a stark contrast to the front of the property: the lawn was kept, the flowerbeds freshly dug and perfectly tidy. He saw the gardening hat of a woman bobbing around in the greenhouse. He approached cautiously as he suddenly became very aware that he was man approaching an unsuspecting older woman from behind, and giving her a fright was not the best ice breaker.

'Mrs ...' He looked down at the note still in his hand, names never stuck for some reason, faces yes, rap sheets definitely, but names escaped him as easy as breathing. '... Keilty?'

Even with the courtesy shout, the woman was still startled. It was clear that she didn't get many visitors.

'My name is Detective Superintendent O'Connor, I'm with the Bristol police, would you mind if we had a little word?' he asked her.

You idiot, Jack, should have brought a female officer with you, too bloody keen again,' he reprimanded himself, but there was no turning back now.

'If that is ok with you, of course.' There, at least he had given her the opportunity to refuse, and if she did he could come back with Officer Smith, people liked her, it must be her smile.

The woman stood with great nimbleness, Jack noticed, she removed her hat and gloves and threw them onto the greenhouse floor.

She smiled half-heartedly. 'I did wonder if you would be paying me a visit, a phone call I made, I presume?'

'Shall we go inside?' Jack gestured towards the back door.

She sighed and headed in, turning abruptly at the step. 'Not allergic to cats, are you? And I only have your bog-standard tea, none of that fancy coffee you youngsters drink.'

Youngster? It had been a long time since anyone has referred to him as that.

'A nice brew would be lovely, thank you.'

Jack waited on the small, doily-covered sofa in the living room while Mrs Keilty busied herself in the kitchen, making the construction of a cup of tea sound like a brass orchestra warming up.

It was apparent that the woman took tea-making very seriously and may be a while, so he decided to allow himself a small, investigative look around. The traditional sideboard was adorned with small silver frames, all of which were full of smiling children's faces. The flock wallpaper, peeling in places, was so old that it was probably back in fashion – not that he had a clue about fashion anymore. One of his favourite quotes, which his wife had taught him, came to mind.

'It's by Oscar Wilde,' she had told him. 'Fashion is a form of ugliness so intolerable that we have to alter it every six months.'

She had said it whilst trying on a summer dress and modelling it for him. They were so young, they still cared about how they were presenting themselves, still trying to influence their surroundings.

Jack continued around the room. A curtain hung from the stairs creating a cupboard-like space. Peering behind it, Jack spotted some old radio equipment and dozens of small tapes, the kind that voice recorders used.

'Two sugars, wasn't it?' Mrs Keilty called from the back room.

Jack sat back down again, he almost felt like an intrusive child close to being caught. Strange, really, as he hadn't felt that way for a few years now. Before his borderline personality treatment he had often felt like a child in a room full of adults. It was one of the more complicated symptoms he had discovered during his therapy, 'a child that dresses in adult's armour' he had read in one of the many informative books.

'Yes please, or three if you're feeling generous.'

The older woman laughed. 'Man after my own heart. We never really grow up, do we, Detective?' She carried a cup and saucer in to him.

'We sure as hell try not to,' he replied, receiving his beverage gratefully.

Mrs Keilty sat opposite him and they both took a courtesy sip of their tea.

'So, you want to talk about the murdered girl, then, Detective?' the woman said, quite unabashed.

Jack was thrown slightly off-kilter by her bluntness, but after the initial shock had subsided he actually felt rather grateful to her – grateful that he didn't have to sweat his way through the niceties any longer.

He placed his tea on the side table, ensuring he used a coaster even though he had a saucer. 'In your phone call, you described a woman being stabbed in some woods.'

He pointed down at his copy of the printed manuscript and left a long pause in the air.

This silence was usually so unbearable, to the point of destruction in most people, that it would only take a second or two before they confessed. This time, however, the woman smiled sweetly back at him.

'O'Connor, nice Irish name, strong Irish name.'

Jack realised they were back to niceties once more. 'Only Irish by name, my great grandfather was Irish but the rest of us are English, born and bred.'

Jack noticed a cut on her hand. The blood had hardly been cleaned away, if she had even attempted to at all. The brown, dry substance stood out on the woman's pale, freckled skin.

'That's a nasty cut you have there.'

Her gentle face looked interested in him all of a sudden. 'Nasty? Unpleasant or repugnant in nature. What an interesting word to use, Detective.'

'It is just a word, Mrs Keilty, nothing more.'

Her lips met her cup fleetingly. 'No, it isn't, it personifies something negatively. Don't get me wrong, Detective, it isn't wrong to do as such, no, not at all – just interesting. Are you religious, Detective?'

'No, Mrs Keilty, I'm not. Would you mind if we stayed on topic, please?'

She smiled gently to him once more. 'Oh, I am, Detective. I am not overly religious either. I mean, I have faith, but it doesn't sit within ghastly religious boundaries. Your young lady was murdered last night, not for sex, or money, or jealousy – but for fun. You see, Detective, the demons in this world enjoy our suffering, and they seek it out and pleasure themselves with it. Your young girl was taken because she could be, no righteous reasoning in it whatsoever. *Nasty*, isn't it?'

'What do you mean by demons? Do you mean bad people? Bad men? You know the type of people I mean, don't you, Mrs Keilty? Are there any of those kinds of people you want to tell me about?'

'Oh yes, Detective, they take the form of men,' she took another sip, 'and women. Even children, at times, when they really want to torment people. Nothing like a lost child to break the heart. But the truth of it, Detective, is that they don't even know what they are.'

Jack felt confused. 'And what are they?' he asked slowly, dreading the answer.

Mrs Keilty looked at him blankly. 'I just told you, Detective, they're demons. They come and they take. They take their bodies, break them up inside and then destroy their soul. That's why I made the phone call, she needed help, that poor girl. There was no way she could have fought a demon alone. In the end, she was so alone.'

Jack's heart sank, just another nut job, a time-waster with games to play to satisfy some disturbed version of Munchausen syndrome.

He stood to leave. 'Thank you, Mrs Keilty, but I think I have heard quite enough already, thank you for the tea.'

'She was scared, Detective, so very scared, and when she couldn't breathe, well, she knew she was dying, and the knife, its blades were terrifying.'

Jack headed to the door. 'Mrs Keilty, I do not have time to play these games with you, I have seen the radio equipment under the stairs, if I hear that you are making these phone calls after listening into police radio stations again, I will have you arrested, do you understand? Wasting police time is a much greater offence than you might think.'

The woman now had tears running down her face. 'I never asked you to believe, you wanted to know so I'm telling you. She felt every stab of that weapon, every blow as it pierced her, Detective, and I saw it happen, I saw the pain and misery and if you do not stop him he will do it again.'

Jack lost his temper, he already felt on the edge of psychosis and he wasn't going to be dragged there by a crazy woman wanting attention.

'Mrs Keilty, you heard stab victim on the radio, yes, well there wasn't one knife involved so whatever you saw was not our incident, perhaps it was all in your twisted imagination. I have a murderer out there, I do not have the time to indulge you in your godforsaken fantasies.'

The woman stood quickly, sending her tea cascading to the threadbare carpet. She erased the distance between them with so much ease, Jack actually stepped backward with surprise. Her face contorted awkwardly, her green eyes pierced into his with searing concentration.

'It was one knife, it was long and had a blade at either end of a leather-bound handle. I know it was leather-clad, Detective, as I felt it under the skin of my hand as it was plunged through her skin, I felt the blood trickle down the top blade onto my hand and I smiled with joy and I will murder again, Detective. The S shape of the blade made for such interesting stab marks, I quite enjoyed the randomness of it all.'

Mrs Keilty's hand reached out and grabbed his forearm tightly, he tried to shake it off but the woman had an iron grip. Her body jerked a little.

'The shame in you, Jack. You weren't there to help them, were you? You were at work, putting your career on top of that pedestal. Was it worth it, Jack, was it worth loving your job more than your family? Knowing that they would still be alive if you had just cared a little? And now, and now you are alone, just as you should be. You know this, don't you, Jack? You know they were taken from you because you didn't deserve them.'

The old woman froze, unblinking, eyes looking through Jack, as if he wasn't there, and then slowly tears formed in them again. Her hand dropped from his arm and she took one long stride backwards, away from him.

'Time for you to leave, Detective, I assume you can see your own way out.'

Jack watched as Mrs Keilty silently left the room to slip into the kitchen, back out of sight.

SHOOTING IN CLIFTON

'Fucking nut job,' he told himself as he drove back to Bristol. *'Should have the old crow arrested.'* But a paltry amount of doubt creeped in at the corners, the dark recesses of his subconscious, giving shadowy spaces for the thoughts to grow. Demons started dancing through his mind in wild and wonderful shades of red and black, and plasma seeped in through people's ears, taking them over like something from a movie. Jack laughed at himself, at his own wild, ridiculous imagination.

Heavy raindrops obscured the windscreen, the wipers could barely cope with the amount falling and the car's heating system, being as antiquated as it was, meant that each window now wore a layer of condensation.

Jack started to slip back into a mixture of tiredness and irritation – the common standpoint of his when things didn't go his own way. His breathing became heavy and laboured, the headlights from oncoming cars were the only way of knowing where his side of the road was.

It was just the same, the same as all those years before when he had been rushing home. He had heard the call on the radio that night.

'Shooting in Clifton, Apsley Rd.'

He had been doing paperwork at the time, the call had

been on another officer's radio. He had reached his car and was tearing his way up Park Street in a matter of minutes, wheels spinning over puddles, losing traction, and still it had felt so slow, like a dream that no matter how hard you tried, you were stuck in a reality that worked on a different timescale.

When he had reached his house, officers were already holding people back while paramedics lifted his wife and daughter's bodies into the ambulance. Even a reporter had managed to beat him there. He had torn the flashing camera out of the man's hands, wrenching the strap from around his neck and sending him to the floor as he threw it down the road as far as he could.

It had taken three officers to stop him tearing the door off the ambulance and, again, this was something he would never forgive himself for. If he had been calm, the paramedics would have let him in the vehicle to travel with them, he may have seen the last bit of life in his family before they departed. But then again, if he had been calm, he wouldn't have been Jack.

PISSING IN THE WIND

Jack's eyes were sore when he realised he had arrived back at the police station, he wasn't sure if it was from crying or from holding the tears back.

The incident room was full of everyone comparing notes, discussing which direction may yield some more clues, everyone having different, opposing ideas, all ringing like out of tune church bells in his head when he had only been there a matter of seconds.

This did not bode well.

'Quiet down, hush now,' he instructed the room.

The familiar faces took up their usual positions.

He looked at his watch. 'It's been well over twelve hours now since our victim was killed, I want to know who did this, I want to be right on their arse, and I want you lot to tell me where I can find them.'

He looked at Kapoor and Peters, the first had his notebook ready to hand.

'Nothing, sarge, nothing on cameras in the local areas or roads leading away. All the plates we found at the exact time of the murder and around it were accounted for. Most were taxis, all of which carried fares, and all went through the company's office, so they couldn't have done it. Thinking of stretching the camera search area up to the motorway, the top of Whiteladies Road and around the zoo possibly. My theory is they are local and know the area well enough to avoid most cameras, bearing in mind that most murderers don't shit on their own doorstep, I don't think he'll be from the Leigh Woods area, but could be from slightly further afield.'

Jack was impressed, good initiative shown.

'What about interviews, what have we discovered there?'

Officer Laurel Smith stepped forward – she would often do that, it was a trick that Jack had taught her. As liberal as the police force now was, some of the old firm still gave women a hard time and stepping forward to speak showed a certain air of confidence, whether it was there or not.

'The family seem to think she had been going running there for a week or so, giving our killer plenty of time to scope out where she would most likely be, but on interviewing the dog walkers, no one out of the ordinary had been seen there. What "out of the ordinary" might be, I'm unsure. Seems like all sorts of people use it for different things. Bird watching, horse riding, schools—'

Jack interrupted her, 'Doesn't mean he wasn't there, but a large man walking the woods without a dog or binoculars, well, that would stand out, surely? There were no dog pawprints at the scene either, except that of the one belonging to woman who found the body. No, it doesn't feel right for it to have been calculated, it was too messy.'

Jack wrote his words up on the board, it was a lot to ask his team to take his gut feeling on things as fact, but they never did question him.

Aubrie knocked gently on the door and walked in.

'Please give us something, anything will do,' Jack pleaded with her.

She shook her head. 'Not a single discernible fibre. Part of the handprint on the tree has been identified as being leather, and we assume it was a full coat, protecting the other clothing. We shaved her head, nothing there that shouldn't be there either. Sorry, Jack.'

The detective deflated. 'Ok, no, that's fine. Right, I want someone to get on to social media, maybe there is something there. See if she had a stalker sending her messages, or maybe a stalker that she didn't know about, hack her accounts if you have to. And someone else get a warrant for it, if you can.'

Officer Nitin Kapoor stood and headed out of the room. 'Leave that with me,' he told him confidently.

Jack took a moment to run his hands over his short hair. *'Where next? Where should I look now?'* he asked himself as he paced in front of his team.

He thought his day couldn't get any worse when the worst came swooping in. It was his superior. Detective Chief Superintendent Alison McQuade pushed her way in, knocking Aubrie sideways a little.

'Jack, tell me we nearly have the bastard? You have the full resources you need, just use them and get him in a cell ASAP.' She examined the board, looked at the faces of Jack's team and then turned back to the man himself. 'We have something, right?'

Jack played this game well, he had sparred with Alison many times before, and sometimes he even came out on top.

'No, ma'am, we don't have anything so far, he's done a good job on us, I'm afraid. We need some more time and we need to shake a few more trees and—'

His superior shot across him. 'Outside.'

It wasn't a question, it was an order, one that was for theatrics only – if she had really wanted to speak in private they would have gone much further from the rest of his team than the one foot outside the door where they currently stood.

'Shake more trees? Don't give me that bull, I know that means keep asking questions until someone cocks up.

Shake enough trees you might just get a lot of bloody leaves. I've got the press breathing down my neck and you're pissing in the wind. I'm going to have to make an appeal – if you don't get anything soon I won't have a bloody choice.'

'You can't, you might as well piss in your own face let alone the wind if you do that.' He could tell that perhaps that last analogy had gone a little too far. 'What I mean is, that's exactly what this killer wants to see. If we start putting out an appeal he'll know that we don't have anything on him, he'll know exactly what creek we are up without a paddle, and worse still, he'll go underground and we will never catch him. It's too soon, let him stew, let him wonder what we know, how close we are and he'll be so busy looking over his shoulder, he'll make a mistake.'

McQuade looked as though her insides were working on nitrogen instead of air, she took huge, nasal breaths before conceding, 'You know this means we are offering up the whole city as his next victim? I'm assuming there probably will be a next victim seeing as you have nothing on any of her family or friends?'

'I think that's quite likely, it's not a crime of love or passion, it, it doesn't feel like a one-off, if you know what I mean?'

McQuade sighed, unfortunately, she didn't know what he meant, but she trusted that he did.

'You need to give me something soon, Jack, I can't keep the vultures at bay indefinitely. Get your team set, get officers on the streets and bloody hell, Jack, get some sleep, won't you? You look like shit.'

'Yes, ma'am, I'll get as much rest as I can. I'm giving everything to this case, don't you worry.'

His commander looked dubiously at him. 'That, Detective, is exactly what I am afraid of.'

He re-entered the room and set all of his team off on their tasks. He ordered Officer Smith to get patrols in usual areas. 'If our man likes woods, make sure Ashton

Court, The Downs and the woods where we found our girl have people on the ground around the clock. The rest of you, do what you have to do, go home, sleep and be here with all the energy you can muster tomorrow. Am I understood?'

He received general murmurs of agreement and watched as phones were lifted and coats became worn. He took one more long look at the board; so far it offered nothing, no clues or hints, just a hell of a lot of nothing.

TANYA RED

He ran his hand over the velvet sofa, brushing it this way and that, changing the colour of it as the fibres picked up the light from different angles. The small, secluded room was what Jack could describe only as tacky, its plush furnishings trying to hide what the true nature of the environment was. It smelt of alcohol and piss, but then so did every old club since the smoking ban had been enforced – one thing the government hadn't accounted for. The newer, upmarket bars in Bristol were some of the most pleasant places he had ever spent evenings, but this was not one of those places. The rhythmic drum of dance music playing off on the dance floor offended his ears, and every one of his senses struggled here. The spotlight above him was there to ensure he could enjoy the show, but Jack just wanted it turned off, there was nothing here that he was interested in viewing in that much detail. The long red curtains parted and the small figure of a woman stepped inside. She wore a corset with long fishnet stockings and red high heels, the kind not designed for walking in. Her tight, pitch-black bob swished deliberately as she turned to face him. She was carrying two short glasses with a dark liquid filling them halfway to the top. She offered one to Jack, downed her own and sat herself seductively beside him. The detective finished his drink in one, suppressed the burning it caused in the top of his stomach and placed his glass on the small table.

'Would you like your usual, sir, would you like me to tell you that I have been a very naughty little schoolgirl and that I need spanking? Or perhaps you would like to hear about when my step daddy touched me and I liked it?' she said smoothly into Jack's ear, making an innocent childlike face and pouting her lips in mock submission.

'Jesus Christ, Tanya, that the sort of thing they ask for here, is it? I thought it was just a dance, flash of a nipple and away they go?'

The young woman laughed, tore off her wig and slumped back beside him. 'You would be surprised some of the shit that goes on in these luxury suites.'

She flicked off her shoes and cuddled up to Jack's arm. 'How you doing, Jack? I know what day it is, it can't be easy, well, obviously, you wouldn't be here if it was, would you?'

Jack burped a small amount of fiery gas into his mouth, the liquor had been stronger than he had thought.

'Why do you still do this, you own the goddamn club, you own about ten businesses, that I know of, you're bloody rich, girl, why don't you live like it?'

Tanya Red was twenty-five, five foot two and one of the most dangerous people Jack had ever encountered. The majority of people he would liken her reputation to were built like shit brick houses and smelt like them too.

Jack met this innocent, young girl aged twenty-one, at the scene of a hideous crime. By all accounts, she had appeared to be a victim. Eleven men had been brutally murdered and mutilated in a quiet little suburb of Bristol, nine of whom had been part of a sex ring and the remaining two their clients.

Six very young, very innocent girls had been at the scene, all had been drugged and all had been raped – bar one, Tanya Red. The girl had an excuse for every reasoning that Jack had thrown at her: she hadn't been drugged as she had been compliant and not put up a fuss, she hadn't been raped as it was her first time being brought to the house. Even when Jack discovered that the college at which all the other girls had attended was in fact eight miles away from the university that she was a student at, he still had no evidence that the young girl in front of him had committed any crime whatsoever. She had successfully managed to cover herself in blood from each victim and contaminated every body, she cried when she was supposed to, looked sad throughout and had everyone fooled. Everyone but Jack. Only when he asked her to indulge him in taking an IQ test and she scored well over one hundred and eighty did her, up until then faultless, act waver.

Indulging in her narcissism had worked, had teased her out of her performance and placed her somewhere near honesty. It infuriated her how Jack had known, worked it all out against impossible odds. She had enjoyed the torment of their emotional and mental sparring.

Her fascination had piqued when he had presented her with something she had not been expecting. Jack had shown her a picture of one of the male victim's mutilated genitals, where a thin, white-hot poker had been inserted down the urethra, exploding the shaft. She had examined the photograph, given Jack a devilish smile and replied, 'How unfortunate for the rapist.'

He had nothing to convict her with, and even if he had a shred of evidence, he doubted it would have proven any worth in court seeing as the only people who were dead most people would have gladly handed the death penalty to.

This made him often wonder if capital punishment would have any effect on today's society if it were to be reintroduced. He suspected it wouldn't, so didn't give it too much thought. And that's where it started; a very unusual, very unconventional friendship was born – if that's what you could really call it. It was difficult at first, but it soon became apparent that a brain that didn't work within the usual parameters, like Jack's, found it impossible to have relationships with others whose brains did work normally.

The young woman sighed. 'Oh Jack, everyone has to have a hobby, besides drinking and catching bad guys. So why don't you take up golf or something trivial like that? Anyway, as far as anyone else knows, Brian "The Butcher of Bristol" owns this place, I'm but an assistant to his higher cause.'

Jack knew that Brian 'The Butcher of Bristol' owned many businesses across the city, he also ran a small drug cartel and was a rather successful loan shark. He also knew that none of his employees could tell you what he looked like exactly, and those who thought they had a clue all gave conflicting descriptions. The man was about as real as Harry Potter, and what he could do without ever actually being seen was just as magical.

'Seriously, girl, you need to look after yourself, it's a dirty world you are mixed up in.'

Tanya laughed. 'It's the same one as you, only I'm on the other side of it. Anyway, you seem to feel quite comfortable in places like this, why shouldn't I? Is it because I'm but a little woman?'

Jack saw her put on her pouty face again, suddenly she was that twenty-one-year-old again when they had first met.

'I just needed to escape for a few hours, having a crap day,' he told her.

'Yes, I heard about your girl in the woods, I don't know anything about it, you know that, don't you?' she said, looking earnestly into his eyes.

Jack nodded. 'That's not why I'm here, and I trust you enough to know an innocent girl would have nothing to do with you.'

Jack remembered the drugs from early that morning, he pulled the packet from his breast pocket.

'This might have something to do with you, though. Know anything about cheap drugs coming onto the market?'

'Now, Jack, you know I only deal with high-end clients – the kind that pay through the nose for the same stuff everyone else pays pennies for. I don't deal in cheap, it's not my nature.' She took the bag from him, examined it closely, and then handed it back. 'I'll ask around, see if someone is trying to flood the market to get people hooked on it. It's been done before, normally by a gang. What they do is push out a vast amount of stock at non-profit prices, get people to enjoy it, so much so that they want more, and then whack the prices up.'

She saw the indignation on Jack's face. 'It's commonplace in other industries, snacks and things like that, it was only a matter of time before the technique moved into illegal territories.'

'I guess all businessmen are crooks then, argh!' Jack threw himself back against the soft sofa.

A searing pain gripped him, images of the fallen murder victim flashed in the front of his mind, followed by more stabbing pains. Memories of his wife and daughter tried to reach themselves into focus, but he fought them back, tried not to think, the pain ripping at his brain once more.

'Seriously, Jack, talk about me having to look after myself, what about you?'

She reached over to him and lifted one of his tightly closed eyelids, he didn't know what she was looking for as she peered as closely as she could into his eye.

He banged his head deliberately backwards against the wall as his back arched, the pain throwing it into spasm.

'You haven't been taking your medication, have you? Here.' She spent a moment taking a small plastic bag, similar to the one Jack had handled moments before, from inside her bra.

Jack's knuckles turned a pale pink as he gripped the upholstery beneath his legs. The pain was hot inside him, hotter than the alcohol he had consumed, hot enough to make him pass out at any moment.

His mouth started to spit and his teeth ground so tightly they felt as though they might fuse.

Tanya pulled a tab from her own small bag and placed it on his lips. 'Take it,' she insisted.

Jack let the paper absorb away on his tongue.

'What is it?' he managed to ask between the puncturing afflictions.

Tanya took one herself, Jack wasn't sure if this was an act to reassure him or not, but it helped.

'Prescription drugs, mainly, my own mix. It's ok, let it take you away, it'll take you somewhere the pain can't reach you.'

Jack's head felt as though it had suddenly been filled with oxygen and was expanding like a balloon. He toppled over onto Tanya's lap where she stroked his head. A tickling sensation started in the pit of his stomach, it seemed to effervesce and gradually grew up inside him, enveloping his heart and lungs. The strange sensation felt warm, like trickling water, it flushed his cheeks and finally his eyes rolled back in his head. The darkness was inviting, it looked like a space where he could hide away, a safe space where he could disappear for a while away from the world,   and   so   he   did.

SHARPENED TIPS

Her vision was cloudy. No, wait, not all of her vision, just the peripheral, hazy and obscured, tunnelled somewhat.

'Oh, sweet god, look at her face, look at how scared she is, poor girl.'

Why can't she stop her hand, the tightening on her flesh? Stop herself from crushing the windpipe and doing it with such ease. With every pathetic gasp of air, spit oozing from the young woman's mouth, she squeezed tighter. She was killing her but she knew that, at this very second, this young victim would never be so close to being completely alive.

'Look how easy it is to destroy you, look how powerful I am, giving and taking this from you,' the old woman thought in the darkest niches of her mind. The centre of her confused vision watched, almost as if as a bystander, as what she thought was her own hand gripped the leather bindings on the weapon. The girl had passed out this time before the fun had truly started, but that didn't bother her as she plunged the cold metal into warm flesh. It didn't snag nearly as much on the skin this time, the smooth insertion only faltered as it hit and ground along bone. Straight through the pretty little abdomen until only the spine was left between the sharpened tips and the exit through her

back.

And the blade certainly had been sharpened, all that work with a whetstone had been worth it, it had been a job worth doing for the difference it had made. Her arms had ached after the constant rubbing down of these edges, but now it was her perfect killing companion – a workman is only as good as his tools, after all.

The murderer took a deep breath and inhaled unseen water, she choked and sat up, and she was alone in her bath. Her hands had gripped the sides of the tub so tightly with her hallucination that two of her fingernails had been ripped off. Her fresh pink blood marbled the cold water.

'How long have I been in there?' she wondered as she stood up and looked out of the window at the night sky. Various parts of her body had pruned and turned a death-like grey. She stood in front of the bathroom cabinet for a moment, examining her own face, ensuring it was the same one as before. There was no change except the blood trickling from her nose. Two red streaks ran from the nostrils, across her lips and dripped from her chin.

The cat awoke on the bathroom mat and purred loudly. She wasn't sure how, but they always seemed to be there for her, whenever she needed them to be, whenever the demons   appeared.

NICE PYJAMAS

The thumping in Jack's head was replaced with the sound of flesh on wood. His eyes, congealed with seepage, took a moment or two to open. More knocks came from his door, they sounded hurried, like an emergency was happening without him, which was his usual type of emergency.

'Alright, give me a minute.'

He recognised that, against the odds, he was in his own bed. He always thought it funny how his brain had been trained to navigate a path home, whatever inebriated state it might find itself in. He supposed that all creatures must be related in one form or another, so that must be his homing pigeon strand of DNA in action.

The covers were unusually tight; someone had tucked them in at the sides and it was with some difficulty that he unrestrained himself from them. He shoved his hands into his lower back, forced himself upright with a loud stretch and caught his reflection in the full-length mirror.

'What the—' His mouth dropped open.

He was standing still, in shock, wearing stripy, button-up pyjamas. The type only worn by old men on TV in the seventies.

He looked up and down his canal boat to find the

perpetrator of this crime against fashion and his reputation, but he was alone – bar the moccasin slippers waiting neatly beside the bed. Tanya's idea of a joke, no doubt.

He opened the door to see a very disgruntled face that nearly managed to hide the smirk at seeing his outfit, but not quite.

'Where the bloody hell have you been? Five hours I have been trying to contact you, oh, and nice pyjamas, by the way.' Aubrie pushed her way past him and into the kitchen area of the narrow boat.

'Sorry, it's my meds, they knock me out sometimes.' Well, it was almost true.

Aubrie eyed him with suspicion.

'She would make a good detective if she ever gets bored of the dead,' he thought as she examined him from a distance.

'What are you on? Or meant to be on, at least?'

'Think, what's that one with the name you can hardly pronounce?'

'Quetiapine, one hundred milligrams a day.'

She seemed satisfied with the answer and flicked on the kettle. 'I'm making coffee, you get dressed, and we've had a murder.'

Jack leant back against the wall and rubbed more sleep from his eyes. 'I know, and I also know we've got sod all to go on and she will still be dead whatever time I would have woken up.'

'Another one, Jack – we've got another body.'

The shower was hot, too hot, but it was only to wash the smell of strip club off, he'd bear it. In the back of his mind he knew punishing himself under the boiling hot water was trying to enact some penance for being comatose while someone else was having their life cut short, but he couldn't think that way, he didn't need the voice of his therapist in his head, not today.

He applied shaving foam to his face quickly above the basin.

Lifting his head, Jack had a sight in front of him, shocking enough to cause him to jump and topple back onto the toilet.

His heart raced and his mouth filled with unneeded adrenaline.

In front of him stood Tanya Red, looking as though she had just walked in from a gentle stroll in the park. She raised a finger to her mouth to indicate him to be quiet, but it was too late – he had already yelped like a frightened girl.

'Everything ok in there?' Aubrie called from a mere six feet or so away.

Tanya just smiled with amusement. She perched herself on a wicker wash basket and was clearly enjoying waiting to see what Jack was going to reply with.

'Err, yeah, just cut myself shaving, I will be two minutes.'

The girl with the red hair gave him a silent, mock round of applause, before standing up and straddling his lap. She took a cutthroat razor from her pocket and began shaving him. She moved his head around gently and wiped the blade of its excess foam in the sink with care. When she had finished, Jack pointed an accusing finger at the pyjamas on the floor and then at her. Tanya shrugged and kissed him softly on the forehead before climbing with unnerving ease out of the small window. Her capabilities never ceased to terrify him.

'Here, bring this.' Aubrie handed him a mug of coffee. 'You can drink that on the way.'

Jack was surprised, not that he had been given a coffee, but that there were the three ingredients needed to make it in his cupboards and fridge. He couldn't remember the last time he had drunk a hot drink at home, let alone bought the stuff to make one.

'It's tidier in here than I was expecting, at least,' Aubrie said, casting a look over the lounge area, 'and I have picked out a suit and shirt for you, all of which were pressed and ironed, so I am impressed, Mr Detective, maybe you're not such a domestically lost cause after all.'

Jesus Christ, what has Tanya done?

Aubrie was right, the place was much tidier than it ever had been, and the cupboards were full of food within their sell by dates, too, by the looks of it. Jack knew that, as kind as these gestures were, it was all a game to Tanya, one to mess with his head a little.

Jack took a sip of his coffee as he slipped his feet into his shoes, at least they were still a little scruffy, would have looked ridiculous if they had been polished, seeing as he had worn them every day for six years and never cared once about their appearance.

'Wow, what is in this?' he asked Aubrie as took a deep sniff of the contents of his mug.

Aubrie laughed. 'Hair of the dog. Trust me, I'm a doctor, it works. It was meant to be an Irish coffee but you were out of whisky.'

'So what did you use, air freshener?'

'No, peach schnapps and Malibu. Now, hold your nose and drink it, you've had worse.'

It was true, Jack had indeed drunk worse – at this time of the morning too, no less – so he slurped it back as he sat in the passenger seat of Aubrie's white Mini. She filled him in with what had happened with the newest murder. It was a young lady again, and the same weapons had been used. The scene was essentially the same and only one mile from the first victim. It had occurred at around two in the morning at The Downs up in Clifton.

'A stone's throw from my house,' Jack allowed himself to think for a moment. He still owned the house – it was paid off, in fact – but now he rented it to a posh couple and their family who had moved from Surrey to work in the city. He had stepped in it less than half a dozen times since the murders, and hadn't been in there at all in the last

twelve months. He hadn't ever had an inclination towards living on a canal boat in his life before, but finding property in Bristol city centre with a price tag that didn't make you laugh had proven to be trickier than he had imagined. When the boat had come up for sale and the mooring fees turned out to be cheaper than renting a garage, it didn't take a detective to realise the opportunity.

No point heading to the crime scene, it was ten o'clock – everything that could have been done there, would have been – so instead he told her to drive straight to the station.

The same faces were waiting for him as the day previous. The Jack of five years ago would have been embarrassed at turning up over five hours late for an investigation and would be doing all he could to get his team back on side. Not the Jack of today though, today's detective thought about one person when entering that room, and usually they were the one no longer alive.

Jack was just heading into the room at the same time as Officer Laurel Smith. 'Another one less than twenty-four hours later. Can't believe it, sarge, can you? Another poor innocent girl. Did you get anything from that caller from the other night?'

Jack knew that she was most likely asking as she kept abreast of everyone's work, and she probably knew that the rest of the team had nothing of much worth to go on.

'No, it was a prank call. Some old woman with an old radio kit, listening into the police radio sets as it was called in. Waste of time.'

They both entered the room together.

'Really? I thought all the handsets and radios went digital a couple of years ago,' Officer Smith said as she took her seat.

'Olivia Harris, aged twenty-three, a nurse at the BRI, murdered between the hour of one thirty and two thirty AM. Same murder weapon, almost the exact same scene as the night previous. That's what I know, now tell me what I don't,' Jack said.

The room of people were quiet.

Aubrie spoke up first, 'Same knives, less wounds but they are all much deeper than before, nearly every blow was down to the hilt. Longer sweeping movements, I think, than before, but not enough of a difference to suggest a different killer. No forensics on the body again and no fingerprints at the points of strangulation this time – the killer was wearing gloves. That's all we have to go on at the moment from the body.'

Officer Kapoor opened his notebook. 'We have her on camera leaving the hospital, walking up Whiteladies Road and then heading off towards her house. She house shares with two other nurses, one of which was home and said that Olivia changed and took the dog out for a walk immediately on returning, at around one. No witnesses around The Downs at the time of the murder.'

Jack digested the information, it was all messed up.

'No witnesses at all? It was Friday night, there are always people at that spot, there's always middle-aged men hanging around in the bushes, there must be someone. I thought I asked for patrols around these areas, where were we when this took place, for god's sake?' Jack felt a marble of guilt drop into his tummy, he knew where he had been, and it was not out stopping murderers.

Laurel spoke again. 'You did, sarge, and we did. We had four officers in and around that area, probably a realistic reason for why we don't have any witnesses – I think all the doggers were put off and gave up.'

He knew she was right, putting those uniforms there would have cleared away any of the usual crowed that inhabited the area.

'So it happened right under our noses. Brilliant.' Jack thought quickly, quicker than his brain had been used in months. 'Peters, check the same cameras as the night before, cross-check the plates that you can find, if there is no match, look at same makes and colours. Our killer wasn't lucky, he's good, so he may have switched plates. Any two of the same model and colour, run their plates and make sure they are legit. The bastard can't fly, and he must have left somehow. Smith, get down to the crime scene, interview anyone who shows any interest, pay special attention to anyone who's over six foot. He's enjoying himself, he won't want to stop and he'll want to know how we are getting on. I'll bet my arse that he's been down there already this morning at least once. I want everyone's alibis to be airtight, or they will be seeing me. That's two teams, take as many officers with you as you need, any of them don't like it, tell them to come to me. Right, this timeframe, we can't assume anything from it. He's not in our system because this is his first offence, he's been opportunistic, and it just so happens his two opportunities were on consecutive days. Normally, a suspect killing at this rate is erratic, hurried, panicked, but our man is none of those. There would also normally be an escalation – something bigger and better than before to satisfy the thrill – but these murders are essentially identical. Sure, the second was more efficient,' he looked at Aubrie who confirmed with a nod, 'but that's to be expected. No tattoos on the bodies?'

Aubrie shook her head. 'Hardly any piercings, either.'

Jack wondered if she had read his mind. 'No, I noticed that too. I wondered if our killer had a fetish, or perhaps judged our girls and was killing righteously, but that doesn't fit either. Olivia was fully clothed, hair tied back still from work, hardly slutty looking, is she? There's no lust here for either of them – not as women, anyway, as fragile victims, maybe.'

He paced the floor, it wasn't enough, it wasn't even a fart in a tornado of shit and Jack knew it. He needed something specific, a real lead to go on, not shots in the dark with a little bit of hope thrown into the pot. The tornado of shit just got worse with the formidable sight of

McQuade   entering   the   room.

THE FAIR ASSASSIN

'O'Connor, my office, now.'

The second the door closed behind him the barrage began. 'Less than twenty-four hours later, an identical murder, and less than a mile from the first. "Don't do an appeal," he says, "we don't want them to go undercover." Well, is this what you wanted, another girl's blood on our hands? And trust me when I say it's *our* hands – the whole force is a laughing stock. And I don't know if you have noticed, Jack, but you and I are fairly high up this tree, which means we have the furthest to fall. Get your god damn arse in gear and show me you're worth the pain in my arse you are slowly becoming.'

He stood there quietly. He had no way of knowing the killer would be this bloodthirsty, but from the other side he had to admit it appeared as though his team had done less than nothing – they had even cleared the area ready for the killer to strike.

McQuade sat behind her desk and put her head in her hands before composing herself. 'I know you won't like it, Jack, but you have nothing to go on – not one viable clue. I will have to make an appeal for witnesses to come forward.'

'No, he'll be watching, that's what he'll be waiting for, a

clear signal of that we have nothing on him. Ma'am, I know it doesn't look like we have achieved anything but we are doing all we can, we don't want to aid him anymore.'

His superior sighed. 'You're acting as though I have a choice, Jack, the press want blood and it might as well be mine before they turn on you again.'

He knew she was right – the moment the papers found out it was him that was investigating the murders they would have a field day. Managing to stay under the radar had taken a steep learning curve for the infamous Detective O'Connor and his unorthodox approach to things.

'Give me a day. If I don't have a decent enough lead by then, well, I guess we will be out of options.'

She moved uncomfortably in her seat before conceding. 'It's eleven now, you have till seven AM – that's twenty hours, which is about nineteen and a half more than you deserve. Now get out and don't come back empty handed.'

He returned to the incident room, the added jeopardy fuelling him, filling him up, pushing his muscles, especially the one behind his eyes, into a gear long forgotten.

His team sat and looked at him as he paced the small space, he breathed heavily. Something was there, something was peeking out at him from the bushes, what the hell was it?

'Weapon? I said "weapon", singular, not "weapons", plural. Why?' He closed his eyes in dread of what he was about to do, he'd had some crazy hunches before, but none had been this ridiculous. He hurriedly wiped a space clear on the whiteboard and picked up a pen.

'Does this mean anything to anyone?' He started to draw.

'This is a leather-bound handle.'

He drew a curved knife upward, with one jagged edge

and two points on the tip. He then drew another blade coming off the bottom of the handle, he curved it down with a sharp edge and tip.

'And these are two blades. One knife, two different edges. That would work, wouldn't it?' he turned and asked Aubrie. 'That would explain how he handled it while restraining our victims? The pattern of the stab wounds.'

Aubrie took a step closer to look at the haphazard drawing.

Her lips pursed as she considered it. 'Yes, I guess so. Would explain the consistency of strength, both blades with the same hand, most stabs coming up with one blade then also down with another. Would explain the width of them at the hilt too, if they were moulded to the handle so it was all one piece. Sure, I can see that.'

Officer Kapoor punched Officer Peters on the arm knowingly. 'The Fair Assassin, mate.'

Jack looked round, he hadn't understood what his officer had said but it felt like he had stumbled on something.

'What? Do you recognise it?' he asked the two male officers who were both now looking somewhat more hopeful.

Peters cleared his throat. 'It's from a computer game, sarge, a pretty new game, actually, only released about a week ago.'

Nitin Kapoor tapped his fingers on his phone before holding it up for everyone to see.

It was an anime image of a young girl, a samurai sword in each hand, her hair cut into a short bob-style haircut that swept across her face. And then there it was in the background. A double ended knife, flying through the air towards the female in the foreground. *The Fair Assassin* was written in stylish black writing with a single bead of blood hanging from one of the letter Ss.

'Is that it? Is that the hunch irritating me down inside my core?'

'That's our weapon, ladies and gentleman. Peters, Kapoor, you seem to know more than the rest of us about these gaming things, set a team up on the cameras and then go and find me where that knife has come from. Peters, you know Dave down on the Cheltenham Road, yeah?' The large officer nodded. 'He deals with a lot of imported paraphernalia and he owes me a favour or two, remind him of that. Officer Smith?'

'Yes, sarge?' she replied, not even slightly startled by her boss shouting her name.

'Get on to our records, look at anyone we may have arrested or who has any connection with replica weapons, would you? Follow up anything that doesn't smell right.'

Jack drew a line to the image he had drawn and labelled it with *The Fair Assassin.*

'That's it, shift. Move, move, move, we have a twenty-hour window to get on with this before the press start poking their beaks in and fucking it all up for us.'

'Sarge, there's a couple of gaming and book shops that sometimes sell replicas, I'll get on to them, too.' Kapoor said, swinging his coat over his shoulder.

'You mean the graphic novel shop you and your mates hang out in?' Officer Smith teased him as they all departed for a few hour's hard graph.

Jack had one more thing to organise, though.

'Do you need to go back to the lab? Only, I could do with some help – it's a science thing.' He asked Aubrie before she could find her way back to what Jack often thought of as a cold dungeon.

'No, I guess not, what is it?'

Jack put the pen onto the table. 'You ok to drive? I'll explain   on   the   way.'

DILUTING THE ACHE

Aubrie put her hand on Jack's arm to stop him from getting out of the car as they arrived at the small, inconspicuous cottage in Glastonbury.

'Jack, please, you cannot be serious about all this, you cannot really believe in demons doing this?'

He felt annoyed with her, annoyed that she couldn't just believe him and come with him without asking questions, but that was why she was there, wasn't it? To provide a rational explanation for all of this.

'I don't know what I believe anymore, that's why I need you to come with me. I trust your judgment far more than my own. Just come with me, listen to what she has to say and tell me how she knows what she does, and we can put this to bed.'

Aubrie let go of his arm, now looking, if anything, like an angry mother.

'There is a murderer out there, Jack, and you want to drive around playing chase the ghosts? I thought you were better than this.'

Maybe she's right, maybe I am just running about chasing shadows because I don't know how to catch this person,' he thought.

'You're right, we don't have time to waste, we will just make sure that she isn't listening in on police communications and leave. How does that sound?'

He saw that as a safe halfway meeting of opinions, and was glad when she agreed without sending him too many daggers in her look.

The old-fashioned doorbell rang and after a couple of seconds the occupant's voice could be heard on the other side of the door.

She was talking to her cats.

'Get out of the way, Jasper, I don't know why you insist on sleeping on the doormat.' The door swung open and Mrs Keilty stood before them, looking completely unimpressed at their arrival.

'Mrs Keilty—' Jack began.

'Call me Florence, love, wipe your feet when you come in, won't you.' She turned her back on them and walked to the kitchen. 'I'll stick the kettle on.'

Jack diligently wiped his feet. 'We can't stay long, I just wanted to apologise for my outburst yesterday.'

The older woman reappeared in the doorway. 'Really? I assumed you were here to talk about the other woman who has been killed.' Her tone was flat and unapologetic. 'Milk no sugar, love?' she asked Aubrie.

Aubrie stuttered with surprise, 'Yes, how did you know?'

'I have a knack with tea, dear. Take a seat and I'll be through shortly.'

The pair of police officers were sat on the small sofa trying not to ruffle the protectors on the arms when Mrs Keilty returned with what Aubrie thought was a rather quaint tea trolley, judging by the cute smile she gave it.

The pot was covered with a tea cosy shaped just like the cottage they were sat in and a small plate of biscuits was on the shelf below.

'Sweet, isn't it? It was my mother's trolley for entertaining, and it never gets used anymore so I thought it would be a nice treat for us.'

'Thank you,' Jack and Aubrie both said in return for their cups of tea.

'Mrs Keilty, this is Dr Sellers, she is working with me on the murder investigation and I explained about our conversation yesterday.'

The older woman laughed. 'And she told you not to believe in such nonsense, I should imagine, and please, dear, call me Florence. Call me Mrs Keilty in my obituary and not before, if you please.'

She turned to Aubrie with a heart-warming smile that started in her cheeks and appeared to have no end.

'It's perfectly ok not to believe, dear, I wish I didn't, maybe that way they would leave me be, but for now I'm stuck with the bastards – pardon my French. But you are a doctor, and that is where your faith lies, in the science of it all. My faith stands on those boundaries we place upon ourselves, sometimes it's difficult to know which category I am going to fall in. But if you would like to speak to me about the second attack, I will tell you all I know, but I will not be questioned and I will not be harassed, not in my own home, is that understood?'

Aubrie nodded, she felt awfully like she had been reprimanded before doing anything wrong.

Mrs Keilty took a large bite of a digestive biscuit and waved her hand to Jack to encourage him to speak.

'Yes, right, well, as you already seem to know there has been a second attack, another young girl has been murdered, and we are investigating several avenues and leads but I wondered if you had any information that could help with our ongoing investigations?'

Jack cleared his throat, it felt uncomfortably foreign using protocol and diplomatic questioning, he'd much rather just say what he wanted to say and be done with it, and if Aubrie hadn't been there, he probably would have.

'I can tell you what I know, which, Detective, is that a young girl was choked then stabbed to death with the same weapon as before. It happened around one in the morning, I think, and was again in some woods but I'm not sure if was the same spot as before, but seeing as it was less than twenty-four hours after, I have assumed not. And that's what I know, which I should imagine is less than you. Is it not?'

Jack conceded and nodded to show as much.

'However, I could tell you what I saw instead, but I ask that you not question me, not question what I describe to you, but rather just accept that it is what happened.'

The room fell quiet, all three parties pondering what this may entail.

Aubrie broke the silence, she turned to look directly at Jack. 'I'm sorry, Jack, I don't think I can do this, all this quackery, it's ridiculous, and I don't want to be a part of it.'

If she had meant to offend the woman who was currently eating the last of her biscuits, it hadn't worked.

'I'm sorry, Mrs Keilty, but I suspect that you have been listening in to police communications on the radio equipment that Jack spotted last time he was here. Failing that, I think you may know someone who is working in or around the case who is feeding you very up-to-date information. Unless you can prove otherwise, I will be forced to report you and you will face questioning.'

Florence stood up and walked over to the where the recording equipment and other electrical objects sat behind the curtain.

She revealed it. 'This is over fifty years old and hasn't been used in more than thirty.'

The older woman picked up a wire. 'Look, it doesn't even have a plug on it, I used that for my hair curlers in the eighties. And as for having someone feeding me information, dear, I have no one, not a soul has visited me here in over three years, and now I've had two visits in as many days and been insulted as many times again. If you do not want to listen, then leave. If you do not wish to leave, then stop being so bloody narrow-minded for two seconds and listen.'

The woman's eyes looked old to Aubrie then, much older than her years should allow, and far more honest than ones she was used to. She knew that the way people looked was often misleading and charlatans spent years, sometimes decades, practicing at looking that innocent, but she still felt herself being fooled somewhat by them.

'An intelligent person knows that they know a lot, Doctor, a wise person realises that they know very little at all. In that respect, I am proud to claim myself as being very wise indeed. I only wish to help you, my dear.'

She dropped the cable and returned to her seat.

Jack took Aubrie by the hand, something he wasn't sure if he had ever done before.

'That lead we have about the murder weapon, it was Mrs Keilty here – sorry, Florence – who told me about it. It's the only thing we have to go on and it's not even my idea. We owe her the courtesy of listening, don't you think?'

The younger of the two women sighed. 'Jack, that game has been plastered everywhere, you probably picked it up subconsciously. And as for Mrs Keilty linking our murders to it, well, everyone has been discussing how games influence people to commit crimes, and it's a natural assumption.'

Jack nodded. 'You are probably right, nevertheless, it was with her help that we got this far. I'm willing to try anything to stop this maniac, aren't you?'

He felt guilty for manipulating her like that, but it was true that he would do anything, even if that meant selling his soul to the devil. He would recognise later that he had used his borderline personality disorder to push Aubrie in the direction that he had wanted, and perhaps that would be a sobering enough realisation to convince him to take his medication but right at this moment he didn't care.

'Fine, but I'm not doing a Ouija board or anything like

that.'

The old woman laughed. 'I can't contact the dead, my dear. People who say they can are crooks, preying on people's hopes and fleecing them.'

'You don't say,' Aubrie replied tartly.

'What I see is what they see, the demons, and what they see is what their host sees. It normally occurs at night, generally when I am sleeping or in a sort of dream state. You know those dreams you have that seem so real and after a moment or two real life kicks back in? Well, these images stay with me and they never leave. I need the room dark to help me concentrate, I need to recall every image, sensation, even smell if I'm to be of any use to you.'

She walked across to the windows, closing the curtains as she went.

Aubrie pulled out a notepad and wrote 'crazy woman' at the top, underlining it twice in full view of Jack.

Mrs Keilty sat very still, perched on the edge of the sofa, and closed her eyes and cleared her throat with an exaggerated cough for effect.

'I saw a woman, in the woods, as I said. Thicker shrubbery though, smaller trees, the edge of some playing fields or something like that, maybe.'

Aubrie scribbled down notes while rolling her eyes.

'Ok, let me get into this, one of my hands is full, it's holding the knife as before but I feel differently about it now, excited to use it, maybe. Yes, that's it, I'm excited. I can see her, too. She's walking straight towards me with a dog, stupid, yappy little thing scurrying along. Looks more like a big rat.'

Aubrie looked up quickly as the other woman's voice seemed to adopt a new cadence and tone. It wasn't a big change, just enough to suggest a different accent, or a younger age, maybe.

The pathologist scribbled down the small details, a new lease of life brought into her feelings about their current situation.

'I have to look directly at her, the outskirts of my vision aren't working, and my eyes feel different. There's a pressure around my head but I don't mind, it feels comforting and protective.'

Mrs Keilty took some deep breaths as if she had been exercising.

'I've grabbed her by the throat and I'm squeezing her, but I can't feel her skin. Why can't I feel her skin? Ok, I'm wearing gloves, new leather gloves, I can't feel her pulse like the other girl. She's unconscious now, I've squeezed the life out of her, she was weak, a rather pathetic creature. And so I stab her, nice and easy, smooth, like a fish through water.' She paused and caught her breath.

'I'm sorry, that's all I got, or that's all I can remember, at least. I don't know what you were hoping for, Detective. Like I said, I can only see what they see, so unless they look in a mirror or at something specific I can't give you a description,' Mrs Keilty confessed, her voice completely her own again.

Jack took a deep breath of air, he hadn't known what he had truly expected. Had he actually thought that she was going to be able to provide him with a profile?

'It's fine, Florence, if you can think of anything else, just give me a call. Can I borrow that?' Jack took the notebook from Aubrie and wrote down his number for her.

'Yes of course. You know that I see it as it happens, Detective, I can't predict it, and I can't help you to stop them from happening unless you catch them first.'

The police officers stood to leave.

'Maybe this was a waste of time, precious time even, while there is a killer out there looking for their next victim.'

'Detective O'Connor, before you go would you mind awfully putting a plug back on my radio equipment for me, see if the old girl is still running? I may be able to use it to help.'

Five minutes later and the pair were back in the car,

heading straight to the station.

'I'm sorry, Aubrie, it's the only lead we had, you've got to understand I had to follow it up.'

Jack was deflated, they hadn't learnt anything they didn't already know and worst of all he had dragged her away from the lab, and if there was any evidence to find it would most likely be on the bodies.

'Its fine, Jack, I know why you wanted to believe in that sort of thing, it's natural when you've lost people, especially the way that you did.'

If those words had been spoken by anyone else he would have broken their jaw, but he knew her intentions were as decent as they came.

But she was wrong, it had nothing to do with Jessica and Felicity's murders, or anything to do with catching their killer. And there it was, the real disgrace in it all. At no point had he thought about using the seemingly supernatural ability this woman had to help him catch their killer. Why not, why were they no longer his first thought? Had it been long enough now for it not to hurt like it once had, is that how grief worked? Did time water it down, diluting the ache in his heart?

'It wasn't a complete loss, Jack, she said he was wearing gloves, we didn't have any prints on the second body, it would make sense, don't you think?'

Jack knew that Aubrie didn't believe what she was saying, she was just trying to ease his burden.

'Its fine, I'll get her friends and family looked into. You're probably right, she's most likely getting inside information and coming to her own conclusions. Fuck, maybe she should be leading the investigation instead of me. She's doing a damn sight better job than me at the moment. Could you drop me off in Ashton? Need some air and to gather my thoughts.'

Aubrie wasn't happy about it, but she agreed, she'd clearly worked out that arguing with him was frivolous and a waste of both their time.

'Call me if you get anything, yeah?' he said as she drove off in the direction of the mortuary where the bodies were being   examined.

SLIPPED BETWEEN THE BARS

Jack walked some of the backstreets of Bristol, using the unusual architecture to distract himself from the horrors in his head. The biggest horror being that his luck had run out, he felt like a fraud with every investigation, as if luck had helped him to solve it, guesses surmised from his imagination.

Pictures of the bloodstained torsos, the glazed eyes looking out into nothingness, swam across his thoughts. What if he couldn't solve this, what if the murderer was smarter than him, smarter than all of them, smart enough to simply commit these atrocities and then stop and disappear?

The detective stopped at a convenience shop, picked up a small bottle of rum and added it to half a bottle of coke. He didn't know why but to think more clearly he always needed to stop thinking for a while first. The dull light of afternoon creeped in, greying the city.

'This is Bristol's true colour,' he thought.

He walked until he came to a self-storage facility. It had indoor storage rooms over four storeys and large shipping containers out the back on a plot of land. This is where he kept some of his most valuable possessions, ones that even he conceded would strike most people as worthless.

The security guard nodded him through and called out to let him know that a different colleague would be taking over from him shortly. Jack pulled back the large steel door to one of the storage containers, flicked on a set of lights that he had convinced one of the guards to hook up to the mains for him and walked over to a desk.

The large, industrial crate was full of memories, most of which hurt Jack, and he concluded that using these reinforced walls was the only way to keep them at bay. He had a large desk above which were dozens of pieces of paper, all held fast to the walls with magnets. There were paper cuttings, crime scene photos, notes, witness statements and small threads of string linking them all. This was Jack's most vicious unsolved case until late. It was that of his wife and daughter. This is where he would escape to when he was feeling strong or particularly macabre. He had lost count of the number of hours he had spent poring over the disgusting details. Each and every time his heart would break and he would poison his liver a little more.

Also in the lock up were innocuous household items. His daughter Felicity's bed lay on top of cardboard boxes, all the covers and sheets had been chewed away by mice, probably making a better bed for them than it would ever be for another person. In the corner, a pile of toys gathered dust, only the child's bike discernible from the mound, all of which disguised the family car behind.

It all lived here. Jack not having the heart to get rid of it or to use it meant it lived in a kind of limbo, somewhere between obsolete and existence.

Long swigs from the bottle calmed his nerves as he pored over the case notes, all of which he had paid for in cash. It had taken three attempts to find someone who had been working the case who was willing to risk everything by putting all of the evidence through the photocopier. He had some suspects, all of which had motive for destroying a copper's life, all of which had alibis, all of which had been questioned twice over. The guilt he felt for not solving this case outweighed any that he could feel for his current investigations. Perhaps that was why he was there, to escape the reality to something that was more important.

Deep down in his subconscious pits nothing mattered apart from finding the killer of his wife and daughter. Nothing was important, not really, not while he sat here with all this evidence pointing in contradictory directions.

For all intents and purposes it looked to be a crime of passion – he knew if he had been on the case the only person who would have really stood out as a suspect was himself.

He dropped his bottle, it hit his foot and skidded away from him. It took more effort than it should have done to bend down without falling over. He might live on a boat but those sea legs were alcohol induced.

A shadow appeared in the crack of the door, just above the bottom hinge. The crease of dull light from outside of the crate was now obscured, and just as suddenly it opened back up again. Someone had been watching him through the slim gap, and now their footsteps were sounding on the gravel, and they were quick.

Jack grabbed at something off the floor to use as a weapon and ran out into the evening air. He heard the person fleeing down behind another of the large metal storage units. Running after them, he couldn't help but bounce sideways off of the corrugated walls to keep himself upright as he navigated the sharp turns. He rounded a corner just in time to see the back of a black hoody take a left turning. He ran as fast as his legs would allow, the alcohol permitting him to recover long enough for the chase. Adrenaline was his fuel of choice and it powered him as he took sudden left and right-hand turns between the shipping containers, as if in stuck in a tin maze.

The assailant was trapped as they reached the tall, outer

fencing.

The detective was closing in on them when, all of a sudden, they slipped between the bars with ease.

By the time Jack reached the perimeter it was too late, they were gone, the dark-coloured clothing offering them the perfect camouflage as they disappeared into the long evening shadows.

Jack looked along the bottom rail of the fence. He found it, the one with a bolt missing, he pushed it and it gave way to the side. He could have squeezed himself through, but it really would have been a squeeze, and catching whoever it was now would be impossible. He knew the field just passed under the dual carriageway and it was normally frequented by junkies looking for somewhere discreet to take a hit.

He bent down and looked closer at the hole with the missing bolt. This was to catch his breath and also examine how long this entrance had been in use. The bolt lay on the floor, its rounded top was not something that a standard toolkit could have removed. The nut was missing, however, and the sharp edge left on the thread led him to conclude that it had actually been ground off.

It could just be the work of junkies, looking for something to rob and sell for their next bag of gear, but they weren't usually the type with the forethought to bring heavy-duty tools with them. He pondered this as he returned to his storage container. He entered it and opened one of the drawers to replace what he had picked up as a weapon. He hadn't noticed until he was returning it, but it had in fact been a torch. It was the metal naval torch that his grandfather had given him and he had in turn given to his daughter. She had been scared once while they had gone camping and only by telling her that it was Grandad's magic torch had he gotten her to go to sleep. It hadn't had any meaning before, now it needed to be put safe, something else to hide from himself until he was strong   enough   to   hold   it   again.

HAS PREVIOUS

The next morning brought a hangover but new hope for Jack. He could think clearer and his gut instinct was saying that today was the day for the case to move forward.

It had been static for twenty-four hours and that was too long. His memories from the night before were hazy at best, considered whether this was a kind of reboot for his brain, having it chemically switched off and on again.

He wasn't sure when he had become a cliché cop, with alcohol and family issues, but he was fully aware that he was verging on becoming a Columbo-esque character, and he couldn't care less.

As usual, he was the last in the incident room but, unlike usual, he was also the chirpiest, the life and soul of the investigation rather than the ball and chain that he felt like he usually was. His positivity was verging on mania, something the therapist had gone into great length about avoiding. The difficult thing with mania for him was recognising it, it was not that far removed from general happiness. So, in the past, once he actually realised that he was manic, it was normally too late and he was off spending money on things he neither needed nor wanted.

Now that being genuinely happy was out of the question, all he was left with was the reality he despised or the mania, so a brief window of calm amidst the depression was something to be nurtured.

He knew his therapist would never agree to it, but deciding to use the mania to encourage progression of any sorts was the obvious conclusion. It never lasted long in borderline personality disorder, it never quite reached psychosis – a fact that he had come to loathe, slipping away from everything for a while always sounded so appealing.

Jack tossed the pen in the air, spinning it enthusiastically, he could feel his energy pulsating into the room.

'So, where are we with the lead on the weapon then?' he asked the two officers that had been sent on the trail.

'Not brilliant, sarge, but we are getting there, narrowing down the possibilities.'

Officer Kapoor opened his notebook. 'You were right about old dodgy Dave, he did have some of these, but they were confiscated almost as soon as he got them. He thinks he sold one or two, but not to anyone matching our suspect's description. He bought them from a Polish gang working out of a car park near the centre, we're going to follow that up today.' He flipped a page and huffed loudly, already setting the tone for bleak news. 'Legal imports of this particular knife are a no go area, we asked two comic book shops about the products and *The Fair Assassin* official merchandise isn't going to be released here for another two weeks. It's been released in Japan, China and the States, however, so perhaps we can have a group of tech support going through eBay and all the usual avenues of buying in from them. Until we speak to the Poles, that's about as far as we can go for now. It's starting to seem like a very specific item, though, so finding out how it got into the city should just be a case of knocking on enough doors.'

Officer Peters cleared his throat. 'That Dave was civil

enough in the end, I gave him a hint that helping us would be in his best interest. I'm sure if we went through his business we could find something to pin on him, and I think he knows it.'

Jack scribbled some notes up on the wall beside the picture of the murder weapon. *Import, probably illegal.*

'Good work, lads, let's keep doing what we do, spread our net that way and see if we can snag anything. Watch out with that gang, if it's who I'm thinking of I've had previous with them, they don't take too kindly to us showing our faces down that way, bad for business. Right, what about CCTV, do we have anything worth writing home about there?'

Jack could hear his voice in his head, and it belonged to him, true enough, but the words were all wrong. He had never used the phrase 'worth writing home about' in his life, and he hadn't intended on turning into someone who only speaks in old-fashioned sayings just yet. He started to feel a hint of self-hatred creep in.

Just ignore it, Jack, we don't need that side of you, not now, not yet. You can drown your sorrows in self-pity and whisky later,' he told himself.

Officer Peters' hand shook slightly as he produced a list of names, and then another list. 'All the cars and their owners that were on camera within a five-mile radius between the hours specified on the first night.' He shook the other piece of paper. 'And this is a list from the second night. One name came up twice, a Mr A. Jeremy, I had a patrol car go to his house to pick him up, but he has no previous and is in his late seventies.'

Jack opened his mouth to move the investigation in another direction but, to his surprise, Peters spoke first.

'But I noticed that on one camera we weren't picking up all of the number plates, it had a two second time delay between pictures. So I went through each car individually and I got this.'

He pulled a third piece of paper out of his folder. 'It is

a 2003 Vauxhall Vectra using a spare wheel – one of those thin wheels that are designed for short distances.'

He pointed to the first picture, the rest of the room could see the car, the back of it with the temporary wheel on it and a number plate that was completely out of focus. 'This car then reappears on the second night, here.' He pointed to another picture of the car below, this time its plate clearly readable.

'It's the same car, both within two miles of each murder, each within an hour of the ETD of our victims. This car is owned by a Jonathan Thompson and, get this, he has previous for general assault, ABH, and he spent thirteen months inside for GBH that involved a woman – his wife.'

The young woman officer, Laurel Smith, spoke next, sounding harassed. 'Did you say Jonathan Thompson? Shit.' She picked up her iPad and hurriedly rushed through documents on it. 'You were right, sarge, he was at the scene yesterday, took down his details, even took a picture of his driving licence for ID. He matched our suspect's description except for the shoe size, right cocky bastard he was, even tried it on.'

Jack stopped flipping the pen for a moment. Was it this simple, after such a meticulous crime scene, could he really have been this stupid?

'But he has previous, right?' Jack asked Peters.

'Right, sarge. A list as long as your … well, as long as your whatsit.'

'So why didn't his prints come back positive for a match? Why was there no evidence at the crime scene? Something isn't right, by all means go and get him, and go in hard. I want this wife beater to know we are serious, but something doesn't quite taste right in the water here.'

Officer Kapoor gathered his things. 'I'll stick on the weapon, sarge, we need it if we want to tie this to Thompson. Maybe he had an accomplice, maybe the handprint was someone off record.'

'What, no criminal past whatsoever, straight into multiple murder? Doesn't sound right to me.'

'Maybe they rapped before and never got caught. Maybe Thompson coerced them into it. Look, I don't know, sarge, but it feels like we are getting somewhere.'

All the officers got up and left, leaving Jack alone in the room.

'Getting somewhere the murderer wants us to be, maybe.'

He looked over the board, at the pieces of evidence. They looked like pieces of unsolved jigsaw puzzles, only he wasn't even sure if they made up the same picture.

'Sir?' Officer Smith re-entered the room. 'Just got a message from the front desk, there's a Mrs Keilty here to see you.'

'Oh Jesus. Ok, thanks. Hang on, before you go, could you get a message to Dr Sellers to meet me and Mrs Keilty?'

Jack left what he now considered to be the room of death, the place inhabited by young, murdered women, and headed towards the front desk.

'Jack, in here, now.'

He knew he shouldn't have gone that way, it was the shortest route but it went directly past DCSI McQuade's office.

He closed the door behind him. He couldn't help noticing that the blinds had already been shut. Was that from the last DI in here who had received a grilling, or some foresight for his arrival?

'Jack, I'm calling a press conference for tomorrow. I'm sorry, you had more than enough time and you have no sound leads. My hands are tied on this, I hope you understand.'

Jack's insides twisted with a childlike rebellion, but on the surface he hid it.

'Ma'am, with all due respect we have a lead and—'

McQuade laughed. 'All due respect? You haven't respected me for one moment these last couple of years, and I let you get away with it on the most part. And as for calling me ma'am, I'm not the Queen, so don't do it, it sounds petulant, especially coming from you. It's going to be tomorrow afternoon, the parents of the two girls will be there and I need to know that you can behave yourself.'

Jack looked down at a nonspecific coffee stain on the already brown carpet, it was futile to argue, and especially when his only current lead couldn't even convince him it was their man.

'I'll do my best. We do have a couple of strong leads, though, one on the murder weapon and one a suspect on CCTV on both nights.'

McQuade smiled, it looked so out of place even Jack felt uncomfortable at its appearance.

'Well then, you might even catch them before we need to let the press get their greasy paws on it. Go, do detective work, tick off the boxes until there's only one left, and that's where you'll find them.'

'That sounded almost poetic, ma'am.'

'Fuck off, Jack.'

Jack got to the front desk and the police officer there pointed him in the direction of a small room just off the reception. Inside sat Mrs Keilty, with what Jack referred to as an OAP shopping trolley and Aubrie, with what Jack referred to as a face like thunder.

'An emergency, Jack, Officer Smith said you said it was an emergency! This here,' she pointed her finger at the entire room and settled it on the old woman, 'is not a bloody emergency, Jack.'

'Calm down, you have to be my voice of reason here, so get your head reasonable.'

The doctor blew hair from her face, it had become untidy with her frantic anger at him.

Jack moved past her and shook Mrs Keilty's hand. 'Nice to see you again, Mrs Keilty.'

'It's Florence, dear, I won't tell you again. Sorry if I have come at a bad time.'

She looked over his shoulder at Aubrie, who was sporting a frustrated shade of red beneath the freckles on her cheek.

'It's just a stressful time for us here, with the murders and what not. Anyway, what can I help you with?'

Jack didn't sit down, he was hoping that this was going to be a short conversation, if not only to save him from the wrath of Aubrie Sellers. The old woman pulled the radio equipment that had been stored, until recently, under her stairs from her trolley and put it on the coffee table.

'It's about this, you might want to sit down, dear, mine's   white   with   two   sugars.'

COME AND GET ME

Jack placed three plastic cups of tea on the table. Aubrie now sat opposite Mrs Keilty, arms folded and looking up at the ceiling at something interesting that only she could see.

'Ok, Mrs Keilty, can you please tell us why you are here, I do have a double murder case to be getting on with, which I know you are fully aware of.'

The old woman sipped her tea and screwed up her face, she placed it back down on the table at a distance that was out of comfortable reach.

'Have you heard of EVP, Detective?'

Aubrie huffed with indignation.

Jack ignored her and replied, 'No, Mrs Keilty, would you care to enlighten me?'

'Well, Detective O'Connor, EVP stands for "electronic voice phenomenon", it was first discovered in the ghostly community around the nineteen seventies. Well, like I said before, I don't believe in any hocus pocus but—'

Dr Sellers couldn't hold herself back any longer, 'Mrs Keilty, EVP isn't hocus pocus, it's hocus *bogus*. The most convincing story of EVP being used was in the eighties by a man called William O'Neil.' She turned and addressed Jack with the facts. 'He claimed to have a built a machine that he could use to communicate with the dead. The machine would only work with him controlling it as it was claimed his "mediumistic capabilities" are what enabled it to work. He even held two-way conversations with a deceased scientist. And do you know what it turned out to be? Well, I will tell you, it turned out that he was a bloody good ventriloquist using an electronic voice box. I'm sorry, Florence,' the sudden address of the women so informally took Jack back for a second, he then realised that she was trying to appeal to the woman's better nature, 'but there is not one shred of evidence that ghosts or spirits can communicate through the white noise or static on a radio. Jack, we have work to do, shouldn't we leave this now?'

Mrs Keilty nodded. 'No, I agree, no dead person can speak from beyond the grave, dear. You know as well as I do once you are dead, you are dead and there's no escaping that. But when I started getting my ...' the old woman searched for the correct word for the situation, '... *visions* well, I thought I would give it a shot, you know, an "it couldn't hurt" type of moment. Every once in a while I would pick up a voice, nothing that distinct and more often than not I couldn't actually make out what they were saying. But, once or twice, there were words I could make out. Well, anyway, I gave it up after a few years and that's when I put this damn thing under the stairs.'

Jack nodded agreeably but he couldn't tell for the life of him where this conversation was going, if anywhere at all.

'So why have you brought it down today?'

'Well, I thought I would give it one last go before chucking it out, and ...' She chewed her top lip uncomfortably. 'There is something you need to hear.'

Jack called through for someone from tech support to meet them. He couldn't use anyone from his team – they already thought of him as being close to crazy, this would surely get them looking for a straitjacket.

A young guy met them. Jack knew that he must have

been new due to the fact that he was at work and was still smiling.

'What can I do you for, boss?' he asked as he started unpacking his laptop and a mess of cables that looked like a mass of snakes all tied together.

Jack slid the radio over to him. 'We have a recording on this, can you play it? And can you identify how it may have got on there?'

The man that Jack felt more comfortable thinking of as a young teenager whistled a long note enthusiastically.

'I genuinely don't know, this should be fun. I mean, once I get it transferred to the computer I have software that'll identify how it was recorded, some of which I designed myself, but …' he spun the old radio around and then back again and ejected the tiny cassette tape from its holder. 'This may take a few minutes.'

The young man started untangling the wires and looked at the ends of them, all of which had different connectors. He inspected the back of the machine again.

'It's pretty basic so the quality is going to be affected, I may be able to render it a little.'

Jack sat beside him. 'Just do what you can.'

'Yes, boss.'

The laptop fired up and, even to Jack with his minimal knowledge of anything with microchips, it was obvious that this particular bit of kit had been customised.

'Well, let's keep it simple for the minute, I'll record it straight off of the auxiliary port here, straight into a sound recognition software program and see what we have.'

'It's about a minute in,' Mrs Keilty told them through a mouthful of hard boiled sweet.

Aubrie sat down on the other side of the tech guy – even if she didn't believe it to be true, she couldn't help but be intrigued.

'Yes, miss,' the young man said, in mock student-to-teacher tones.

'Well, he may even still be at school,' Jack thought to

himself, but he was none the less impressed with the speed that windows opened and closed on the screen in front of him. The detective could type a letter and make a report on a computer and that was all he ever needed. If the force had wanted a computer whiz running his department then they should have given the job to someone else.

The man's fingers stopped tapping the keys, he flexed them together and managed to get three or four good cracks from his knuckles.

'Just recording now, we'll give it ninety seconds, see what we've got, then have a play around with it and see if we can't clean it up.'

He stopped the recording. 'Yeah, there is definitely something there, look at the sound waves at fifty-two seconds.' He pointed to a line on the screen that had spiked, and then hit play.

After a couple of seconds of static, a low mumble came in, a voice-like sound muttering, like an old man speaking not quite under his breath.

'What did that say?' Jack asked, looking at Aubrie.

The tech guy spoke, not realising the question hadn't actually been intended for him, 'Sounded like it said Jack to me. I mean the word Jack, not as in it said jack all.'

'I know what you meant, can we get it a little clearer?' Jack asked the other man.

'Sure, yeah, volume up, background noise down and …' He pressed play again,

and again, a voice could be heard speaking. It was definitely male and definitely speaking English, but it just wasn't quite clear enough to be audible.

'Hang on, wait there, I'll take what we've got, put it through a scrubbing program I've got, bear with me two seconds, and …'

A small box appeared on the screen.

Scrubbing 16%, Scrubbing 38%, Scrubbing 71%, Complete, Importing

'Right, it's done. Ready?' the young man said, confident

in his triumph.

No one answered. Instead, Jack leant over and pressed the play button.

'Hey, that was my bit!' the tech guy protested, but as soon as he did the voice from the computer kicked in.

This time it was very clear, very definitely audible and seemed to speak directly to Jack.

'Detective, are you there? Come and get me, Jack.'

And then the machine went quiet.

'Wow, creepy.' The tech guy blew after speaking as if trying to expel what he had just heard.

Jack looked at Aubrie and then back to the young man. 'How was it recorded?'

The young man looked through a page of data, his fingers flowing effortlessly across his keyboard like tree branches in a turbulent breeze.

'Well, with this old stuff it's tricky. You see, there isn't a computer trail, but as far as I can see it was just your average voice recording, with a mic or something. Hang on, was this recorded on this machine?'

All three looked to Mrs Keilty, who had now removed some knitting from her bag and was halfway through what looked like a baby's cardigan.

'What? Oh, yes, dear, I just pressed record and let the tape run through, and then when I listened again there were those noises.'

'Why, what difference does it make?' Jack asked.

The man looked closely at the machine and then at the old woman. 'Do you know how microphones work?'

'You speak into them and sing into them – not that I've ever sung into one, not my thing, all that karaoke and stuff …' the old woman trailed off when the young man turned his back on her.

'There's only a headphone port on here and speaker connectors. Now, there is a way of turning the headphones into what, essentially, is a microphone, but only if you know what you are doing. Other than that, I don't know how she could have recorded it. If it was a weak radio signal there would be more or less static through the tape, but there isn't, the whole thing stays completely level; even through the speech the static doesn't increase or decrease. I'm almost certain it isn't an external signal.'

Aubrie looked closely at the screen. 'Are you sure?'

The man laughed. 'No, bearing in mind this radio is three times as old as me. But what I also noticed is that it doesn't have an aerial, no antenna at all. Now, is this as weird as I'm starting to think it is? Because I don't mind telling you it's a bit out of my pay grade if it is.'

Jack patted him reassuringly on the back.

'That's brilliant work, help Mrs Keilty to pack it away, will you. Mrs Keilty, thank you very much, are you ok to see yourself home? Only I have a mountain of work to do and a pile of paperwork bigger than that.'

Jack and Aubrie walked out of the room and down the hall, he could feel that she was waiting until they were out of earshot of the room to speak.

Away from the main body of the station, she grabbed his arm.

'Jack, that was strange, I'll admit, but there's—'

Jack pulled his arm away from her grip forcefully. 'I know, a hundred explanations for it. The most obvious being that that little old lady is an evil technological genius who just wants to make things difficult. But she isn't, and don't ask me how I know I just do. And I know what you're thinking, it's some Munchausen thing where she wants to be a part of the investigation for the attention but it's not that either. Christ, she was in her own little world most of the time, let alone trying to impose herself into ours.'

'Jack,' Aubrie sounded wounded, almost, defeated.

Jack shook his head, he knew what she was going to say, he always did.

'It's fine, it isn't helping the case. All I want to do now

is catch this guy, demon or no demon. I'll forget it, for now. Just don't fight me on this anymore, please, just stick to the case with me.'

She nodded and held his arm again. Jack liked the fact that his outbursts never scared her away, he liked that she was not afraid to stay within the firing zone. He knew he would feel guilty in the long run about his behaviour. She was the only person he cared enough about to feel guilty for.

'When was the last time you ate?' she asked him with a heart-warming smile.

Jack thought hard, the question had him off balance momentarily.

'This morning I had a packet of bourbon biscuits.'

'Come on, you've got a tough afternoon ahead of you, lets grab a meal and talk about anything but work, just for half an hour or so. Yeah?'

He didn't have a good enough excuse not to agree and, in truth, his stomach had been objecting most of the day to the fasting.

Aubrie led Jack across the town centre and down through some of the old lanes near the Christmas Steps to a fish and chip restaurant. The buildings there were a small part of old, uncompromising, crooked beauty in an otherwise concrete area.

'I've been told by a colleague these are some of the best fish and chips in Bristol – we were checking the contents of someone's stomach at the time and found a couple of fish bones,' she told him, laughing at his face as he unwrapped the paper.

'Don't worry, it wasn't the fish that had done it, it was the infection in his lungs. So, you're a cod man, are you?'

Jack used his small wooden fork to prod at a bit of fish. 'Yeah. Been a while, though, since I've had any. Bit of treat, to be honest.' He faked interest in the mundane conversation, it was easier than trying to speak about the one hundred and one thoughts currently all jockeying for first place in his mind. 'And you are a battered sausage kind of gal, I see.'

She laughed softly and placed a large piece of food in her mouth.

Jack threw away the thoughts in his head for a minute and observed their surroundings. They sat on a bench outside a pub. The building itself leaned in so many different directions, in truth it was a feat of engineering genius that it still stood. He remembered drinking in there a couple of times when he had first joined the force. The tiny spaces inside were better geared towards romantic couples having a quiet drink rather than the rowdy group of coppers after twelve-hour shifts that it had been subjected to. But the bar staff never complained and the drinks had been well-priced for being so close to the centre. What a different person he had been then, full of hopes, dreams and ambition. And now, well, he had achieved those ambitions without even trying and he no longer cared.

'Even Bristol has its beautiful parts, you know? I know we only see the ugly parts for a lot of the time, but it doesn't hurt to remember the good parts when we get a chance, or visit them once in a while,' Aubrie said softly.

Jack had a feeling that Aubrie was not just talking about the city, he recognised the parallel with life. Maybe she was right, maybe spending so much time in the bowels of life could make you feel sick of it all. She was right about beauty, at least. He wasn't blind, he knew what all the other officers said about her and she was beautiful and kind and she had brains to spare. But this was him now, alone was better, and alone was safe and reliable, especially in a world that could be so desolate and cold. Even if it wasn't true for the rest of the population, it was true enough in his world that he couldn't drag anyone else into it, it wouldn't be fair.

A chip hit him between the eyes and fell onto his lap,

Aubrie laughed heartily and nearly choked on her food.

'Cheer up, Mr serious,' she said to him. Her infectious smile warmed Jack's heart. He skewered a small piece of fish onto his fork and pulled it back, making a mini trebuchet. He was just about to fire when his phone vibrated in his pocket, and he dropped his missile onto his lap also.

Aubrie laughed once more as he pulled the ringing phone from his pocket.

'Saved by the bell, you were lucky,' he told her, sliding his finger across the screen and answering. 'O'Connor.'

'Yes, I am lucky,' she said under her breath.

She smiled at Jack, who was now engrossed in his conversation.

'Ok, sure, I'll be there in ten minutes.' He slid the electronic device into his breast pocket. 'They've brought in my suspects.'

Aubrie's eyebrows lifted. 'Suspects, more than one then?'

'Well, one is a seventy-something-year-old man who served in the armed forces with no previous convictions, and the other is a known woman beater, emphasis on the known, because he's a violent bloody idiot. Not what you would call a calculated, intelligent killer, but nonetheless he fits the bill better than anyone else we've got.'

Jack shovelled a few chips into his cheeks and stood to leave. Aubrie joined him but decided to carry her meal with her to eat on the way.

'Oh, Jack, I found something on the second victim. Within the stab wounds I found some very small stone particles. Only in the wounds, though, and they don't match anything from the locations of the victims.'

Jack closed his eyes, it may have been confusing to someone analysing the facts, these small foreign bodies appearing out of nowhere, but not to him. Not when the murderer's psyche was slowing revealing itself to him.

'Let me guess, a sedimentary type of stone, possible wet

or covered in an oil?'

The pathologist literally stopped in her tracks. 'How could you possibly know that? Yes, they were damp and not from blood or other bodily fluids, but an oily substance, like you said. Seriously, Jack, how did you know that?'

'The conflict escalation in murders theory. We assumed that it would be the violence, you know, more stab wounds, more frenzied. But not our murderer. It seemed like it was going backwards, almost, but there was one area of intensification, and that was efficiency. The stone particles are from some kind of whetstone. Whet meaning to sharpen – he sharpened the weapon, it was too blunt, he needed to kill better.' Jack turned to look at Aubrie. 'No, not kill better, to be a better killer. That's why he did it right under our noses, it was a better kill than before, and you can't deny that.'

GET ME MY LAWYER

Jack entered a small room with a heavy locked door that slammed convincingly behind him. Officer Smith was already sat at the desk opposite the frail-looking man.

Jack put his cup of coffee down, placed a thin, cardboard folder on the table and sat down.

'Mr Arnold Jeremy, how are you? Would you like a drink?'

The old man shook his head, clearly nervous to be sat opposite two police officers. 'No, thank you, this young lady here got me a cup of tea when I arrived.'

Jack opened the folder, there was only one piece of paper contained.

'Yes, Officer Smith is good like that. Has she informed you of why you are here?'

The old man nodded. 'My car was on that close network tele thingy when those girls were murdered.'

Jack expelled a large lungful of air.

'Does everyone know about these murders, is there any point doing an appeal when everyone and their dog already knows exactly what's happened?'

Jack refocused. 'Yes, Mr Jeremy, that's correct. Now, I would like to ask you a few questions—'

But Jack didn't get a chance.

The old man started speaking in short, panicked sentences.

'I'm sorry, I know I shouldn't have done it. But times are so hard, and my pension doesn't cover it anymore. I'm sorry, I was just trying to provide for my wife, she has dementia so I can only go out at night, I'm looking after her all day otherwise.'

Jack raised his hands to calm the old man. 'Whoa, whoa, whoa, Mr Jeremy, calm down. What were you doing on those nights? Let's start with that.'

The old man looked right at the two officers, one after another, clearly terrified of the consequences of his confession.

'Mr Jeremy, *Arnold*, it's fine, you won't be in trouble if you just explain what you were doing. We can help you,' the female officer reassured him.

His jaw twitched and his hands pulled his flat cap from his head, wringing it like a naughty Victorian school boy might.

He finally spoke. 'I was taxi driving, just a few trips a night, just to make up some grocery money, you know. I know I shouldn't have done it, but when you don't have money you just have to do these things sometimes. My wife is so ill now I'm doing everything.'

Jack closed the folder. 'Mr Jeremy, you served for your country, you look after your poorly wife, you deserve better treatment than this. Officer Smith, get this man a warm meal, give him a hundred pounds from petty cash and the help and support he needs. Speak to social services about what he is entitled to and get it sorted fast. As for you, Arnold, no more late-night taxi driving, you're too long in the tooth for that sort of stuff. It's a rough place out there, you stay home and spend some quality time with your wife, and that's an order.'

Jack stood, picked up the folder, threw it into the bin and headed for the door.

'Excuse me, sir,' the old man called for his attention.

He promptly stood up and saluted Jack.

The police officer smiled and left the room. He headed for the toilets before going to the next interview.

Jack locked himself in a cubicle and sat on the unopened toilet seat. His heart thumped inside his chest. The world was offering up one of his emotional days, the ones where love could be seen all around him and it tasted like a sharp reminder of what he once had, what he had cherished all those years before. The old man he had just met was so frail, so underweight, and it was in no doubt due to the fact that he was putting his wife's needs before his own. To spend your whole life loving someone, even once their mind was gone, how could someone do that?

Jacks eyes filled with tears, and the small, salty droplets ran to his mouth. He knew this was part of his borderline personality disorder, it would give him these enlightened days, sometimes, when every sense was heightened and uncontrollable. Music became the sound the world would make, rain became a cool reminder of being alive and the sun beating down on his skin was euphoria.

Even though Jack knew it was all in his head, knowing something did not automatically make it easy to control. He punched the toilet roll holder, cracking the plastic case, and started giving himself a pep talk.

This isn't the Jack you need to be today, you have a possible murderer in the next room and you need to deal with him, you need to knock him off his guard and get him to confess, or at least get him to admit he's an evil git, that way you can get the truth out of him. Come on, Jack, pull yourself together, for god's sake.'

He took long, rhythmic breaths, calming himself from the inside out, and left the toilets for the second interview room.

The suspect was a large man, indeed fitting their description so far. He was rocking back and forth confidently on his chair. His folder was already on the table behind which Officer Nitin Kapoor sat, reading it.

The officer closed the folder. 'Sarge. I haven't started yet, he's been read his rights, just waiting for you.'

'Good man, how did the arrest go?' Jack asked him.

The scoff from the large man on the other side of the room indicated his opinion of it.

'As smooth as can be expected, sarge. Mr Thompson here became very familiar with Officer Edmonds.'

Jack allowed himself a small chuckle; it was fake, but it was enough to have the desired effect on the man waiting to be interrogated.

'Getting him riled up will be easy,' Jack thought. And he knew from experience that getting someone angry was a much easier and quicker route to the truth than trying to befriend them.

He sat slowly and adjusted his seat several times before hitting the record button on the tape recorder, all of which was to add some more weight to the resentment the large man was already feeling.

'The date is September the twelfth, the time, two fifteen PM. Interview with Mr John Thompson, Detective Superintendent O'Connor and Officer Kapoor present. My name is Detective O'Connor, you have obviously waived your right to have a lawyer present, any reason for that?'

The man crossed his arms and rolled his eyes.

That's it, have total contempt for me, you piece of dirt, I'll reel you in anyway, don't you worry.' Jack smiled sweetly at the suspect, leaving that silence between them, the kind that screamed 'fill me'.

'Because I don't need one,' the man spoke finally, his thick Bristolian accent extending the vowels here and there and dropping the odd consonant. 'I only have one when I'm guilty of something, they get you out of right tricky spots, them weasels.'

Thick as pig's muck, he's just admitted on tape that he only has a lawyer present when he's guilty, that'll come back to haunt him.'

'That's fine by us,' Kapoor said, making a note on a

piece of paper.

Jack pulled the man's file towards him and opened it, he skim-read a few pages, giving a few small whistle noises and exaggerated humming, showing that he was thoroughly entertained by the rap sheet.

'What an interesting past you have had, Mr Thompson. A prison stint, community service – a hundred and seventy-eight hours, no less. You have even punched a police horse, well, that is something. I was wondering, Mr Thompson, all this history here, all this violence, you seem to be such an angry man. How angry can you get, Mr Thompson, hmm? I wonder if you could get angry enough to hit me, Mr Thompson, finally rise to the challenge of picking on someone your own size. Well, almost your own size,' Jack said, patting his considerably smaller stomach.

The suspect's demeanour didn't falter, his calm exterior remained as cool and collected as ever, and his smile was just as icy.

'I do like a challenge, Detective, perhaps under different circumstances we can see how it might pan out,' the man replied, tipping his weight back on the chair again.

Jack grinned, perhaps they would, only he wouldn't be a punching bag like the rest of them. The fight in this dog was to the death, something John Thompson had not experienced before.

'Oh good, I am glad to hear that, I thought it might only be women and animals you enjoy knocking about.'

The chair rocked forward and the two front legs slammed into the concrete floor. 'Cheap shot, Detective, very cheap. I'll let you have that one, for now. So, why am I here then? Your lot finished rounding up all the celebrity rapists from the seventies?'

Was that a chink in his armour? Is that what those women did, questioned his manhood, questioned his superiority?' Jack wondered as he took in the man's aura.

'Murder, two accounts, two women. I don't think you did it. But what I think doesn't count for much – the evidence does, so I'll go by that. Here, Mr Thompson, is this your car, heading away from the crime scene, just minutes after the first murder took place? And here again, look, can't quite see your number plate in this one but, as you can see from this wheel here, it is clearly your car, oh, and it's heading away from our other crime scene within an hour of the crime. Does anyone else have access to your car, Mr Thompson? Or is this you driving?'

Jack had given him an out. Given him the chance to say it wasn't him driving.

'Let's see how quick you can think on your feet, then. Who are you going to say was driving?'

The large detainee looked closely at the pictures and pushed them away.

'Yeah, I was driving it. Driving isn't a crime so you'll have to do better than that, mate.' His reply was straight, not arrogant, and not lying either. This was a new one.

'Looks more like fleeing than driving to me, sarge,' Kapoor joined in, he also knew shaking this particular tree was bound to loosen something.

The man shrugged and looked around the room idly.

'Right, ok, I get it, you didn't want a lawyer because you're innocent, so why not just explain what you were doing in these areas, have an alibi to back it up and then we can all get on with our lives,' Jack said, closing his folder and resting his hands on top of it. 'I know you didn't do it, you know you didn't do it, but I have an entire force here that says you did; they'll find some evidence on you eventually unless you give me something, John.'

The man looked as though he was considering this option. 'Second thoughts, get me my lawyer.'

Jack's head and hopes dropped, this going quickly and smoothly was now out of the question.

'This interview is being concluded at,' he checked his watch, 'two twenty PM exactly.' He switched off the recording   machine.

PIECE OF CRAP

The two officers left the man alone in the room, his temperament still that of someone who was waiting for a bus and was only mildly disappointed at its lateness.

'You don't think he did it, sarge, do you?'

Jack sighed with frustration. 'Our killer is clever, so far smarter than us. Get a warrant and search his home, he's hiding something for sure, but no, I don't think he's our murderer. I mean, come on, the guy's an idiot. No, he's worse. He's a gloating idiot. Get him in a cell and give some food, make sure its salad and couscous or something like that.'

Officer Kapoor looked baffled. 'Why, sarge?'

'Our man in there looks like he likes a meal or three, get him hungry and you'll get him uncomfortable – he'll confess to whatever we ask him to then.'

The younger officer looked uncomfortable at this suggestion.

'Don't worry, I don't want to fit him up, I just want him out of this investigation quickly, he's muddying the waters at the moment.'

Officer Kapoor allowed a small laugh to ease the moment back into regulated territory.

'You take policing to another level, sarge, you always do.'

Jack was momentarily paralysed at that, long after the other policeman had walked away and the sound of him barking orders into the radio had died out, Jack still remained rooted to the spot.

'Another level, is that what I'm doing, taking it to another level each time?'

Officer Peters turned the corner and looked pleased to see his superior for once. 'Sarge, how did you get on? Did he do it?'

Jack didn't even hear him, he just about acknowledged the man in front of him. 'What? No, no he didn't. Can you get me one of the confiscated knives? The murder weapon, I mean. You said that dodgy Dave had them taken from the shop, right?'

Officer Peters nodded

'Good, I want to get a feel for it. Get it here by tomorrow morning, the afternoon is no good, I've got a press conference to assist with. Good man.' He walked away, he didn't want an answer, just for it to be done with no exception.

That afternoon found Jack in enemy territory, or at least he saw it that way. Hordes of shoppers passed him and surged with such ferocity he considered that perhaps his riot gear wouldn't have gone amiss. His police ID always made a slight sticking noise when he opened it due to the fact that it was rarely used. It was as good as the day it was printed and helped him to jump queues – this particular one was at least twenty teenage boys long. The store clerk found Jack's goods for him and was particularly amused at the way they were asked for. Apparently, it was considered uncouth to ask for a particular computer game followed by 'one of those bloody expensive machines to play it on.'

They took his money all the same and didn't even

complain at his swearing when he was informed of the total price. Between navigating the consumers and the afternoon traffic, the night sky now wore its dull purple colours and Jack knew he was in for another cold night on the boat.

Jack hadn't realised when buying the portable house just quite how cold it was going to be, so much so that he had even considered a onesie one particularly cold winter night. The image of him standing in something so ridiculous was nauseating even to him, a man whose wardrobe consisted of the boat floor, and sniffing the items of clothing was the only discernible way of telling if they were clean enough to wear or not.

He pulled up at the docks and grabbed his new console from the boot, thinking about how it was too light to be worth the money he had just coughed up for it and that he should at least be able to drive it for that sort of money as he slammed the boot shut.

'Does this mean I need contents insurance now?' he asked himself as he locked the car, nearly dropping his shopping in a puddle. Maybe he should upgrade to a newer car, for the central locking alone.

'Detective? Detective O'Connor?' a young voice called him, it sounded feminine but not quite.

He looked around to see a male, somewhere between a boy, a man and a good meal. He was runty and his clothes hung off him like one of those 'after' photos of a successful weight loss programme member. It was a shock to be addressed here, at his home, especially so politely – the odd paparazzi would find him when he was in the news for one of his usual noteworthy escapades, but this young man was definitely not one of them.

'Who's asking?' Jack replied in his usual kneejerk way. He looked around to see which one of the 'ups' this was – a wind up or a set up.

'Sorry, you probably don't recognise me, I was a little worse for wear last time you saw me,' the young lad said.

Jack searched his mind, hoping that this wasn't one of those 'you're my long-lost daddy' moments.

'Sorry, kid, you've got the wrong person.'

The skinny kid rushed forward to stop Jack from walking down the gangplank to his boat. 'No, the other night – well, actually, it was morning – I was at the club on Gloucester Road. You put me in a taxi and paid for it.'

His face became familiar. 'Oh yeah, the kid with the Nirvana t-shirt, I remember you. You got home ok then, good. Now, I know I don't look it, but I'm actually quite busy.'

'Is that with them dead girls?' the boy asked keenly.

For fuck's sake, is nothing sacred in this city?'

'I can't say. Anyway, good to see you again.'

The boy looked scorned. 'I was just giving you your money back for the taxi. Here, I've only got fifteen pound, I don't know if that covers it.'

Jack turned back to face him and placed his bags on the floor, he took the money from the kid, turned it over to examine both sides and handed it back.

'No, it's not mine, I've never seen it before. How the hell did you find me, anyway?' the detective said, handing back the notes.

The boy in front of Jack now looked guilty, far more so than anyone else he had seen that day.

'I went back to the club. The barman told me what happened cos I sort of blacked out, he told me your name, so I went to the library and looked you up. I found an address for you, so I went there and the tenants were there and they told me you lived on a boat. So I asked at the marina office and they pointed me down here and said you would be driving an old piece of crap car, and then I saw you pull up.'

Jack gestured that he had the gist of it. 'Alright, well, there is no accounting for taste. It's a classic, actually, what would they know about classic cars anyway? And you thought you would come all this way just to give me some money back, did you?'

The young man looked at his feet. 'No one's ever helped me like that before so I wanted to say thanks. I brought pizza with me.' He pointed at a bench where two pizza boxes lay.

Jack looked from the boy to his shopping, to the boxes and then at his boat.

'I'm probably going to live to regret this, but, do you know how to set up a PlayStation thing?'

The boy nodded in response.

'Fine, grab the food and give me a hand with this, and then   you   have   to   go.   Got   it?'

COMPLETE, BEGIN GETAWAY

Jack sat on the step at the end of his canal boat, watching as the skinny kid disappeared behind his TV. After exclaiming how cool it was to live on a boat more times than Jack had managed to count, the young lad began setting up the new PlayStation.

'So, what do I call you anyway?' Jack asked him while kicking off his work shoes.

The kid, as Jack had been calling him in his head, pushed the TV back into place, switched on the console and sat on the small sofa opposite.

'My name's Daniel, you can call me Danny, though, if you want. Right, here we go, you don't seem to have Wi-Fi so we'll skip all this bit, and you just want that game on, right?'

Jack lifted a lid on the one of the pizza boxes. 'Daniel will be fine, I think.' He didn't want the kid to get too comfortable. 'Yeah, just the game, none of that online gaming crap.'

The old man, as he was now calling himself in his head, lifted a slice of pizza out and took a huge bite. His stomach grumbled gladly and his taste buds thanked him for providing something that wasn't designed for burning them off.

'What the hell is on this?' Jack spoke with a mouth full of pizza, bad manners, he knew, but thankfully he wasn't this kid's dad so far as he knew, so what did it matter?

Danny smiled. 'I work at the pizza place and it's my own invention. The sauce is a mix of BBQ and sweet chilli and it has ten different kinds of meat on it. Don't you like it? Oh, yeah, your tenants told me to tell you something. They're moving out tomorrow and you haven't contacted them about keys or anything.'

Jack tried to reply but he had just taken another huge bite. 'Oh, crap, yeah, forgot about that.'

Then the ten different meats dawned on him. He wasn't even sure if he could name ten different meats. By the time he had thought of five, one of which was black pudding, he was on his second slice. The game loaded and the beginning credits started to play.

They showed a petite Japanese woman slaying around thirty men dressed in suits, all of whom were attacking her ineptly, and then it switched to the home screen.

Danny's fingers moved the joy sticks around the screen and clicked *Start*.

'You have to choose your character first. Look here, you press left and right and they switch.' The kid tried to hand the controller to the old man but his hands were full with pizza and a bottle of open beer he had just found tucked away in a corner.

'You do it, I'll just break the damn thing.'

The boy smiled and turned back to the screen. 'I'll go through them you just tell me when to stop.' He flicked the characters in and out of shot.

The first was a man in a black suit. He looked like your typical Hollywood hitman, like something Jason Statham would play.

Jack swigged his beer.

The next was a Chinese woman with long blonde hair down to the floor, she was dressed in white and had two guns, one on each hip.

'Well, that's just impractical,' the police officer in Jack's head analysed as he shoved an entire crust in his mouth at once.

The next one was a man, tall and stocky and dressed in bike leathers.

'Stop,' Jack managed to splutter, spitting crumbs almost as far as the TV. 'That's the one, head to toe in leather, that's why there was no forensic evidence.'

Danny clicked on the profile, and another screen popped up.

'This is the same but you choose the weapons now, see.'

And again the object in view skirted away to be replaced by another one.

'Is this about those murders? Is someone copying the game?'

Jack looked at him. Between working out where Jack lived and finding him in one night and now instantly working out that this game was linked to the crimes, this kid could be a detective, probably a damn sight better than some on his team.

'Yes it is, but I didn't tell you that. And you were never here either, by all accounts.'

The kid flicked through a couple of swords and knives. 'Mum's the word.'

'Speaking of which, where is your mum? Does she know you are out chasing down policemen? Wait, stop.' The suspected murder weapon was on the screen. 'That one, choose that one. Why aren't there any guns, that other character had guns?'

The kid clicked the weapon and they waited for the game to load again.

'I think you have to unlock them, you know, as you complete levels more things open up. As for my mum, your guess is as good as mine, I live with my dad, fucking waste of space he is, and my sister. She's the clever one in the family. Ok, Level One starts now.'

Jack looked hard at the TV, the page filled with script but his eyes were too strained to focus on it.

'I need to wash, can you complete this level and explain to me what all this is about?'

Danny replied but looked anxious, 'I don't know, I've never had a console before, I'll give it a go.'

Jack look bemused for a moment at the thought of a young boy not owning a games console and then walked down the boat for the bathroom.

'They're designed to work in your hands, not these old crusty things of mine, you'll be fine. I'll be back in ten minutes.'

Jack chucked water at his face, constituting a wash, and put a t-shirt on before returning to the main galley of the boat.

'How you getting on?' he asked, grabbing two beers from the fridge and slapping the tops of the lids on the kitchen side, removing the caps cleanly.

The young man took the drink and swigged it gently. 'Yeah, I've got the gist of it. I have to kill the daughter of a gang boss. You earn money from doing the job and then some upgrades. It's in some woods. Is that like the murders?'

Jack scratched an itchy bit of scalp behind his ear. 'Exactly like it. Wait, go back a bit, go and stand by that big tree there in that clearing.'

Danny made the computer character do as the detective wished. There was a light purple glow behind one side of the tree, as soon as the digital assassin stood on it, the camera angle changed. It showed an image of a young woman running through the woodland area, she was panicking and kept looking over her shoulder. It switched back to where Danny had control of the game again and the young woman came past his location. Danny punched a few buttons on the controller, more in the hope that it would do something than any real grasp of the actions the character could produce, but it worked; the assassin pounced on the young woman and stabbed her a couple of times, it then kicked her to the ground and big, red writing flashed on the screen reading *Complete, begin getaway*. Danny obliged and sent the small figure in the game sprawling off between trees.

'It's a bit easy, it tells you what to do!' Jack exclaimed.

Danny saw another patch on the screen glowing, this time it was a warming green colour, the colour to say you had completed what you were asked to do.

'I think this is just like tutorial levels. Probably a couple of these and then the game will get a bit trickier.'

'Alright, well I've got work tomorrow and it's a school night. Get yourself home, get a goodnight's sleep and when you can, get back here and see if you can do a few more levels, yeah?'

Danny froze the screen, looked for a way to save the game and switched off the console.

'Thanks for letting me come over. It beats being at home with Dad any day.'

Jack patted him on the shoulder and led him to the door. 'Well, I didn't have much of a choice, now, did I? And don't forget he's the only dad you'll have. Some kids aren't lucky enough to have one.'

Danny laughed. 'Hah, they're welcome to him, he's a loser.' He paused at the end of the gangplank. 'I need to check on my sister after college and then I'll come over.'

Jack noticed a sound of dread in his voice. What was so wrong with checking on your sister? Then he remembered how he and his brothers had fought constantly well into their late teens, and how civil sibling rivalry could be anything but civil. He certainly would never feel like he had to check on either of his brothers, but perhaps that's the difference between having a sister to a brother – you actually care if they're ok or not.

Jack brought his new snippets of information to the incident room the next morning, explaining about the motorbike outfit.

'So, Peters, I need you to get back on the cameras, take as many people as you need and look at any motorbikes you can find in and around the city centre, look at the motorway too, there couldn't have been many bikes on the road at that time of night.'

Jack paced the room in his usual rhythm.

'The thing with bikes is they don't have to stick to the roads, do they? They can pretty much go where they like, and if our killer is as smart as I fear he may be, he'll know where all the cameras are. Smith, can you check to see if we had any nuisance callers in regards to bikes being ridden across fields, through farms, down footpaths – that sort of thing. Kapoor, could you hang around the phones, pick out any useful bits of information. We have the press conference at lunchtime and then we can meet here again this afternoon. The rest of you, hit up informants and try some more canvassing. We need to push this on now, we've had sod all for long enough. Let's get something – *anything* – concrete in the bag.'

The incident room had been more docile than the previous couple of days, everyone in the room was aware of the odds of new information turning up, and they weren't good. The entire team also knew that a press conference being needed meant that they had already failed. A room full of volunteers would be needed after it, all of them manning phones, taking calls, gathering piles of useless information that the team would be forced to sift through. It was the long and clumpy way of finding information – not detective work at all, not what they were trained for.

Jack sat alone in his small office, prodding his way around a keyboard, looking at all of the information they had. He was paying close attention to Aubrie's post-mortem reports but amongst the long medical terms and phrases there was no information at all. Jack hated himself for thinking it, but he was even considering going back to

Mrs Keilty's house – at least in her presence something had happened. Right now he was deserted and deflated. As the head of the investigation he would be expected to be at the press conference but perhaps he could just stand in the background and look stern, not say a word, and not have the opportunity to put his foot in his mouth.

THE COWARD KILLER

The large room was busy. A long table had been set up at one end, it had police colours and insignia draped over it. The back wall had also been covered in white and blue block patterns and the phone number for the helpline was written in a large, black, easy-to-understand font. The press occupied the lines of chairs and the back of the room on their feet, all awkwardly balancing notepads and mobile phones set to voice record. Large cameras had been arranged strategically also, all with two people operating them. McQuade spoke with the parents of the two dead girls, her body language the perfect example of what she would have been taught in her family liaison training.

'What are they doing here?' Jack asked himself. *'The girls are dead, start mourning, stay away from this circus, for Christ's sake. These people aren't here because they care, they're here so they can get as much filth as possible to sell their papers.'*

'And this is Detective O'Connor, he is in charge of bringing our suspect to justice. He's the best detective I know so rest assured, after today it will only be a matter of time until he is found.' McQuade introduced Jack to the grateful couples. They looked reassured at his superior's words, again, she used the playbook well.

If only they knew how little they had.

'I'm sorry for your loss, we are doing all we can.' Jack spoke from the only page of text from his training that he could remember. This seemed to please them enough and the families departed out the rear doors, both husbands with their arms draped over the grieving mothers' shoulders.

'Bloody hell, Jack, you could have sounded a little sincere.' McQuade scolded.

Jack didn't answer but instead watched as she sat at the table, ready to address the hordes from the papers and TV channels.

Jack stood behind, his hands nestled in the small of his back; he knew from experience that this made him look attentive even when his mind was drifting to dark places.

He heard her begin to speak but he wasn't listening to the words. He could see out of the corner of his consciousness that she was reading from a piece of paper, a pre-written speech, ready to encourage and reassure the public, galvanising them into helping. Jack looked at the faces opposite them.

The pace of the conference changed, it went back and forth and occasionally the crowd would become raucous as they all tried to speak at once.

Jack was hardly there, he was thinking over and over about the timeline. Two murders in two days and then nothing. It felt contrived, not panicked or messy like other killing sprees. Was that it, two swift murders with no evidence left and then nothing, just drop out of existence and slip back into society unchallenged?

'Jack, Jack, they are asking you a question.' McQuade had her hand over the microphone and was calling him through gritted teeth.

Jack was suddenly dropped back into reality with a thump. 'What, why?'

'Detective O'Connor, can you just answer the question, please?' one of the reporters shouted above the rest.

McQuade looked put out but she relinquished her seat

and pulled Jack towards it by his forearm. She leant in close to his ear. 'Don't fuck this up.'

He sat down and straightened his jacket and tie and leaned in towards the microphone. 'Sorry, what was the question?'

The reporter that had just spoken shouted at the top of his voice, 'I *said*, are you going to be using any of your *unorthodox procedures* in the investigation, Detective?'

'Two girls are dead, more to come, possibly, and all these filths are thinking about is selling as many papers as they can.'

They would relish the chance to put him back on the front page, doing something a policeman shouldn't, trying to accuse him of being a vigilante of some sort, or just inept. He had battled this way with the press enough times to know that he didn't stand a chance, not when they could manipulate any word he said to fit their headlines better. That's the problem with a free press, they have the right to print whatever nonsense they see fit.

Jack contemplated his answer for a moment, and whispered under his breath so no one would hear.

'If I can't beat them.' He cleared his throat before continuing, 'No, I will not be using any, as you put it, *unorthodox procedures*. Just good old, hard police work, like we usually do. Bristol is a big city but it has surprisingly few hiding places.'

A different journalist to his left addressed him. 'So, do you think your killer will do it again?'

Jack allowed himself a very slight smile, he knew that what he was about to do would earn him a lifetime of pain from McQuade. 'Yes, I am afraid to say I think our murderer will kill again. I fear for all the young women out there as they will be prime targets for him. You see, we think our killer is a large male, over six feet tall, and I think he is going to prey on the weak and vulnerable. So far, he has only picked on people that he was sure to overpower. Some of our officers have dubbed him the "Coward Killer" because of such.'

Jack watched as the room fell into stunned silence – no one knew what to make of his revelations. He was giving them publicity gold and not a single pen scribbled on paper.

'If you are male and of reasonable size, I should imagine you are safe as our killer doesn't want a challenge, he doesn't want a fight with anyone of his own size as there is a strong chance he will lose. Anyway, my name is Detective O'Connor, I can be found and contacted at Bristol police station on that number there,' he pointed at the boards behind him, 'and if anyone would like to come and visit me in person, I shall be at the station.'

Another moment of silence strung out before suddenly bursting into an eruption of chaos.

McQuade pulled on his shoulders and Jack stood up and followed his superior from the room.

He knew this was going to hurt so he braced himself; he wouldn't even be that surprised if McQuade slapped him. Actually, a womanly slap wouldn't be her style, a swift knee to the nether regions, maybe.

'The "Coward Killer"? Really, is that the best you could come up with?' she asked him, not even sounding that angry.

Jack shrugged. 'I was thinking on my feet, it's the best I could do.'

McQuade gave a sarcastic laugh. '"Thinking on your feet", I'm not sure you were actually engaging that brain of yours, O'Connor. Anyway, I know what you were doing, it's done, and I can't change that now. If it works then maybe you'll be up for another promotion – my job may be up for grabs in six months – but if it doesn't, well, it will be the end of both our careers. We had a good run, hey, Jack? Now get back to work, and do your job. You still have Jonathan Thompson in a cell, go and squeeze something of use out of him.'

'Yes ma'am.' Jack headed back to the cells as quickly as he could; McQuade was being unnervingly relaxed about the pile of crap he had just dumped on the pair of them.

'*Best to avoid reading the newspapers for a couple of days,*' he thought.

'Sir.' Officer Kapoor came running around a corner. 'Sir, I've got something on Thompson. He has a storage unit at a lock-up, you know, down by the river in Ashton.'

Jack knew the place too well and didn't like where the coincidence was heading.

'Well, while you've been busy I got a warrant to check it and sent a team down there, and well, we found some drugs. Now I know it doesn't help us find our murderer but it should be enough to get him to open up, sarge.'

'So what are you saying? It's a lot of drugs?' Jack asked.

Kapoor nodded eagerly. 'A shitload, sarge, biggest find in eight years. A few million pounds' worth.'

Jack was stunned. Surely a drug dealer on that scale didn't live in a council house in Bristol. Or drive a crap car with a dodgy wheel.

'Really? Well, that should help our Mr Thompson to cooperate, now, shouldn't it?'

Jack arrived at the duty desk, arranged for the second interview with their suspect, and waited for Officer Smith to join him.

Mr Thompson had a lawyer present with him on this occasion. It was a man Jack recognised, he had represented some teenage drug dealers a year or so before.

'Interesting choice of representative, Mr Thompson.' Jack flicked on the tape recorder and ran through the usual rigmarole.

'Now, Mr Thompson, as you know, my colleagues and I are investigating two counts of murder.'

The suspected spat as he spoke, 'Yeah, I fucking know, and I also fucking know you don't have fuck all on me. And you know how I know? Cos I didn't fucking do it.'

The man's lawyer typed something onto a laptop, the skinny, suited man had obviously decided to remain a spectator for the time being.

'Mr Thompson, the sad thing is, I actually believe you. I know, shocking, isn't it? But the problem we have is the only real evidence we have points at you and you haven't actually told us what you were doing in either location on the night of the murders in question. So, from our point of view, you can see why that is somewhat suspicious, can't you?'

Mr Thompson moved uncomfortably in his chair but looked determined to remain silent.

'You can say no comment, if you want to, I really don't mind.' Jack bit his lip as he looked down at his paperwork, seemingly intrigued. 'However, you should know that we were granted access to your storage unit at the secure lock-up facility in Ashton. You should also know that we have found a large stack of, shall we say, *incriminating evidence.*'

The man's cool approach to their situation dissipated quickly. The lawyer stopped typing but didn't have the nerve to look at his client directly.

'So, if you would like to avoid spending the remainder of your life in prison, I suggest you cooperate.'

The proverbial penny had dropped, along with the man's hopes of leaving the station.

'It's not my lock-up, I mean, it is mine, but I don't use it, I didn't know what they were using it for. I knew it was dodgy but they paid me not to ask questions.'

Mr Thompson slammed his elbows down on the table and pushed his head into his hands. 'I assumed it was drugs, is it drugs? Is it bad?'

Jack shifted his weight to sit more comfortably. 'I'm not at liberty to say right now what it is that we have found, but yes, Mr Thompson, it is bad, really bad, and believe me when I tell you it would be in your best interest to spill as much information as you can, because you see, Mr Thompson, I do not have the time, nor the inclination, to waste any more time on you. Do you understand?'

The man lifted his head from his hands and nodded.

His legal representative raised a finger and began to

interject.

'Don't bother,' Mr Thompson spat at him. 'I'm in a load of shit here and you aren't going to help me out of this one. I'll tell you what I was doing those nights, but it stays in this room, do you understand?' His panicky voice did nothing to endear Jack to him.

'You are in no position to bargain with me, Mr Thompson, but by law, unless it is used in a court of law, everything in this room is confidential to those on a must-see basis.' The suspect tried to protest, but Jack knew his kind well, and knew what to say to stop him from instantly clamming up. 'So that means your wife and friends will not find out about your late-night excursions. The lock-up, however, well, that will be up to another policeman. I'm only interested in crossing your name from my murder investigation list. I may, however, be able to put in a good word for you, though.'

The scared man raised his eyes to the ceiling before closing them and then, after a moment or two, spoke quietly, 'I was out looking for … I was looking for sex.'

Jack had known this, he had suspected it from the moment the man had decided not to cooperate.

'And can anyone back that up?'

Jack knew this was most likely doubtful, but he needed to tie this loose end up, double knotted if he could, and to his surprise Mr Thompson nodded. The large man had a couple of tears appearing now. Jack had not been prepared for this – shouting, spitting, maybe even the odd headbutt attempt, but not this.

'Not for the first night, but there is someone on the second night. They can tell you where I was. I was with them for most of the night at their house. I don't know their full name but I can tell you where they live. Their name is, it's Clive.'

Jack motioned to Officer Smith to write down the name.

'Give my officer his address and a brief description and

you'll be dropped from the murder investigation, Mr Thompson.'

The crying man looked at the officer in front of him, clearly shocked at how little the reaction his confession had created.

'Mr Thompson, your sexuality is of no consequence to anyone other than yourself and possibly your wife,' the policeman paused to think if that statement was accurate, and then amended it, 'yourself, your wife and this Clive.'

Mr Thompson looked Jack right in the eye. 'I'm not gay.'

Jack returned a smile. 'We have had people in this very room claim to be asexual, non-gender specific, you name it, we've had it. And my answer every time is I couldn't care less. Now, Officer Smith here will be following up your alibi. For now, though, you will be going back to a cell, a new officer will be taking over, most likely from our narcotics team, and hopefully we won't be meeting again.'

The man looked crestfallen. 'Can't you do it? Can't I have you handle my case?'

Jack stood and walked to the door. 'I've wasted more than enough time on you, Mr Thompson, all our officers are more than capable. Mark my words, they will deal with you thoroughly.'

Officer Smith met Jack outside of the room. 'Not a murderer, then. Just a bit stupid and pervy.'

He returned a slight smile. 'Each to their own. You ok to sort that out? Take a picture of our Mr John Thompson with you and—'

'I know, I know, make sure he can identify him before telling him his name, in case he is being paid to give a false alibi. I've got this, sarge, I'll see what else I can dig up back at the incident room too.' Smith beat him to it.

'Don't work too hard, can't be dealing without you on the team if you burn yourself out.'

The young officer scurried off. Jack checked his watch. It had been at least an hour since the press conference, plenty of time for something to have come up, he could go straight to the phone room, grab whatever they had and take it back to the incident room. It would be quiet in there now, everyone would be out following leads – what little they had, at least.

'Sarge.' Officer Peters rounded the corner carrying a large holdall with him.

'I've got our murder weapon.'

'What, how?' Jack was shocked, but then Peters turned a rich, red colour.

'Sorry, sarge, I mean one like our murder weapon. You asked me to pick one up from the lot that had been confiscated.'

Jack inhaled deeply and let it out, this was the best he could do to disguise his annoyance. 'Yes, of course, good job.'

He took the bag and inspected the weapon inside, it was heavier than he had thought it would be.

'And there is one other thing, sarge, there is someone who wants to speak with you, I have put him in room thirty-four.'

Jack was confused. 'That's an interview room, isn't it? Am I questioning him?'

The large officer looked uncomfortable. 'I think you might want to, sarge, yes, his name is Yanislav Ivanovic and he is the head of the Polish gang.'

OVERDOSE

Jack walked into the interview room and threw the holdall onto the table in front of the man. He was tall, broad and had various tattoos dotted over his body. His head was shaven short and showed off even more tattoos on his scalp. He smiled at Jack warmly, baring a gold tooth. Hs tight leather jacket creaked as he offered a hand for the detective to shake.

'We don't need niceties, Mr Ivanovic. As you can imagine, I am a very busy man,' Jack told him, he didn't even bother to sit down. 'So, state your piece so I can get back to work.'

The man retracted his hand and smiled even more broadly, he spoke good English but in a thick, eastern European accent.

'I saw you on the news earlier, I had already decided to make contact with the head of this investigation, but after seeing what you did on live television, I knew you were the man for me. Crazy man, yes, but the right one no less. As your colleague would have informed you, I am the head of an organisation, one of which would like to do some mutual arrangements with you.'

The detective looked at the man in front of him, he had no doubt that he was who he said he was, he was just sceptical of his reasons for being there. It's not every day that gang lords walk into a police station – of their own free will, anyway. Jack didn't speak, he had no intention of making this easy for him.

'I have many people in and around this city, Mr O'Connor.'

'Detective,' Jack shot back at him.

Again, the man smiled. 'Indeed, Detective. As I was saying, I have lots of people in places where perhaps your officers are unable to go. They see many things and hear much, I would like to offer my people up to your service. It would not take us long to identify who is killing these young girls.'

Jack gave a cynical laugh. 'And in return, what? You would like me to turn a blind eye to say, a shipment of goods coming in, help a few of your friends find asylum here?'

'No, nothing as horrid as these things you suggest. I am a business man, Detective, and someone is tampering with my business, and it is someone within your organisation. You see some of our …' the gang man waved a hand as he searched in his second language for the correct word, '*produce*, was found and taken by colleagues of yours.'

'We are policemen, you do something illegal, we stop you. You have contraband, we take it, it's what we do, and it's called the law.'

Yanislav nodded in agreement. 'You are in one business, I am in another, and I appreciate this, Detective. We have contingencies for this, you find our stock, you take it and so on and so forth. This is the nature of our businesses, but you see, what we do not have a contingency plan for is our products being taken and then being distributed amongst our regular customers. Can you see why I have a business problem now, Detective O'Connor? Someone from your side of the fence is playing for both teams.'

Jack rubbed at his chin, there would usually be stubble to play with as he set his mind to work, another day or two and he should be back to his usual, dishevelled self.

He pulled the drugs Steven at the club had given him and threw them onto the table. 'Is this the stock in question?'

Yanislav picked it up and, to Jack's surprise, he pulled out some reading glasses and a notebook. He looked at something on the package that Jack had not noticed before, some small writing, printed straight onto the plastic surface. He flicked his way through his notebook, held it open and turned it around for the detective to read.

'The numbers on the bag are the batch number, and the colour square beside it coincides with the colour printed on the product, and this word here,' he pointed in a column besides the small, neat writing, 'that word is what we use to refer to when our stock has been impounded. It means captured.'

The gang lord recognised the look of bemusement on Jack's face.

'Like I have said, Detective, I am a businessman, I must ensure that I organise myself as such. When this country opens its eyes and legalises drugs, this will all become common practice. We will be doing your job for you, even paying tax for you.'

'That's not likely to happen any time soon, so for now it is very much illegal, Mr Ivanovic. Speaking of illegal, you do realise that I have someone in my custody who may be a concern of yours? Now, isn't that a coincidence?'

The foreign man smiled. 'I know that you have Mr Thompson here, yes, and I can corroborate his story. The man knew nothing of what was being stored in his name, nor did he have any connection with the buying and selling of it. He is just someone who likes to cooperate with us.'

Jack picked up the drugs from the table, just in case they were to go missing. 'Well, unfortunately for him, partaking in illegal activities doesn't have an ignorance get out clause. Do you actually have any proof that it is a police officer selling what you call your stock? Because you understand that is what you need to take action against someone, factual evidence?'

The gang member chewed the inside of his mouth, he clearly didn't like Jack's tone. 'Only whispers of rumours, I am afraid, if I had certain proof of who it might be … well, I usually like to handle my operations myself.'

Jack knew what the gang man was offering, and he wasn't wrong, they probably could find a killer quicker than his team were able, but he didn't like their methods. Torture was just a means to an end for these people, and they didn't discriminate on who they turned their attentions to.

Jack opened the bag on the table. 'Tell me what you know about this weapon, please, Mr Ivanovic.'

The man was clearly vexed at being made to make a diversion from the current conversation. He peered into the bag and narrowed his eyes at Jack. 'It is a piece of crap, we had a few with some other stock, and we pushed them all onto a buyer.'

'Did you sell any individually?' Jack persisted.

'Your men have spoken with mine about this already, please, Detective, if we could get back to why I have come to see you today.'

The man's warm demeanour was gone, and that smile he had shown Jack before was non-existent.

'Mr Ivanovic, I am surprised you had the arrogance to come in here. Did you really think that I was going to cut a deal with a man who makes a living by breaking the laws that I am paid to uphold? Did you honestly believe that I would see you as anything other than a criminal? Listen carefully to what I am about to say because I do not want you to misunderstand how serious I am. If you interfere with my investigation in any way I will arrest you, if any of your men get in my way, I will arrest you, if you even so much as look at me in the street, I will arrest you. Now, I hope I have made myself completely clear.'

Jack saw the frustrated rage in the eyes of the other man behind his reading glasses, which he yanked from the bridge of his nose. Jack also saw that he was about to open his mouth and shoot a tirade in his direction, but he wasn't about to give him the satisfaction. Jack swiftly picked up the bag containing the weapon, spun on his heels, and left the room.

Doing all he could to catch up, Officer Peters came spilling out of another door and chased after him.

'You sure told him, sarge,' he said, noticeably out of breath.

But Jack hardly heard him, something had changed inside of him. He knew this feeling, recognised it for what it was, and it was rage, uncontrollable rage. The lights in the station all of a sudden seemed intrusively bright and felt like needles scratching at his corneas. He covered his eyes with his hands and kneaded his forehead once again.

Peters took a hesitant step towards his commanding officer. 'Sarge, you don't look too good.'

Jack was getting hot and flustered, he had to get away from this idiot, and just being near him was all of a sudden unbearable. He was irritating him by just standing there.

'Just get on to finding that motorbike, will you.'

'But, sarge—'

That was it, the beast snarled and snapped. 'Just fucking do it, will you? I've got to go.'

Jack marched out of the building, ignoring two officers who tried to ask how the investigation was going and if there was anything that they could do to help. He stepped out into the afternoon sunshine, it was low and, again, was painfully bright. Even the weather was against him now, the whole world had turned on him.

Jack noticed his tie constricting his airways, he hooked the knot with a strong finger and grappled it loose.

'Fucking sunlight.' He turned his back on the low sun, only to have it reflected off of shop windows, bouncing in such a way it made itself feel like a physical assault to him.

'Stop panicking, Jack,' he whispered to himself as he marched down the street, trying to escape something he couldn't quite place his finger on. Escape *himself*, was it? Escape his borderline personality disorder, which was filling his head, leaving no room for rational thought?

Jack took a second to look at his surroundings, shading his eyes from as much of the sky as he could.

'The morgue,' he said, reassuring himself that he could find some respite at last.

Even the lobby provided enough cover for him to start to get a grip on himself. The young man behind the desk smiled and greeted him.

'Wasn't expecting you down here, sir.'

Jack looked around uncomfortably, his mind still wasn't on an even keel. 'I just need somewhere to rest for a few minutes, do you … do you know what I mean?'

The receptionist smiled and nodded. 'Go down that corridor, take the second left and then straight down to the end. It's the viewing gallery, a couple of the pathologists are working at the moment which means it should be quiet, it is a little cold down there, though, is that ok?'

Jack sighed with what felt like to him an unmeasurable amount of gratitude. 'That's more than ok, I'm a bit hot and bothered, to tell you the truth. Work, you know, gets a bit heavy sometimes.'

The young man smiled and allowed Jack to walk off, also allowing him to save face somewhat.

Jack found a couple of soft seats that looked down on the mortuary through a large window. He imagined that this feeling of looking down on the people below must be similar to that of the viewing galleries in death row prisons in America, only without the truly horrible bit in between being alive and dead.

Jack watched one of the pathologists at work, a tall, broad man who had an assistant with a camera watching his every move closely and documenting it with a flash from his equipment. It took Jack a moment to realise that behind the table at which they were working stood Aubrie. She too had an assistant helping her with a grey, lifeless body. There were only four people actually alive in the room yet it seemed to be excessively busy, Jack couldn't ever remember it feeling so much like a real place of work. It normally seemed so removed from what was normal that it was easy to forget that it was somewhere a job needed to be completed.

Jack controlled his breathing, slowing it down so much that he found himself becoming tired. He shook this from his body and stepped forward so as to flick a switch on a small control panel. He knew it was the switch to allow him to hear what was happening in the cutting room, he didn't, however, count on it alerting the occupants to his arrival. The large pathologist glared at him before returning to his work whereas Aubrie smiled sweetly and raised a hand to wave to him, realising just in time that she had a slice of liver still in her grasp. She shared an awkward look with him as she replaced the dark red meat back onto the examining table.

He watched the masters of the silent witness at work, listening intently to everything being shared between them across the room, giving himself a point for each time he understood what they were discussing.

Forty-five minutes passed before Aubrie gestured for Jack to enter the room, and reluctantly he did so.

It was on entering the room that Jack realised that there was a third corpse lurking on a gurney in the corner.

'Wow, busy day, hey?' he said, turning his nose up at the organs in bags Aubrie was putting into a freezer.

She laughed at his squeamishness. 'The big, brave detective afraid of a little blood? Yes, well, no – these actually came in three days ago, but your case bumped them down the list. Three in two days, all suspected overdoses, not unheard of, but not our usual consignment for one weekend.' She removed her gloves and tucked a strand of hair behind her ear. 'What are you doing down here, anyway? I thought you would be all tied up with being a celebrity now.'

Jack looked confused.

'I saw you on TV, you really nailed it – whatever it was you were going for.'

'Oh, right, that. The only thing I nailed was my own coffin shut, I think. No, I just needed to clear my head, nothing seems to be adding up, it's all confused.'

Jack followed Aubrie to her office. 'Let's see if we can figure out a way to simplify it, then, maybe if we write out the facts, well, it might make a bit more sense,' she said, flicking on the strip lighting and picking up a black marker pen.

She walked over to the smart board on her wall and wrote in the top right hand corner the word *Facts*.

'So, we have two murder victims,' she said, drawing two circles and writing a letter *V* inside of each of them. 'You have your suspect.' She drew another circle and put a large *S* inside of it. 'And your murder weapon.' She filled this circle with the letters *MW*. She connected all of the circles up with lines. 'So, what else do we need to put up?'

Jack took the pen and drew a separate circle representing Yanislav, and connected both the murder weapon to him, and the suspect circle.

Jack then explained about how he couldn't connect either him or John Thompson to the murders.

Aubrie wiped away the two lines that Jack had drawn. 'There, see, it's simple? You have nothing connecting them to the murders, so pass them on to someone else and concentrate yourself. Sometimes you have to just follow the evidence, Jack.'

Jack laughed pointedly. 'That's the problem, I don't have any, and what I thought I did have you just took an eraser to.'

The word evidence sparked his mind to travel down a new alleyway of thought. 'What did you say your three youths died of, overdose?'

'Yes, why?'

He pulled out the packet of drugs from the club and handed them to her. 'Test the tox reports against these, I'll bet ten pounds they are a match.'

Aubrie looked closely at the packet. 'I did find traces of sugar paper in two of them. It could be the same. Where did you get these?'

'A friend of mine runs a club, he said he was worried about some gear being sold cheap in there.'

The pathologist gave Jack a scorning look. 'Concerned of the price it's being sold at? Shouldn't he be concerned that it's being sold at all?'

Jack should have expected that, how could she have a realistic view of what happened in the dark parts of the city when she was cooped up in a lab with dead people all day?

'You can't stop people doing what they want to do, ultimately they will do it regardless, but you can try and manage the way that they do it, if nothing else.'

'I guess,' Aubrie conceded, looking uncomfortable as she did so.

Jack checked his watch, he could leave for home now, seeing as he had nothing to go on and nothing more to contribute. Aubrie told him that she would be there for at least another two hours writing up reports and, as always, he admired her with self-loathing and guilt. Maybe if he was more astute with his work this killer would have been caught already. But then again, you could only do the work that was put in front of you, and while his caseload felt heavy, he seemed to have met an immovable impasse.

He picked up his car from the station and fought the afternoon rush back to the boat. He was always thankful about having bought that rust bucket – he was as central as you could get without being a billionaire and it was as quiet as living in the Lake District, just the odd river ferry carrying people up to the SS Great Britain and back. His other house was in one of the arguably more sought after areas of the city, but it attracted a new battalion of students each year and, while he had nothing against educated people, he just knew that he wasn't one of them. Jack's intellect always seemed to him to occupy a different space to everyone else's. He once held a conversation for nearly two hours with a scientist he met working on a case up at the university about string theory and how dark matter was proven to exist in many ways by its absence. But he never felt on a level playing field, his attention span for any one subject was negligible. No, he would never be the one with letters after his name, never accepted into the elite of the world, but he understood how they ticked just enough so as to camouflage himself amongst them for short stints at a time. He always found it amusing how his fickleness to those looking in must seem like a weak characteristic of his but, to him, it was the only thing that had kept him alive on the inside all this time.

SHOOT HIM NOW?

Jack was walking the gangplank when he noticed the door to the boat was half open. He stepped silently towards the open hatch and reached up onto the roof, pulling down a nine iron he had hidden up there for exactly this type of event. He then toyed with the idea of ditching the golf club and removing the huge knife from the bag he was carrying, but even to Jack this seemed an excessive move.

He heard a voice inside, it was excited and shouting.

'Oh man, this is awesome. Wow, ha-ha, take that.'

Jack's heart rate eased off as the voice of Daniel carried down the galley.

The golf club got replaced as he entered through the small doorway.

'How the hell did you get in here?'

The boy with strawberry blonde hair paused the computer game and smiled. 'You left the door open.'

Jack knew that he was probably telling the truth. 'Yeah, that does sound like me, leaving it unlocked.'

The boy shook his head. 'No, you left it open – wide open. I thought you were in here, then when I realised you weren't I had a quick look around to see if anything was stolen, but it doesn't look like it. This would have been the first thing to go.' He pointed at the computer console as

142

he walked over to it, ejecting the game he had been playing and inserting a different disc. 'I borrowed a game from a friend, it's an old one for the older console, but this machine is backwards compatible so it still runs ok. You don't mind, do you?'

Jack threw his coat and the black bag with the weapon in onto the small breakfast counter at the end of the kitchen portion of the boat.

'I didn't understand a word of that, and no, I don't mind.'

The boy's face changed from a look of unsure over-familiarity to one of positive joy. 'I'll just load the game now, see if we can figure out who the next victim is going to be. You do think there will be another victim, don't you?'

Jack loosened the knot in his tie completely and dropped his bodyweight onto the sofa. It creaked as he did so, reminding Jack that it wasn't just his body that was starting to show signs of ageing.

'I think so, all the profiling I know of says he will. There's no connection between the girls and he seemed to enjoy it. There isn't a lot to stop him at the moment, either.'

Daniel's face now took on a look of sobriety. This surprised Jack – he thought kids loved blood and gore these days, the more dangerous the world, the better.

'Well, I know you'll get him, you're the smartest person I know. It's loading from the last place we left it,' Daniel said as he started manoeuvre the joy sticks.

A circle appeared in the middle of the screen below the flashing of the word *Loading*.

Some images suddenly sprang into life and even Jack could tell that this isn't what was known as 'gameplay footage', he knew this phrasing of words from the many computer game adverts that stated it at the bottom of the screen.

The character that Daniel had been using in the game

appeared to be strapped to a chair in a dark, industrial-type setting. The computer assassin was surrounded by inhumanly large men in suits and a smaller man who was using the bound figure as a punching bag.

'That is the guy whose daughters we killed. The girls were sisters and his rival paid us off to kill them,' Daniel explained to Jack.

The small man on the TV spoke to the one tied up. Jack only half listened, he knew the boy would be taking it all in so he gave his mind some breathing space, let it wander in and out of the mundane, stretching its legs after a hard day's thinking.

'Right, apparently, we have to kill the man who hired us before and this gang guy here might let us live. It's a pretty cool story so far – kill or be killed and all that.'

Jack brought himself back into the room. 'So the target is a man, then? I wasn't expecting that.'

The game switched to player mode and he watched as Daniel figured out where he needed to go. The setting was different to the previous levels, the tall trees had been replaced with urban blocks of flats and rows of garages.

'Hang on, wait, look.' He pressed a button on the controller and brought up the weapon selection screen. 'I've got a sniper rifle now, look, it's got a long sight on it, guess I have to use this to kill him. Oh, it's only got one bullet with it. I guess I'll have to make sure I don't miss.'

Jack took more of an interest, performing the ritual of scratching his chin. 'Right, well, if you are meant to use that you'll need to get up high, on a roof or something. Can you get into those flats there?' Jack pointed at the tallest of the concrete tower of homes.

Daniel made the figure kick in the doors and start running its way up the many stairs.

Jack again rested his mind, it was one of the skills he hadn't imagined that he would have picked up from his years on the force – the ability to let the useless pass him by and at the same time allow the small pieces of useful goings on to hit him somewhere in the front of his mind.

While the boy continued on with the game, Jack put himself in a partial coma, just about registering that the computer character had reached a purple haze, where it began to lay down and fix parts of the sniper rifle together.

The angle of the screen changed and it was now in first player mode, looking down a scope.

'Cool, look,' Daniel said, without realising he was squinting through one eye just as a real sniper might. 'When I put the scope on people it tells me who they are. Wow! And what convictions they have and stuff. Can you get guns that actually do that?'

Jack refocused himself and shook his head. 'No, that's just fiction. I wonder if that will bother our killer – not being able to do it accurately. I guess we will find out soon.'

Daniel jostled the joy sticks until the screen flashed up green. 'Ah, look, it says *Target* now. I've only got one bullet;   shall   I   shoot   him   now?'

TRIGGER

A few miles away, an old woman looked down the sight of her very own sniper rifle. This one was not like the game and she knew it. A simple cross with small measurements along the lines was all she had.

'*No, this isn't my gun,*' she told herself, but this was of no comfort as she felt her fingertip on the cold steel of the trigger.

No gloves this time – no need, killing from this distance was much easier, much less chance of being caught and much less personal. The woman's breathing slowed as she scanned a quiet car park, the excitement needed to be controlled, utilised, used to assist the weapon. A few men walked into view and there he was, victim number three, lighting a roll up cigarette and laughing with the rest of them.

'*Shall I do it now?*' she asked herself. '*No, it's not me, I'm not doing it, but I want to do it.*'

The woman battled with herself as her eyes focused down through the glass lens. Two younger men – no, wait, boys, not men – walked into the car park and straight up to the target. They handed over some money and took a couple of small packages.

'*Now,*' she ordered herself, her finger twitching and her

shoulder feeling the recoil hit firmly right where she expected it to. She watched as the two boys stood rigid, blood splatter covering both their faces, and then chaos breaking out amongst the other men.

She rolled away and began taking the gun apart, feeling content, a warm, satisfied tide washed over her. It was enough to keep her happy, but only just. The *EastEnders* theme tune played and the rooftop faded to give way to her comfortable living room. One moment she had been watching her usual soaps, the next she had been high up in the air, looking down on a city. She rubbed her hands up the back of her arms for moment, self-comforting as she waited for reality to set in, it was an hour or so before she was convinced of who she really was.

BRASS KNUCKLEDUSTER

Daniel left just as Jack's phone rang, it took a short moment for him to work out who was calling him as it was unusual for it to be anyone other than work. He stepped outside the boat into the cool air to get a better signal.

'Mrs Keilty, how are you?'

He didn't have time to find out if the woman was indeed ok, because the world around him took a strange turn. His legs became heavy and weak and refused to bear his weight at exactly the same time as his eyes unfocused and rolled back in his head. Jack didn't know what was happening to his body until he came back to consciousness, a dark material hugged his face and restricted his breathing as he tried to pull air in through his nose. The back of his head hurt and a warm trickle going down his neck told him that he was bleeding. He reached his hands up to his head and tore the bag from it, half relieved, half surprised that he hadn't been bound.

The bright lights from a van hampered his sight, he could only make out a figure in front of him, sitting calmly on a chair and smoking a cigarette.

'Detective, glad to see you are back from the land of nod.'

Jack recognised the thick accent of Yanislav Ivanovic –

even if he hadn't spoken to him that much, the thick, growling accent was difficult to mistake. Circling Jack were half a dozen men, Jack instantly became aware of how much this scene reflected that of the computer game.

'Nice to see you too, Yanislav,' Jack replied, squinting his eyes and flexing his vision to become acclimatised to the headlamps glaring at them.

Yanislav didn't recognise Jack's tone as a slight, or, if he had, it was unnoticeable because he walked straight up to the detective, stony-faced.

'My brother met with a police officer this afternoon, a sit down to converse over information. Two hours later and my brother is dead.'

The large Polish gang member brought his fist into the air. Jack instinctively looked at it and instantly wished he hadn't. It came down like a hammer, connecting with his jaw. Jack half leapt from the chair, catching his weight on his hands as they fell to the concrete floor.

Jesus, he hits like an iron bar,' Jack thought as he righted himself and sat back in the chair. And then he knew why. The light from the van glinted off of a brass knuckleduster.

'Now you know I am not playing games with you, I want to know who has killed him, and I would like this information now.'

Jack spat blood from his mouth, feeling something hard leave with it that he guessed was a tooth. He looked around, he really was in a heap of shit and there was no way out of this one – no way out still breathing, at any rate.

'Let me guess, single rifle shot to the head? Probably from on top of a nearby building?'

Again a huge blow pounded against the same side of his face, causing a cracking noise. The only reason Jack was still in his chair was that he had half been expecting this one and had grabbed the plastic seat in anticipation.

'Jesus Christ.' Jack spat even more blood out, his vision hazy due to his left eye beginning to close up. 'I don't know who did, I just know how.'

The large, standing man removed the weapon from his hand and flexed his fingers.

'And how do you know this, when it happened less than an hour ago?'

Jack would normally have never given any information up – it was the most valuable thing he owned – but given these circumstances, he didn't have a choice.

'It's the same killer – the same as the two girls. It's this computer game killer, it was the next level.'

Yanislav placed the heavy piece of metal back in his hand and approached Jack.

'You are telling the truth?'

Jack coughed and choked on more of his own blood. 'I swear.'

The punch-happy man stopped and kneaded the knuckle duster into a tight grip. 'If you are lying …'

'I'm not lying.' Jack sensed an opening, a tiny window of opportunity to get out of this situation alive. 'I need to get back out there and find this killer – your brother's killer.'

The gangster laughed. 'You have no evidence, you have nothing, and I know this.'

Jack risked raising his hand to feel the damage done to his face. 'I do now. I have the bullet in your brother that will tell me all I need to know. Sniper rifles are easy to track, I can find him, and I can bring him to justice.'

'You are not having my brother's body, he must be buried at home, and I am taking him home.'

'Do that, and we may never find the murderer. Just let me do my job, I will put this person away for a very long time. You'll have justice.'

Yanislav turned his back on the officer for the first time and paced from side to side, evidently considering what Jack had said. He spoke to one of his men who had been standing closest in a language that the detective didn't recognise.

'No, you will not have his body or deliver your inferior justice. I will allow you to examine his body, and take your evidence and then you will let the person who did this be mine.'

Jack shook his head, feeling an ache in his jaw. 'I can't do that, you know I can't.'

The standing man walked back over to the one sitting, pulled a small knife from his pocket and flicked it open. He leaned in close to Jack's shoulder and spoke softly as the knife was brought up to his neck. 'What I know, Detective, is that you have not much to live for.' The blade pushed against his skin, threatening to split it open. 'But I also know who you are friends with and who is left for you to care about, and I know that you would very much like them to continue living. Now you need to know, Detective, that I have no problem in slitting their throats in front of you, letting you watch as they bleed out slowly, begging for their lives. I am a man of my word, Detective, please do not underestimate this. Now, I believe I know where there may be a newly vacant lock-up available, assuming all of the contraband has been removed?'

Jack knew that the hours between Mr Thompson being arrested and now was plenty of time for the forensic team to have been and gone, so he nodded.

'Good, then I will meet you there at three o'clock in the morning. Please bring one of your doctors. You can have twenty minutes with my brother's body to gather your evidence. I offered you my hand in helping with your investigation and you turned it down, now my brother is dead. Refuse my cooperation again and it will be your last opportunity to do so.'

Even under this immense pressure, Jack made two mental notes, the first being that Yanislav had assured him that he was a man of his word, and the second being that he used the word 'cooperation'. Exactly the word Jack would be reminding him of if things began to turn into the wind again.

'Fine,' the policeman replied, and the blade was lowered.

BLOODY SINEWS

The van ride back to the docks was an uncomfortable one. While the thugs were permitted to stand, he was ordered to remain flat on his back and he felt every bump in the road like another small punch to his injured jaw, but his unwillingness to show weakness was resolute. His phone lay where it had landed after he had been struck on the head, a lucky couple of inches from the edge of the jetty. He phoned Aubrie without a thought for what time of night it was. It was only when she answered still half asleep that he had become intrigued as to how long he had been unconscious for. Only after he had asked her to come right away and bring some of the tools of her trade had he taken a look at the small, digital clock on the home screen of his phone.

'Wow, they must have it me hard,' he said, registering that it was now almost two in the morning.

Aubrie arrived within half an hour, and even though she had been rudely awaken, she still looked as prim and proper as she always did.

'What is going on, Jack?' she asked, hiding a small yawn behind a fist. 'And what the hell happened to your face?'

'Long story, I'll tell you in the car. You ok to drive? I think I might have broken a wrist too.'

He explained about Yanislav, and how this was going to be the most unorthodox post-mortem she would ever have done.

'So we are working outside of the law now, are we?' she asked him, speeding the car around a corner.

Jack winced in pain as the car shoved his weight up against the door, he had a suspicion that she had done it on purpose, but was not about to start an argument over it.

'Like I have a choice. You've seen the state of my face. Either I catch the killer in the right way, which might take long enough for the Polish to get bored and lose faith in me, in which case you'll be performing *my* post-mortem. Or I can do it in the wrong way, which means I can catch the killer quicker and maybe stay alive. Or I could refuse to do anything at all and run away to the Maldives.'

Aubrie took another sharp turn much faster than was necessary.

'Yeah, this is a time for jokes, Jack.'

Who said I was joking?' he thought to himself as he saw the barbed wire of the lock-up ahead of them.

Jack was glad that Aubrie had been anxiously scanning their surroundings as they entered – it meant that she didn't notice that the night guard that had let them in had actually known Jack by name.

Three men stood outside of a large, green shipping container, opening the doors as the pair approached. Inside was Yanislav and one other man, which Jack thought was rather a small entourage, considering the situation. There was also a body, already undressed and waiting for the pathologist on a cold stainless steel table.

'Oh, the irony,' Jack mused in his own head. *The very table they used to cut their drugs on, with god knows what, is the same place where the drug dealer is now about to be cut apart.'*

The container was brightly lit with lamps, powered by a small generator. Jack couldn't help but feel impressed at the gang's efficiency and attention to detail. Aubrie held rubber gloves to her mouth and breathed into them so they inflated before pulling them on to her hands with a snap.

Yanislav grabbed the pathologist's hands as she pushed the dead man's head from side to side.

'Take only the evidence you need and that is it. My brother deserves to be laid to rest.'

Tugging her hand from his grip, Aubrie returned to the job at hand. 'I don't know what evidence there is to take yet, not until I have done a thorough examination.'

Jack recognised the fury in the Polish man's face and, fearing that she may receive the same treatment that he had been given, he stepped into the conversation.

'Just look at the gun wound, Aubrie, it was a rifle killing, and there won't be anything else on the body.'

She turned her head to scorn him, but she didn't argue.

Jack noticed just how hardened Yanislav had become as he watched the skin on his brother's head be pulled back to reveal the skull.

What makes a man this cold?' he thought, but then realised that you didn't become leader of a gang like that without seeing or doing far worse.

Bloody sinews stretched and snapped as a large piece of skull was prized away by the hands of the pathologist.

Even to Jack's untrained eye, the brain damage was clearly extensive. Aubrie had to remove large parts, which she dropped into what would normally be used as evidence bags.

'Usually this would all be weighed and catalogued, you know, done properly.'

Jack covered his mouth as she dug a pair of tweezers in deep to the part of the brain remaining. 'You're doing a fine job.'

She looked up at him, clearly angry at his attempt of flattery.

A small squelching noise spluttered from deep inside the dead man's head and with it the tweezers emerged, holding a small bullet.

'Ok, this is about as good as it's going to get,' she said, placing the bullet in a clean evidence bag. She went to put it in her case when the brother of the deceased grabbed her wrist again. This time Jack intervened, pulling him from her and standing between the two.

'She needs to take it for analysis. Anything we find, I will pass on to you. After all, you are a man of your word, and so am I.' Jack hadn't given him a choice, the Polish gang member had to agree, allowing Aubrie to place the small fragment of metal into her reinforced briefcase, which she closed with a thump.

Jack and Aubrie returned to the car, leaving the entirety of the body behind. Aubrie had offered to close and stitch him up, but Yanislav had told them that no more steel was to touch his brother.

'Thanks for doing this,' Jack said to her as she drove him home.

She scoffed, 'Like I had a choice.' She paused in thought, Jack knew she was weighing up the options and was thankful that she was smart enough to come to the same conclusion that he had, which was that neither of them really had a choice. 'I have an ex who works in ballistics. I'm sure I can convince him to do this on the quiet for us.'

To Jack's surprise, he felt a small hit of jealousy settle inside him at the mention of an ex, but it soon passed. It had been a long time since he had thought about relationships and how they worked. He wasn't sure if he even knew how they functioned. Being alone felt natural, it felt like the only way of being. You got up, went to work, spent the money on things a single man with no outside interests spends money on, and then you went to sleep. He hadn't even considered retirement, what he would do with himself when the work dried up, or if he dried up even sooner than that. He had his house as his nest egg for when all the police work was done and dusted, at least.

That reminded him that the current tenants had moved out and it wouldn't be long until squatters took up residence.

'I'll advertise it for rent online when I get a chance – if I ever get a chance.'

His thoughts turned to how quickly life was coming and going and, when all was said and done, how little he had actually achieved – after all, you are only as good as your last case and, right now, this was feeling like it would soon become his last case.

'Don't take me home, drop me to the centre. I want to see where our shooter was positioned,' he told her as the weight of his future began feeling heavy.

'Fine, but I'm coming with you,' Aubrie replied tartly.

Jack laughed, hurting his jaw all over again. 'You are kidding, if we both get out of this car it will be nicked in no time.'

'I'm not letting you walk around injured and vulnerable like that by yourself.'

Jack opened his mouth to protest, but didn't get a chance.

'It's non-negotiable. Now, for once, do as you're told, Detective.'

NO JOY

The building that the shooter had used was situated in the heart of Easton, a part of Bristol that Jack avoided whenever possible, a part of the city he had certainly never been to willingly, only when the work had called for it. It was a tall block of offices that had long been forgotten and now offered a dry place for the homeless and needy to hide from the weather and, normally, the law.

'Just stick close to me, won't you?' Jack asked Aubrie as her expression divulged her sense of horror as they entered the building.

They walked through a nearly pitch black lower level, its open plan gave shadows the opportunity to stretch far, making ugly distorted shapes. Three men lay on blankets against one wall, they were huddled around an upturned crate with a burning candle on top, its flame dancing in the gusts running through.

Aubrie gripped at the elbow of his jacket.

'Don't worry, they are probably on a different planet to us at the moment.' He was meant to sound reassuring, but even to himself he could hear a tone of menace. Whether it was real or just distorted contempt for the lower lives of some of the city, he wasn't sure.

They made their way up a couple of spiral staircases

that swayed under their weight like ship masts in the wind until they came to the door to the roof. It had been kicked in; half of the frame was spilled across the floor, the padlock still hanging from the latch that clung to the wood by the tips of the screws. The rooftop shingle was deep gravel and moss and felt spongy under the pair's feet.

'Just span out a little as we cross, yeah? That way if part of it goes only one of us will go through.'

Aubrie nodded and then appeared to notice something significant. 'Look,' she said, pointing at disturbed gravel. 'There's got to be at least a dozen footprints here. And there, look, more indentations.'

Jack knelt to where she was pointing. 'You're right, pretty fresh too, looking at the way the moss has been kicked up. Must have been the Polish, probably wanted to try and find the shooter. He would have been long gone by the time they realised where the shot had come from.'

Jack continued on towards the edge of the building.

This time he spotted the marks on the unstable surface below their feet.

'This is where the shooter was, look, can you see where the moss has been flattened instead of turned up? He must have been flat on his front, barrel just on that lip there.'

Aubrie recognised Jack's tone as being disappointed. 'What's wrong, were you expecting more?'

He shook his head. 'No, well, not exactly. I was expecting it to be … no, not expecting, *hoping* it had been a more difficult shot to pull off,' he told her as he looked over at where the brother had been shot. 'Even I could have made this shot, single bullet or not. Which means I'm not looking for a professional, which means—'

Aubrie spoke at the same time as him, saying, 'It's not narrowed down at all.'

He saw blood splatter on the floor across the road from the building and his eyes became unfocused.

'Come on, Jack, you can do this,' he encouraged himself and, without thinking, he lay down, pressing his stomach

firmly onto the gravel. Jack closed his eyes and concentrated on his breathing, slowing it down just as a sharpshooter would. He let empathy in like before, and let the surroundings wash over him.

He closed his eyes and envisioned a huddle of men down the scope of a rifle.

'Nice and easy, Jack, you have a clean shot, nothing in the way.'

Aubrie watched as Jack's posture mimicked that of someone holding a rifle.

Jack's breathing stopped and his finger twitched at the invisible trigger, he began breathing and rolled on to his back, bringing his hands to his chest.

He felt efficient, he felt like he had just completed something impersonal, work-like almost, but there was no joy. No, he didn't enjoy it, it was necessary to follow the plot, which had not fulfilled something that the first two murders had. There was no hate this time, no anger, no pleasure. Not like when the life had been extinguished under his strong hands. This one had not been enough, this would be the last killing with a gun, whether that followed the game or not.

Jack opened his eyes. 'He's going to murder again and it's going to be soon and it's going to be messy.'

He was glad that Aubrie had been there but more glad that she hadn't pressed him very hard on what he had seen and felt. He knew her opinions on the paranormal and, while Jack knew he was only guessing, only using the empathy that he could feel, he was also fully aware that it was not normal behaviour.

The boat was a welcome relief. After polishing off a packet of pain killers, he managed to get as far as taking his shoes and socks off before falling into a world of dreams.

ARMED POLICE

Jack's dreams always centred around one thing: that night when he came home to his world being destroyed. Sometimes the dream involved him running home, pushing against the floor as hard as he could with his legs but still he was stuck in slow motion, sometimes resulting in him being on all fours, desperately trying to get enough grip to speed up. Or, on the occasion that he did get there in time, he searched for the killer in one room, only to hear the screams come from another, and then he would find the bodies. Once or twice in the last couple of years, the dreams had allowed him to spend a few minutes of time with Jessica and Felicity, but this only added to the hurt on waking, as it took him a few moments to gather reality back in and break his heart all over again. It was one thing to feel guilt for not saving them, but to lose them all over again was soul destroying. This time he woke with enough pain in his face to eliminate most of the thoughts from his sleep; his pillow was covered in blood.

Through his sleepy black eyes he could see his phone lighting up and moving across the floor under its own vibration. Knowing it would be the station, and the only thing they would want to know is where the hell he was, he didn't let it worry him, walking into the station looking like a crash test dummy would keep them off his back for a day or two.

A car tailed him all the way from the dockyard to the station. He didn't recognise the man driving, but the passenger had definitely been at the unorthodox post-mortem.

Jack found McQuade in her office, her eyes narrowed, peering intently through a small pair of reading glasses, which she promptly removed as Jack entered.

'And where the hell have you— What, in Christ's name, happened to your face?'

The anger dropped from her face the moment that she caught sight of him.

'Yeah, this is what I need to talk to you about. I was interrogated last night.'

McQuade's eyes widened with disbelief. '*Interrogated?* More like hit by a sodding truck. Who did this?'

'There has been a third murder – a member of the Polish gang, the brother of Yanislav Ivanovic. They seem to think it was a policeman, but I happen to know that it's our computer game killer. I've been kindly asked to find who has killed him and they made me an offer I couldn't refuse.'

Jack knew that he had just dropped a ton of information in one short sentence, but he was far beyond treading lightly now.

McQuade looked down at her paperwork, folded it back into its cardboard pouch and looked back at Jack, weighing him up.

'You're not going to be able to work from inside here, are you? Let me guess, they have men outside waiting for you as we speak?'

Jack nodded.

'And you are sure it's the same killer?' Jack nodded again. 'So, if you refuse to help them, they will kill you, and if you do find the killer and don't turn him over to them—'

Jack spoke for her, 'They will no doubt kill me, yes.'

'So what are you going to do, Jack? You can't go vigilante, you'll lose your job and you can't do anything to piss them off or you'll lose your life.'

Jack managed a small laugh. 'Right now, staying alive is about all I'm able to do. I don't know what I'm going to do once I find the killer, but I can't let the Polish have him. And you're right, they are watching everything I do, if I have a dump, they'll know how much paper I use to wipe my arse.'

Jack's superior stretched her arms up and placed them on the top of her head; she was clearly as baffled as he was. She stood up and paced behind her desk.

'Are you sure it wasn't that what's his name, the one you interviewed with all the drugs that he didn't know anything about? John Thompson, wasn't it?'

Jack acknowledged that the name was correct. 'Pretty sure, yes, ma'am.'

She sighed. 'Well, I'm going to take at a stab at speaking to him. He sounded perfect for it, I thought we had our man already. Would have been just what we needed.'

She paced the room, absentmindedly tidying the many pieces of office equipment on her desk.

Jack was about to speak when McQuade cleared her throat, her mind had clearly been made up.

'Ok, here is what we are going to do. I'm taking over the investigation here. You pass on whatever information you find directly to me, and only me, do you understand?' He knew that she was asking without asking. 'And I'll pass on anything of interest to you. Here, take this.'

McQuade wrote something down on a small piece of paper and Jack was surprised to see a phone number. 'That's my personal number, this is getting messy so let's at least keep it tidy between us. Walk through the office before you go and make sure that as many people see your face as possible, I'll tell them you need time off to recover.

Jack, this is getting out of hand, we need to get a grip.'

Jack gave another short nod and went to leave the room.

'Oh, and Jack?'

'Yes, ma'am?'

'Stay alive.'

For once I'll do as I'm told,' he briefed himself as he walked past colleagues, all of whom smiled then took a longer than usual glance at his face before finding something on the floor to interest them.

He left the police station and headed into town, thinking of a way of ditching his new, unwanted bodyguards. They had been easy to spot – they were both stood scowling at the entrance of station as if it had offended them and, in some crazy way, it probably had.

Jack's inner monologue started speaking to him. He hated when it did that, it made him feel crazier than Mrs Keilty.

Mrs Keilty? That's right.' He remembered that she had phoned moments before he had been bludgeoned.

'So, how do I lose you two ugly bastards?' he whispered quietly, looking for some way of escaping.

Some lights flicked on in front of him as a result of the grey sky deepening in colour, it was the neon sign of the holiday inn

'Perfect.'

Jack walked straight up to the desk of the hotel and flashed his ID.

'How can I help you, sir?' the young man addressed him as politely as was humanly possible. Jack always hated this, the young guy in front of him was the one doing the job that he would never be able to stomach, which in Jack's mind made him the better person.

'I need your help,' Jack took a look at the gold name badge pinned to the man's smart black jacket, 'Dillan. Two men just followed me in, no, don't look, it's very important that they don't see you noticing them. Do you understand?'

Dillan nodded and looked with all his might directly at Jack.

'Good man, now, I need you to go and phone the police from another room and tell them that Jack O'Connor has informed you of two armed men sitting in your lobby. Can you do that?'

The man gulped. 'Armed?'

'Can you do that for me, Dillan? It is official police work and I'm counting on you, can I count on you, Dillan?'

Jack didn't like manipulating the young lad, or the dozen armed police that turned up less than five minutes later, but on this occasion, it was necessary. He couldn't have them following him to the old lady's house, she didn't deserve that. And after all, they probably were armed.

Jack slipped out the fire exit once he heard the cries of 'Get on the floor!' and the pounding of police boots echoing all around the lobby.

Bristol's new bus station was directly behind the hotel and made for a quick getaway, and, due to the fact that he might still have another tail on him, was the perfect choice.

The bus was half empty and, except for the engine roar, was actually quite peaceful. He rested his head against the glass, allowing the vibration of the bus to soothe him and, without realising, he fell into a more than welcome sleep.

WASTE OF FLESH

'It wasn't enough, I wanted to see his eyes as his life was taken. The scum didn't deserve to die so easily, he needed to suffer. He didn't deserve it to be quick like that, he did deserve more of my time and effort, though. He deserved to know he was going to die, deserved to feel cold metal ripping his insides apart.

'It's done now, no point looking back, just concentrate on the next one. I will take my time with this one, I want to know how their pain tastes at its most great, and I want to see what the fear of death looks like in those fragile human eyes. No one knows how lucky I am, how powerful I am just by seeing these things. No, not seeing — creating.'

'I think it's sharp enough now.'

'So? I'm enjoying sharpening it, it keeps me focused, I get bored too easily.'

'Look out the window, look down on them.'

'No, I'm busy.'

'You're not busy, just fucking look out of the window.'

He wasn't sure when the one voice in his head had turned into two, but it did feel crowded sometimes. He had begun letting the new voice have centre stage more. The blank spaces of time that he couldn't quite remember were becoming longer and more frequent. At other times, he could remember some of what he had been doing, but he couldn't give up this new tag team inside him, it was giving him strength, helping him become more than he had ever been before, more than anyone else around him.

He looked down onto a full street of people.

'Look at him, walking that dog, that pathetic excuse of a dog. And why? Because it's part of the family. What a joke, what a sorry specimen of a living thing, what a waste of creation. Look at that one over there, how she drives that piece of shit car with her hand hanging the cigarette out of the window. What beauty or masterpiece will she ever create? What possible influence will she have on this world?'

'She might have children.'

'So fucking what? They will be just like her: a stupid, on the dole, waste of flesh. We should kill them all and rid this cancer from around us. We are better than them, you are better than them, all of them.'

'Better than the nurse I killed?'

'Don't be pathetic. She worked in a hospital that feeds its patients lies, lets them down, kills more people than you ever could in your lifetime and then they all wash their hands of it. A fucking hospital that has let babies die because their incompetence couldn't even stretch further than their own vanity. Nurses, doctors, even surgeons, they are all the same. They all want their pay check at the end of the month and none of them want the responsibility that comes along with it. They are all weak and together we are so strong.'

POSSESSION

'Glastonbury, love, is this your stop?' a gentle voice woke Jack.

In his confused state, for a moment, he had actually thought it was his mother waking him.

He thanked the old lady, stepped around her shopping trolley and off of the bus.

It took him a little while to gather his bearings but Jack recognised the end of Mrs Keilty's road and, once he had gotten over the shock of a small group of druids standing on the corner of it, he walked down the path to her small cottage.

Jack was a few steps up the path when the front door opened and the old woman stood in its frame.

'Detective, come in, I saw you coming. I had been watching those weirdoes in their dressing gowns, look.'

Jack laughed and it felt like it might have been the first time ever. Not necessarily at her comment, but the fact that it had been accompanied by her wearing a crash helmet and marigold gloves.

'Ah, yes, I forgot I was wearing this, dear. Give us a hand with the strap, would you? And I'll get the kettle on.'

Jack allowed himself one smaller laugh before threading the strap of the helmet back through the two metal loops. The common strap-fixing on those old helmets could be tricky, he remembered from his moped days.

'You look like you could have done with one of these yourself, love, what happened?' she asked him, extracting her head and bush of hair.

'Only a business meeting.'

'Really? Well perhaps you should consider business insurance, no?'

Jack smiled warmly to her. He didn't know why but he felt calm here. Was it the house or her? Or a combination of the two? He couldn't tell, but he sat down on one of the armchairs and an unfamiliar sense of safety swept over him.

A few moments of serenity passed and Mrs Keilty re-entered the room with her tea tray laden with biscuits and jam tarts.

'Help yourself, dear, the tarts are homemade. I got worried about you when you didn't call me back. I figured you lost signal or were busy and judging by your face, I figured right.'

Jack finished a jam tart in two bites and spoke as best he could without spraying pastry from his weakened mouth. 'Sorry, I got caught up in things.'

The short woman went to take a sip of her tea but stopped promptly. 'Don't you dare apologise to me, young man. You have work to do, murderers to catch, and you have to have your own life, you know?' she said, gingerly sipping her tea. She looked sad. 'You had another killing last night, didn't you? A young man, shot in the head. So young, bless him.'

Jack started on another of her baked goods. 'He was a drug dealer and a probable human trafficker, Mrs Keilty, I wouldn't worry yourself over the loss of him.'

'Yes, well, a life is still a life, Detective, but maybe it will save others in the future, yes?'

Jack loved the way that she framed statements as little

questions sometimes. It's like she was still looking for answers, still trying to work out the world just the same as he was. He also noticed how desensitised he was now to her in-depth knowledge of the killings with no possible explanation.

'Mrs Keilty?'

'Yes, dear?'

Jack placed the half-eaten jam tart back down. 'Forgive me, but why were you wearing a crash helmet?'

'Ah, well, that is a good question, Detective. When I was having one of my ...' she had to think for a moment as to how to phrase exactly what it was she was having. 'Let's call them funny turns, for the sake of argument. Well, when I was having one of my funny turns, what do you call it, the outsides of what you can see?' She waved a finger around her head.

'Peripheral vision?' Jack offered.

'That's it, well, I thought it was fuzzy, which is different, you see, it's always been clear as ice before, and then it got me thinking. It was reminding me of something but I couldn't place my finger on what it was and when I went out to the garage to find slug pellets, look, it dawned on me. Me and my old man, god bless his soul, used to have a motorbike and sidecar and what I was seeing in my funny turns was the same as when I used to wear the crash helmet, look. So I put it on to see if I were right and then it was quite comfy, so I didn't bother taking it off.'

Jack smiled, his affection for this woman, who, if he were honest, was still close to a stranger, grew like a balloon inside him.

'Yes, that was one of my theories too – that he was wearing biker gear.' Mrs Keilty raised a telling eyebrow so Jack hurriedly added, 'Not the whole helmet thing, no. That was a stroke of genius, Mrs Keilty.'

She smiled. 'Did anyone ever tell you that flattery will get you everywhere, Detective?'

'Not recently, no.' Jack wanted to keep the mood light

so didn't let this comment dwell in the air for too long. 'Did you manage to see anything during this funny turn?'

The old lady nodded and sipped her tea simultaneously like a pro. 'I had two small turns, one right after the other, which is a first for me, too. I didn't get a lot, but what I did get was that he wasn't happy, he hadn't enjoyed it as much as the others. I think part of him felt like it was too easy or something.'

'Part of him?' Jack didn't understand why he noticed that wording, it was a usual turn of phrase, after all, but this time it felt like it had stuck to the wall.

The old woman thought deliberately before speaking. 'It's hard to describe, Detective. Do you ever talk to yourself in your own mind?'

'I guess.'

'Well, imagine that voice is telling you what to do, only it's not your voice, it's like an extra being has taken up residence. Well, it's in your head, isn't it, so why would you question it not being part of you?'

Jack tried to understand. 'You wouldn't question it, and the second voice is still part of you if it's in your own head.'

'Ah, see, that's where the problem lies, look. It isn't them, it's an energy that they let in. For whatever reason it's something that they have accepted as becoming part of them. Normally, it's with the promise of being powerful, getting what they always wanted.'

'So, are we talking possession from a demonic psychopath?'

Mrs Keilty nodded. 'Exactly, Detective. We all have demons inside us at one time or another, Detective, the only difference is how we bargain with them.'

Jack wanted to tell the woman she was wrong, that evil is a creation by evil people, but her theory had legs, he had to admit. When he himself was in a rage, it felt as though something else was taking over him, as if he was now a bystander, just watching and accumulating the guilt from his actions. And he had seen so much murder by people who didn't seem capable – by children, even, who had been so full of hate in the heat of the moment and so broken after, it didn't seem humanly possible to hold such opposing mindsets.

And then Jack remembered his diagnosis: borderline personality disorder. It meant that he was always sitting just out of the reach of psychosis, so close that he could almost taste it in the wind. Dangerous thoughts lay in this way of thinking, he knew, his therapist had made that more than clear on more than one occasion. That's what all of his therapy had been about: controlling his thoughts, changing the course of them and reacting differently. This had been all too easy to say, but breaking the habits of a lifetime meant changing who he was, altering his personality drastically. Jessica had always said how much better he had been after his therapy, how much better he coped with stress and the anxiety of certain situations, but what he had always felt was that he was choosing to be someone else, like he was always pretending and had lost the real him somewhere in that bland room.

The conversation comfortably slipped away from murders and demons to Ireland, where Mrs Keilty had been born and raised as a child, and how she had known a family named O'Connor, and wondered if they had been relations of Jack's. Then to how the Glastonbury Festival should actually be called the Pilton Festival, seeing as that was the village where the farm was that it actually took place on, and how it was actually over six miles away.

Jack couldn't remember the last time he had enjoyed just talking, and having someone listen to him on subjects that his opinion was not all that set on. It was surprising to him that this woman, who was so easy to get along with, whose company was quickly becoming bliss, was still so alone. She had no family left in England, and received no visits from friends or neighbours – or, at least, that was the feeling Jack had gotten from her by the way she spoke. Eccentricity had always been a trait that he had championed, though, and he suspected it may have been in a severe attempt at constructing a world where he could fit in.

Her kindness still prevailed when, on finding out that he had caught the bus to see her, Mrs Keilty, set in motherly mode, insisted on driving Jack back to Bristol.

'When you insisted on dropping me back, Mrs Keilty, I assumed you had a car.'

The older woman handed him a crash helmet, a pair of gloves and a bright-yellow, knitted scarf.

'No, no, this is much better, dear.'

'And when you said we would take the motorbike and sidecar, I assumed your husband had driven it and you had been in the sidecar.'

Jack forced his hips down into the tight space parading as a seat.

Mrs Keilty laughed and kicked the starter on the bike. 'No, he couldn't drive, bless him. Don't worry, you are perfectly safe with me, dear.'

Jack had often found himself in unbelievable situations, but this one was quickly making its way to the top of that particular chart. His hands gripped the frame of the sidecar as he closed his eyes and tried to ignore the fact that he was sitting mere inches off of the tarmac.

COP KILLER

Jack always gave credit where it was due, and the journey home had been no exception. Mrs Keilty had surpassed all of his, albeit low, expectations and within an hour Jack was standing outside his boat. He hadn't let her drop him to the door for her own safety – he was expecting a visitor or two – and the few hundred yards' walk would also allow him to gather himself. While his driver had been capable on the way home, she hadn't exactly made it relaxing for him. Seeing the door on his boat wide open again he felt some relief at ensuring his ride ended early, but not much as he knew that he had to walk on-board alone.

'Well, if it were a trap they would have closed it behind them,' he said to the air as he decided to leave the golf club where it was. If they were armed they would have something that a nine iron would most likely be ineffective against.

He took the two steps on to the rear end of the boat and slowly walked its length.

'I'm sorry, Jack, they just burst in, there was nothing I could do.'

Daniel was sitting obediently on the sofa, his eyes flicking from Jack to someone standing just around the corner in the kitchen area of the boat.

'Ah, Detective, I wondered how long we would have to wait for you. I commend you on losing my men earlier, which was indeed very clever.'

Jack saw the large figure of Yanislav leaning against the kitchen side, eating an apple and holding a gun pointed at the young man.

'Good, it's only you. How are you, Yanislav? How has your day been?' Jack theatrically allowed his gait to be one of calm as he walked over to Daniel, standing deliberately between him and the gun.

He turned and spoke to the boy, 'It's ok, you've done the right thing, nothing's going to happen anyway.'

Daniel nodded in a way that almost convinced Jack that he had believed him.

'Good lad, show that you are strong,' he thought.

'It has been, how you say, fruitful. I have confirmation that it is a police officer leaking our drugs back onto the street. I have witnesses telling me that they have not met the person but that he has confirmed that more produce will be on the way, and that it will be a large amount. Now, the only large amount of this particular product that has been brought into this city was confiscated by some of your men recently.' The gang leader opened his coat and tucked the weapon away. 'However, in the case of my brother's murder, I have not received any information.'

'And that is why I am lucky enough to receive a visit. Well, in regards to your *produce*,' the policeman replied sarcastically, 'that sounds pretty conclusive. I will pass the information on when I can, and there will be an internal investigation, mark my words. But, as you know, you have asked me to work outside of the law on the case of your brother, so I will not be in contact with any of my colleagues until we catch this killer.'

The gang lord nodded and placed the apple core down on the kitchen side. 'You know, we didn't eat much fruit growing up, our long winters were too cold, the frost burned trees and left them bare. No, what we would eat is lots of meat, it is what gives our people their strength. I often hunted red fox and bear in the Ural Mountains, and my grandfather taught me to how to skin animals and gut them. A useful, how do you say, string to my bow. Maybe it is one that I shall practice when you bring this man who has killed my brother to me. It is a skill I would hate to forget.'

Jack took his tone and expanded on it in his mind's eye: if Jack brought the man to him he would be killed like an animal, and if he did not, Jack would take his place – either way, someone was going to be separated into parts.

'I didn't realise there were bears in Poland,' the policeman said, trying desperately to ease the tension.

Yanislav laughed. 'You English are obnoxious. You named me and my men the Polish gang, and then assumed that we were from Poland. Do we all look like plumbers, too?'

The gang lord chuckled to himself before taking a lazy, leisurely walk and exiting the boat, leaving Daniel's heart at double its usual rate.

'Well, he was a nice guy,' the boy joked as he slumped back in the chair, seemingly exhausted.

'Yeah, he's probably got mummy issues. Anyway, mate, probably best you get off.'

Daniel was clearly disappointed, but Jack could sense a storm in the air and he didn't want this kid getting caught up in it.

But then he looked at him properly for the first time. 'What happened to your eye?'

The young guy put his hand to his face. 'Oh, yeah, that. About the same as what happened to your face, I reckon.'

Jack leaned in close to him, he could see burst blood vessels, zig-zagging red streaks across the white of his eye, and blotchy patches on the edge of a deep purple bruise surrounding it.

'Was that your dad?' Jack asked, a hint of rage just edging his voice.

Daniel nodded. 'Yeah, but it's ok, it stopped Carla, my sister, getting any of it.' He changed the subject instinctively. 'I completed the next level for you, and the next target is a policeman. You stab them and then plant evidence on them.'

Jack allowed him to move the conversation away from his injury. 'Policeman? How did you know which one to kill?'

'I didn't, you could choose any, it was to stop a court case happening or something, I wasn't really paying attention to that bit, I thought you would just want to know who he was going to kill next. And that's also when that guy turned up. Is that ok?'

Jack patted him on the back and walked him to the door. 'You did excellent, mate, go home and get some rest. I'll help you sort your dad out another day, ok, once I've cleared this up a bit. Oh, and if you think someone is following you, just circle back round on yourself and come straight back here, ok?'

Daniel smiled. 'Wow, I feel like a spy. No one can follow me on that thing anyway.' He pointed at his moped. 'I go down all sorts of back alleys and secret passageways, I'll be ok.'

Jack waited until he had put his helmet on and sped off along the waterfront before closing the door to the boat.

'Great, now we might have a cop killer on our hands, just when I thought it couldn't get much worse,' he spoke to himself as he poured a large glass of whisky. He looked at the bottle for a second and wondered which one of his last four guests had brought it with them, as he was sure it hadn't been there before, but decided dwelling on it was not as important as drinking it.

Jack found McQuade's number and dialled it on his mobile. He put it on loudspeaker so he could help himself to another drink and search his cupboards for something to eat.

Her voice was short and urgent on answering. 'Jack,

you ok?'

'Yes ma'am, just got some information you need to know. The next victim on the computer game is a police officer; we need to tell any uniformed out on patrol to keep an eye out and stay extra safe, only work in pairs, etcetera.'

'Ok, good work, Jack, we still aren't getting any cooperation from the game manufacturer on that front at the moment, and they are trying to distance themselves as far as possible. They have even denied to the press that we have contacted them at all, which isn't helping. I've got a bit of an update on the motorbike for you also. We had a few witnesses claiming to have seen a bike on the evenings of our murders. Not many, only four, so we questioned all of them and asked them to look through some pictures of bikes. Now, they all chose different bikes but they were all very similar, and all four claim that it was black with this white detailing. Our vehicle experts have said that it is most likely a custom detail job, so I've got Kapoor and Peters following that up as a possible lead.'

'Shit they have done more than me and I'm motivated by my life being on the line.'

'That's great news, ma'am. If I get anything else, I'll be in contact.'

'Same here, I'll speak to you soon. Oh, and Jack?'

'Yes, ma'am?'

'Good to hear you're still alive.'

'Yes, ma'am.'

The phone went dead and Jack grabbed a bowl down and a box of cornflakes. He was just pouring them when the   door   to   the   boat   clicked   open.

MI5

'Daniel? Were you followed?'

No one answered, so he stepped out to look down the boat. A man in a suit stood facing him, with his hands up in classic surrender pose. Jack looked at him and then down at his hand. It was perfectly possible that he could have picked up a weapon and been pointing it at the intruder without realising it, but he hadn't, he only had a spoon in his hand.

The man walked slowly towards him, still holding up his palms and making no sudden movements, and then Jack heard the tell-tale click of the hammer on a gun being slowly released back into safety position.

Tanya Red poked her head from around the man's back.

'Evening, lover, I found this guy snooping around your starboard side and thought he might want to have a meeting with you.'

'Hi, Jack,' the man said calmly, lowering his hands and straightening his cuffs.

'It's ok, Tanya, I know him and he's harmless,' Jack told her, trying not to show too much glee.

Tanya barged past the man, deliberately knocking him, and placed the gun on the kitchen side before sitting on the sofa.

'He may be harmless, but he wasn't armless. That gun is his,' she told Jack as she checked the chipped paintwork on her nails.

'I would say it's good to see you, Collingwood, however Mother told me I mustn't tell lies.' Jack turned to address Tanya, 'It's ok, we were at training together, someone got fast tracked and recruited to MI5 – it pays to be well off, you see.'

The intruder laughed. 'How sour are those grapes, Jack? The fact that I speak four languages and have a degree in social economics may also have given me an edge over some of our lesser-talented colleagues. And this is the infamous Tanya Red. I think you should keep your pit bull on a shorter lead, Jack.'

Tanya bared her teeth and growled at the suited man.

'What the fuck are you doing here? My night has been stressful enough.' Jack was starting to lose his temper as he grabbed for the bottle to have another glass of whisky.

The tall, broad man slicked his hair back and adjusted his collar.

'Jesus Christ, Jack, what happened to you? You showed such promise – a bit underwhelming at times, sure – but not like this. You should try harder at looking after yourself, you know.'

The spy appeared to have far too much pleasure in his tone of voice for Jack's liking. The glass in his hand was soon beginning to feel like quite an acceptable missile.

He spoke through gritted teeth, 'So I have been told. Now, seriously, what do you want? You do realise how much I have going on?'

'What do I want? I want you to start doing your job and stop letting the side down, Jack. I'm here to tell you that your little gallivanting murderer is causing all sorts of havoc for us and it needs to stop. He has already killed an important person of interest and from what I can tell you have a brilliant nothing on him. How is that even possible?

Three murders and not one important piece of evidence – you genuinely could have been doing this job so far with your eyes closed. Get it sorted and get it done quickly, or I'll make sure you will end up on the dole for the rest of your life.' Collingwood picked up the whisky bottle and looked at it in disgust. 'However short the rest of your life may end up being. Do you understand me, Jack?'

Jack didn't answer. He was hardly listening, he had reverted back inside his own head, thinking beyond the facts he was being told, making his conclusions.

'They're not police informants, they are working for you. The Polish are working for the secret service. No wonder they have the balls to do whatever they want and no one has been allowed to touch them. You are fucking protecting them.'

Collingwood laughed. 'Oh, don't be so naïve, Jack, of course they are working for us – well, the major players are, anyway. Don't you understand they have contacts with terrorist organisations, sex traffickers, and major drug lords throughout Europe? They are assistants that we can ill afford to lose, whatever your opinion on their business credentials.'

'They are just a means to a greater good, no matter how many lives they ruin in the process? Have you seen Jack's face, they did that to someone they need *help* from, what do you think they do to people who don't matter to them?' Tanya was focused and on edge, like a cat ready to pounce.

The spy was not bothered by her presence or her words. 'You know, Jack, we have tried to recruit this little feisty one on several occasions, each time she has told the department where to go. Its commendable, it really is, but you must know that you have much less freedom on the outside than you do on the in, Tanya. Anyway,' Collingwood said with a chipper tone to his voice, 'I shall leave you love birds to your cosy night in, but heed my warning, Jack, these scum are actually worth more than you right now.'

The spy picked up his gun and tucked it away while keeping a keen eye on Tanya before turning and walking casually out of the boat.

'How far have you fallen down the rabbit hole with this one, Jack?' Tanya said, getting up off of the sofa.

Jack gave her a small laugh of appreciation. 'I think I may be turning into the Mad Hatter at this rate. It's beginning to get a bit messy.' Jack sat down in the spot that Tanya had just vacated and rubbed the back of his head as he hunched over.

'Right, well, no more drink, I'll get some of your meds and a glass of water. I have something I need to show you. It might make things even more complicated, I'm afraid, but it can't wait.'

Tanya left the boat and returned with a satchel, she looked through the bathroom cupboards for some tablets and, as she said she would, gave them to Jack with a glass of water to help wash them down.

'You should probably have a coffee, too, before I show you this,' she said, eyeing him inquisitively.

'Just get on with it, my head is as clear as it can be, considering everything.'

He stood up to look at what Tanya was now removing from the bag and placing on the side. She placed a protective hand on top of some paperwork.

'Well, if you are sure. It's about Jessica and Felicity's murders. I have these and I think you should look at something.'

THE SOCIETY OF JESUS

Jack pulled the papers towards him, opened the file she removed and saw case notes. They were his case notes, he was sure of it. Anger hit him like a sledge hammer in the gut, he couldn't control it, it was like a wild animal suddenly unleashed from bindings, or like a demon striking up from somewhere deep inside him.

He turned on the small woman and grabbed her by the chin, pushing her to the wall.

'Where did you get these? Did you take them from me? Tell me where you got these *now*,' he shouted at her.

The betrayal, it was tantamount with the murder itself, desecrating all that he had left and clung onto for hope.

Tanya looked him straight in the eyes, placed her hand on top of his and slid it calmly down to her throat, where she pushed his grip on her harder.

Jack felt his hand close her airways slightly and her pulse beating against his palm.

'These are not your copies, Jack, they are the originals.' She squeezed his hand tighter, making sure she could only just breathe. 'And this is where you grab someone when you want to frighten them.' She breathed as heavily as she was able, groaning with the slight pain it brought her.

Jack relinquished his grip suddenly, almost falling

183

backwards to the floor, but just managing to stay upright.

'I'm sorry, I'm so sorry, I don't know …'

Jack was close to tears, he hadn't realised that was in him.

Tanya closed the gap between them and cradled his face with her hands. 'Shush now, it's ok, I understand.'

'I didn't mean to.'

She smiled warmly at him. 'I know you didn't. Please, let me show you.'

Jack agreed and she took hold of his hand and guided him to the kitchen side and the files again.

'This is going to be hard, but there is some evidence you haven't seen.'

Jack shook his head. 'That's impossible, I have copies of everything that was in the files, I'm sure of it.'

Tanya nodded in agreement. 'Yes, you did, but there was something taken out and held for some time in another location.' She spread a few of the files out, for Jack to look at. 'Now, all of these are dated in accordance with each other, all inspected and filed together by the lead detective. And, look, signed and dated again when the case was handed over to cold cases.'

Jack was sure that she was being careful to not let any of the pictures from the scene be displayed.

'Now this, however …' She held a couple of pictures to her chest. 'It's not pretty, Jack.'

'It's fine, please, just show me,' he pleaded.

She gently placed the photos down in front of him. 'Now, these have a much later date on them, a date of return from only a year ago, look. And they are signed but I can't work out whose signature it is. Anyway, that's not important, but what is in them is important.'

Jack looked down at the bodies of his wife and child, taken in two separate pictures. They were from the same angle as the ones that he had in his lock-up but they looked completely different. They were made up of different shades of blue and mauve, and where the rich colour of blood should be, a bright, white substance was present instead.

'What is this? I haven't seen these, and I wasn't told that ultraviolet was used. Why did they keep this from me?' Jack asked, scrutinising every detail in the images, tears filling his eyes again. It was only pictures of their torsos and back, where they had been shot, but that was more than enough to tear him up inside.

'I think this may have gone a bit above anyone's pay grade at the police department,' Tanya replied, placing a comforting hand on his back.

Tears dropped from his eyes now on to the paperwork and he traced his finger down the back of his daughter's spine. It was then that he noticed something, something peculiar that his copy of pictures had never exposed before.

'What the— What is that? Those marks there, I haven't seen them before.'

Tanya pushed the picture of Jack's wife in front of him. 'They are on Jessica also. They are very light bruising – I mean so light they were undetectable to the human eye, but under UV the burst blood vessels are incredibly clear.'

'But how did they get there? They look like some sort of writing. I don't understand. A major clue like this and it was hidden, hidden from the department, kept from me. Why did they do this?' Jack's mind was pinballing from hurt to confusion.

'You're right, it is a language, and it has taken me two months to figure out which one,' Tanya explained.

'You have had this for two months and you haven't told me?' Jack's fury sparked again for a moment.

'Tell you what? There is weird bruising on them and it might be a language? You would only have taken the pictures from me and gotten nowhere with them. Jack, I speak seven languages fluently and have contacts with the best professors in ancient dialects up and down the country. I was the only one able to work this out, so I left it in the best hands available – mine. Hate me if you want, but I just saved you two months of agony and anxiety.' The young woman widened her eyes at Jack's so as to dare him to tell her that she was wrong.

Even Jack was capable of the maths in that equation and she was right, knowing sooner without being able to do anything about it would have driven him to destruction.

'You're right, thank you. So, what language is it?'

Tanya took a deep breath. 'It is one that nearly no one speaks anymore and one that none of my contacts speak, but a professor in Manchester recognised what it was straight away. It's a form of Aramaic, an ancient language that was adapted over time and became what we now know as Arabic in roughly the seventh century.'

Jack shook his head with confusion but allowed Tanya to carry on explaining.

'It's a very rare form of language and only roughly two hundred thousand people speak it. But there is a problem, this particular form of Aramaic is only spoken by a handful of those two hundred thousand, so locating someone has been a little beyond me, but there is something else that can help.'

She flipped the pictures over and pointed at a small, flattened bit of wax.

'That is a seal. You know, the type that was used to seal letters hundreds of years ago. Well, this is only a year old. I have looked at the image on the seal closely, and you're not going to believe this but it's the crest of la Compañía de Jesús, otherwise known as The Society of Jesus.'

Jack shook his head. 'No, means nothing.'

'It shouldn't, but you may have heard of The Army of Jesus – that's what they are normally referred to in the media and things like that. They've been affectionally named as such as they operate in cells all around the globe, waiting and ready to act when given the command. Now, their image is one of cushions and fluffy animals at the moment, which is due to the big effort on the part of the churches to hide their more, shall we say, *sinister* acts.'

Jack was impressed, he didn't realise religion could be this interesting. 'So, what do they claim is their intention, then?'

'Well, all their press stuff talks about how they build schools and help people out of poverty through education, blah, blah, blah. But throughout time this sect – this completely male sect, I might add – have been accused of assassinations, cover ups and even have their own small team of investigators. They look into so-called Catholic miracles. So, from what I can see, they have a public image as do-gooders, and a private one of, well, whatever you can think of.'

Jack looked closely at the wax on the piece of paper. It looked like a small picture of a sun, inside its centre were three letters in capitals, I, H and S, and piercing the crossbar on the middle letter was a tiny cross.

Tanya carried on speaking, 'The members of the society call themselves "Jesuits", and, like I said, it's a completely male gang. They are very secretive and, owing to their complete contempt of women, I thought it would probably be best left for you to approach them. Now, all of the members in this country that I have been able to find are more of a smokescreen, I can't see how any of them hold any power in the society. It would seem that the Vatican keeps the members with real power close.'

'The Vatican?' Jack looked up from the pages in front of him, his neck felt stiff where it had been so rigid with his determination to absorb all that had been presented to him.

'Oh yes, this goes all the way to the top, Jack. I mean, the current pope is a member.'

Jack took a few steps away from the counter and looked wildly around before sitting down on the sofa.

'You have got to be fucking kidding me. In the last twenty-four hours I have got caught up with drug lords, spooks, psychic, motorbike-driving old women, and now the church?'

Tanya laughed. 'Psychic what?'

Jack waved a hand, batting her question away. 'It doesn't matter. I really don't know what to do with this, Tanya, I really don't. I can't go up to the Vatican – Jesus Christ, I have never even been to Rome – and start banging on the pope's door. I've got a murderer in my city that I have nothing on and I'm nowhere near catching, a drug lord who wants my head on a platter so he can bury it next to his dead brother in the fucking mountain tops somewhere, MI5 trying to turn me into a whipping boy, and that's not to mention someone on the force selling confiscated drugs back onto the market.'

The detective's breathing became heavy and frantic, sweat beads decorated the outer edges of his face as he burned from the inside out.

Tanya sat down on the floor in front of him. 'It's ok, Jack, none of this is your responsibility, and no one is asking you to solve all these problems but you. It's ok not to be ok, sometimes, and it's ok to be selfish. This murderer is attacking the city, it's the city's problem, not specifically yours, and you are only one man.'

Tanya gave Jack a moment for her words to settle in.

'I have a name for you, it's a priest who used to be a Jesuit. This is your family we are talking about, Jack, *this* is your problem. I will leave his name and where you can find him on the side. It's ok to concentrate on yourself, Jack, no one else is going to look after you.'

Jack looked down into her big, green eyes. 'You always seem to be looking after me.'

She leaned in close to him, gently holding his head like she always did, and kissed him on the cheek. 'I have to go away for a day or two.'

Jack looked worried, he thought he had just scared her away by being too honest, too open.

Tanya recognised his anxiety. 'No, it's just business. I have to see a dog about a man and sort a couple of arms deals in Northern Ireland. A woman's work is never done, after all,' she joked and walked back to the paperwork. 'I'll write his details on here, and Jack, do whatever you want. After all, that's what everyone else is doing, isn't it?'

FATHER CAMALDO

The boat felt so empty, more than it ever had before. Jack tried to convince himself that it was because that night had seen more people come and go in a matter of hours than had been through its door the whole time that he had been living there, but he knew that wasn't true. It felt more abandoned now because of him being trapped inside it, stuck in a cell where everything and everyone on the other side of the steel hull was against him. The tight walls felt as though he was stuck in a snow globe and the force with which all of this information had hit him was the shake it had needed to send his whole life into a blizzard.

'No, you're not that important, Jack,' he told himself.

He grabbed his coat and headed for the streets. The tall buildings and immense crowds in the city centre were a good way of reminding him just how insignificant he really was.

Jack walked against a rush of people crossing the swing bridge at the end of the docks. The cranes shed huge shadows, stretching across the water and beyond to the concrete amphitheatre of the Lloyds building. The smack of wood on smooth concrete as skateboarders bailed from their high-flying tricks hit Jack's eardrums, reminding him of how small things matter to all people. He watched as a girl landed her feet square on the deck of her skateboard and imagined being her for that moment. That split second in the air where she was unsure if she would land smoothly, that essence of nothing else existing apart from the air beneath her feet, purifying the world into a single, flawless experience.

It had been a long time since he had let the borderline personality disorder in without deconstructing it. It felt like it had been a part of someone else that he had only known in a past life for so long that it was almost like rediscovering an old friend, or an artist picking up a paintbrush after a ten-year sabbatical, who starts creating moments from their dreams and abstract images of how the world should and could be. How could this feeling be wrong? How could *feeling* be wrong? He had been, for all intents and purposes, a walking zombie for years now, letting everything around him deflect off his armour – including love and hope. Now he was full to the brim with it, so much so that it threatened to spill over, flow out of him and show the world his whole existence.

But no, that was the problem. That was why his borderline personality disorder needed to be handled with care, or with unbiased oppression, at least. The world didn't reflect him. Everything that he could become was not the right shaped peg to fit the hole where he belonged, and if you couldn't fit in, you got left out.

'What's the plan, Jack? Got to have a plan,' he said aloud, leaning on the bridge. He knew he had started to block out the borderline personality disorder already as he didn't care about the women looking at him as he spoke to thin air.

Without realising it, his hand was grasping something; it was the piece of paper that Tanya had written on. It seemed amusing to Jack how often he did things without realising. It had started with placing objects in strange places, like his phone in the fridge, or his wallet in a kitchen drawer, but the more that he became accustomed to it, the more elaborate his subconscious had become. He often would realise that he had watched the entirety of a late-night film without knowing he was doing so. He had taken a shower and shaved before while thinking about a case. It only become apparent to him that he had been cleaned and pruned when he pulled on clean clothes. It must have been a survival tactic that he had acquired over the years of battling his mental health pitfalls.

One of the symptoms of many mental health conditions that Jack had been forced to learn about during his diagnosis programme was the rushing, reoccurring negative thoughts. They used to plague him at night, keeping him up for all of it on regular occasions. He could often feel his mind stuck in a high tempo, chasing one thought after another and just not being quite able to catch them and pin them down. He would think so much and for so long he would become physically exhausted from the process, one that was completely undetectable to others and could often result in them calling it laziness. So, Jack's brain turned its excess power to the physical rather than the emotional, allowing him to do things and learn experiences without the need for a constant conscious host.

He unscrewed the ball of paper and read it.

Father Vincenzo Camaldo, Clifton Cathedral.

This surprised Jack, he had lived in Clifton for six years and never known there to be a cathedral, but then again, he hadn't had much of a chance to take relaxing strolls around the neighbourhood. They had chosen to live in the nicest part of Bristol without actually having the time to experience it. His work had been back-to-back cases, and the only time he had been given off was paternity leave, which had consisted of two months of nappy changing and bottle warming. Jessica, even after having Felicity, still

managed to hold down a full-time journalist career –
sometimes this had meant strapping the baby to her and
getting on with it, which Jack had always admired.

'I do need to check on the house,' he convinced himself.

A small, niggling voice in the back of his thoughts told
him not to neglect the murder case – if only to stay alive,
do not neglect the murder case.

*'I don't have anything until we can get a trace on the bullet
anyway,'* the louder voice overruled. He checked his keys to
see if he still had one for the house on the bunch and, on
finding   it,   he   flagged   down   a   taxi.

HEAR THEM RASPING

'Tonight, we will do it tonight. This one will rip through them like a tidal wave through a village, washing grief straight into their hearts. We will enjoy this one, nice and close, nice and personal, close to sexual. Yes, it is like sex, but better, more intense an experience for all of us. We will watch as our blade slides out of them, blood running down it, splattering the ground with a beautiful mess. I can hear them rasping already, pleading with us to save them, to stop what we are doing to them. Their lack of control is our greatest achievement, they can't even take a breath without us letting them, and we will not let them, we will take everything. I want to feel their body against mine, twitching and writhing under the pain and panic, we can press our weight down on them while they are powerless. Shall we pierce them slowly? Shall we gently allow our blade to make its way between muscle and bone? I think we should enjoy every second of this one, our crowning glory up till now.'

Mrs Keilty wiped the tears from her eyes. She was not sad – these had been tears of joy. Tears of eager joy at what was about to come and then she felt sick. She pulled the magazine that she had been reading on her lap out from under the cat who had settled on top of it and placed it aside. She breathed heavily and stroked the ginger moggy, the nauseating thoughts that had flooded her consciousness had been strong. They had come unexpectedly   and   they   had   not   been   her   own.

DEMONS

Jack looked at the picture on his phone of the cathedral and then at the building in front of him.

It occurred to him that he had driven by this building hundreds of times and somehow it had managed to go unnoticed. The *somehow* unnoticed was because, right then, he was considering naming it the ugliest building he had ever seen.

'It looks like it was designed in the seventies by somebody who hates architecture and god equally,' he thought as he walked up the concrete paving slab walkway. The outer walls were more concrete, this time in huge, brown blocks, and had been placed together in a way that left nothing but harsh angles.

He pushed open the doors and was greeted by a huge amphitheatre-like space. It was surprisingly light, seeing as its interior was, again, a masterpiece of pre-formed concrete.

It was completely empty and his footsteps sounded intrusive as they echoed around the large, cavernous area. He decided to do what they did in films, and chose a random pew to sit on as he waited for someone to arrive, asking if he needed guidance. That didn't work and it only took Jack ten minutes to get bored enough to start exploring the rest of the cathedral. A small gold plaque on a discreet door told him that it was the office, he knocked and, to his relief, a voice told him to enter.

'May I help you?' A man dressed in robes looked up at Jack over the top of some small reading spectacles. He was bearded, which made it impossible to tell how old he was. The hairs were grey, which allowed Jack to assume that he was older than him, but the cheeks were full and there were hardly any lines on his face, even though he was smiling warmly.

'I am looking for a Father Vincenzo Camaldo. Sorry, my pronunciation is probably awful,' Jack said, entering the small office.

The man gently placed a pair of half-moon glasses down and stood to shake Jack's hand. 'It is not too awful, and you have found me. How can I help you?'

The priest's accent was thick and Jack instantly recognised it as being that of an Italian man speaking English. It was playful on the ear and interesting to listen to against the backdrop of the usual heavy thumps of the Bristolian take on English.

The people that he normally interviewed treated the English language with as much contempt as an old, beat-up car that they were deliberately trying to run into the ground.

'My name is Detective O'Connor and I am investigating a murder.' Jack thought about how relevant this man's help could be in his professional, as well as personal, search for answers. 'Well, actually, it's multiple murders, and multiple investigations, and I was hoping to ask you some questions. It's ok, you're not a suspect.'

The older man in front of him smiled even more broadly. 'Indeed, I should hope that I am not. But, of course, I will help in any way that I can, Detective. Why don't we leave the confines of this miserable office and talk somewhere more comfortable?'

He led Jack back into the main, large room of the

cathedral and gestured for him to sit in the front row, facing a white, stone altar.

'Now, Detective, what questions would you like to ask of me?' the priest said, making the sign of a cross on his chest.

Jack looked up at the cross on the wall. Usually he hated the symbols of religion. He felt that they held more power than the people following what they stood for, and power out of human hands seemed to be uncontrollable. But today, and he wasn't sure if it was owing to the quiet nature of this particular building, or whether for once a cathedral looked to have been a reasonable price to build, the cross seemed to be a beautiful decoration.

'I need to ask you about the Society of Jesus, if that is ok?'

Jack noticed a slight tightness appear in the priest's, until then, relaxed manner.

'I can talk about the society as a whole, but I am not a part of it anymore – I cannot speak on behalf of them. I hope you can understand this, Detective.'

'I understand, but I am investigating murders so I may be asking uncomfortable questions, and I hope that you will give me the respect of answering. I hope you can understand that?'

The priest turned his body to face Jack directly. 'Yes, Detective, there is no greater crime than murder, I will assist you with no prejudice if I am able.'

Jack was unsure how to take the last statement, but right then his head was with the information that Tanya had given him about the society, and that was enough for him to push this man to get answerers.

'Could you tell me why the Jesuits may be interested in evidence from a murder scene?'

The priest seemed to consider this for a moment. 'I can think of many reasons why certain parts of the Society of Jesus would be interested. If there was extraordinary circumstances – the appearance of a possible miracle, maybe.'

Jack wasn't sure how much honesty he could expect from this man, but he certainly didn't avoid answering.

'Do they have the authority to take evidence? You were part of the organisation, were you not?'

The priest smiled his warm smile again. 'I was a member, a key figure in investigations, in fact, but that was many years ago. Unfortunately, I had ideas that were not coherent with what my peers considered important. You see, Detective, I wanted religion to be transparent for its followers, which is why, as a scientist, I urged all the evidence in our investigations to be made public property. These ideals of mine were not matched and eventually the powers that be saw to it that I was no longer a thorn in their side, as it were.'

Jack was warming up to this man slowly, it was something about the way he had wanted to choose the right path over the usually trodden one.

'As for your question regarding evidence, I would think that, yes, they do have a certain authority. As a police officer, you will be well aware of the term "sleeper agent". Well, the Society had Jesuits in many different places and as many different leading characters in important fields, including the police force. It only takes one phone call or meeting by a high priest and that agent becomes live, and acts according to what is asked of him. If you imagine the type of powerful people that work as part of an organisation like this, then it would not take much to consider that they have that much authority collectively. You seem to be at war with yourself, Detective, is this something close to you? Maybe something a little more specific?' the priest asked.

Jack wanted to be able to trust him, he wanted to be able to ask straight, but currently he couldn't see how anyone was on his side.

'It is close to my heart and, unfortunately, is a matter of confidentiality, so forgive me, Father, if I choose my words very carefully.'

The priest nodded in agreement. 'Confidentiality is what makes the world stand still when it has to, but I understand. We are not so dissimilar, Detective, I, too, used to investigate what others failed to understand, and many a time they did not like the answer I would give them.'

The priest turned away from Jack and leaned back on the chair, relaxing himself against the hard wood. 'Do you know what makes them saints in the eyes of the Catholic Church, Detective?' The priest nodded towards an old painting on the wall. It depicted an elderly man reading from a book. A solid-looking halo sat firmly on his head like a balancing discus.

'Miracles, isn't it?'

'Indeed it is, Detective; if a person performs two miracles, if they are said to have been touched by God twice, then they are to be treated as saints. Have you heard of Saint Drago, Detective?'

Jack shook his head.

'He is the Patron Saint of unattractive people; unbelievable, I know, yet it is true. He vowed his life to God and as he grew older he was afflicted with a disease that caused facial disfigurement. Before he became too ugly for the townspeople to bear he had shed himself of all of his belongings, it is said that this was a form of penance for him, due to his mother dying while giving birth. So his church built him a cell for him to spend the remainder of his life in, so onlookers could be spared from his ugliness . The reason he was granted sainthood was that he was believed to bilocate – people said that he was seen working the fields when others were seeing him at mass. Now, these circumstances today would be seen as, shall we say, *scientifically negotiable*. For example, it may have been that two people in the town had been afflicted with the same growth disorder, a DNA trait, possibly. At the time, the church made the best decision that they felt possible with the information that had been presented to them – and here is where I differ from many of my colleagues, Detective – just because that was the best decision at the time, does not make it the best one now.'

Jack felt like he understood all too well. In his line of work, evidence could change from minute to minute, it could be admissible one moment before being thrown out the next.

'You are wondering why I am telling you this, Detective.'

'To be honest, yes, Father, I am.'

The older man rubbed his knees, obviously feeling some discomfort from sitting still. 'I am trying to let you know, Detective, that I am not afraid to disagree with those powers to which I must answer. If I see a wrong, I will do all in my power to help change it, my belief guides me to the truth – in science and in religion. I have met many troubled men looking for answers in my time, Detective O'Connor, and I can see the anguish in you. If you would let me, I would like to help you.'

Jack wished he could allow someone to relieve his burden slightly, but there were people he had known all his life that he was still protective of his family's memory around. Maybe this tactic had driven him into the rut he was in, maybe trying to carry this alone was why it had become too much of a weight to bear, dragging him further and further into an early grave.

The priest spoke to relieve the room of its silence. 'Alas, faith in people is often the hardest to achieve – perhaps this is a road you must tread alone, Detective.'

No, he owed it to Jessica and Felicity to take risks, to try anything to discover the truth. He had achieved nothing yet, so why not throw everything up into the wind to see where it landed, as long as it didn't blow away?

'My wife and daughter were murdered five years ago. They were shot and the killer was never caught. There was very little evidence until recently. I have discovered pictures that were taken under ultraviolet light.'

The priest made the sign of the cross again before speaking, 'I am sorry for your loss, Detective.'

Father Camaldo breathed heavily and linked his fingers together tightly across his lap, obviously considering what he had heard.

'I know of this technique, it is to allow you to see a truer picture of the patterns of blood, is it not?'

'Usually, yes. It helps determine direction of splatter and sometimes shows where blood had been previously, before being cleaned up. On this occasion, however, it shows bruising on my wife and daughter. Very light bursting of blood vessels, and it is this that I would like to speak to you about.'

The priest looked confused. 'I am a scientist of cosmology, I know very little of the human body in that sense.'

'I appreciate that, Father, but a very reliable source,' Jack winced internally at the thought of Tanya Red being a reliable source, 'has informed me that these bruises are in the shape of a language – an early form of Aramaic, to be exact.'

The old man's posture became rigid again, and his voice was one of shock, 'That is the language of our Lord, it is almost unheard of to see it in this country.'

'And on these pictures is the seal of the Society of Jesus,' Jack said forcefully, hoping to hammer home how important this truly was.

The old man scratched at his beard as he drifted away in thought.

He turned back to Jack and seemed to be examining him once more. 'I believe I can help you. Walk with me, won't you?'

He pointed at the direction of the candles in the corner of the large room and Jack led the way over to them.

The priest took a long splint from a small holder and handed it to Jack. 'Why not light a candle for your daughter and one for your wife.'

Jack carefully held the splint to one of the already lit tea lights and moved the flame to two untouched wicks. For the first time in a while he smiled at the thought of them, at the images of them being alive and well.

'The reason why the Society would be interested in this is very clear. As I said, the language of Jesus is incredibly rare. There are only a handful of scholars, most of whom work at the Vatican itself, that can decipher it. But as well as this, the language of our Lord is said to be indicative of the presence of either a miracle or, I am sorry to say, a demonic habitation. I believe that a full investigation would have been carried out on the murder of your family, Detective, with the sole aim of discovering under which circumstance this writing happened to become – whether it was due to the hand of good or of evil.'

Jack stared at the tiny flames as they stood perfectly still, there was not a single breeze to animate them, they looked rigid and whole, like he could pluck them from the air.

'Demons?' he finally asked, already knowing it to be true.

The priest didn't answer right away, but instead took the splint from the detective and ignited his own candle.

'I have seen evil, Detective, so dark that it defies my beliefs in the natural world. I cannot answer if demons are real in a sense that we can measure or explain, but I know the evil to which they are said to possess is as real as you and I.' To Jack's surprise the priest's warm smile returned. 'And the argument of how real you and I are is one for another day. I can entertain you with my facts about how much of our make-up is, in fact, empty space. But if you would be so kind as to return to speak to me I still have friends in the Vatican, I shall speak with them and see if I can find out some information from them.'

The door to the cathedral opened and two large men, both wearing thick leather jackets, entered. They glared at

Jack and took up seats near the exit.

'Speaking of friends, it would seem that you have brought two of your own. I trust you do not need assistance with this?' the priest asked as he smiled and waved to the two men, who did not return the gesture.

'No, Father, they are just babysitting me for someone very nasty.'

'You get more and more interesting, Detective. I shall speak with you soon.'

Jack left the older man to bow his head so he could pray, and headed out.

'Evening, boys,' he said to his two minders as he passed between them.

They followed him all the way to his house, staying at a professional thirty feet behind, and smoking the customary roll up cigarettes.

Jack entered the house, leaving the two goons to lean against the railings of the small green across the road.

The entrance hall was empty of belongings and its tiled floor was clean, which was as much notice as Jack would allow himself to take.

That was the spot which he had raced to, where he saw the body of his wife being moved on to an ambulance gurney, blood stained. His daughter had already been placed in a body bag and been moved, a sight that Jack was spared, a sight that he thought would have killed him of a broken heart.

He quickly walked through to the living room. Its large windows allowed the waning light to fill the dual-aspect room. Half of the furniture remained; the family that had moved in had tried to keep as much of it in place as possible to save Jack from storing it, but a family of five only had so much space that they could spare, as they brought a large amount of their own belongings with them.

The dining table, however, remained, and on it stood a large bottle of whisky with a card. Jack picked it up and read the words on the front.

They read a brightly coloured *Thank you* and inside the whole family had signed, even the youngest who had been given a red crayon. Jack took the bottle to the kitchen with him, poured himself a large measure into a leftover mug and returned to the room at the front of the house. He closed the wooden, slatted shutters that his late wife had convinced him to buy. He saluted the two men across the road before blocking them out. He had always hated these blinds when Jessica had been alive, it had been a combination of the price, the overenthusiastic saleswoman at John Lewis and the fact that it had taken four trips to the store before the colour was settled upon. Now, though, they were the crowning glory of an otherwise scarce room, and Jessica had been right, the windows were the eyes of the room and they deserved to be appropriately dressed.

He sat in a lonely armchair in the corner and tried to not let the past drill into his psyche.

ON THE MOVE

Her heart pounded with excitement and she could feel the breeze cold on her cheeks. She didn't want the visor down, she wanted to feel everything, wanted to occupy her skin as her environment became more and more electric. The road ahead was clear so she pulled the throttle back, taking a deep breath as her destination closed in on her.

Mrs Keilty opened her eyes. She was half surprised to find herself sitting on the edge of her bed and not powering down a B road on her motorbike. It had been her first attempt at deliberately channelling the visions that had previously plagued her. She was sweating and out of breath, it had felt more physical than emotional to work her way into the mind of this murderer, and she had not gotten far before it had been too much for her to bear.

She stroked one of her ever-present cats.

'He is on the move, and it won't be long now.'

The cat meowed loudly.

'It's ok, mummy's ok now.'

She left the comfort of her bedroom to find her phone and Detective O'Connor's card.

BRITISH ARMY

Jack sat with his head leaning back, facing the ceiling, imitating being asleep. It had been too long since he had last taken his medication, which would usually allow his mind the freedom to shut off completely. It took a while for it to sink in that the vibration in his jacket pocket was his phone ringing. He took it out and it gave the corner he was occupying a cold, white glow. He read the name and answered.

'Hello?'

'Jack, it's me. I've got the report for you,' Aubrie told him.

Jack couldn't quite align what she was saying into his conscious thought. 'Report?'

He heard her sigh over the phone. 'Yes, the report on the bullet that we extracted from a skull at three AM surrounded by thugs. Remember?'

Jack rubbed an eye, he didn't feel tired but he must have been to be very far away from where Aubrie had expected him to be.

'Yes, of course, sorry. What's the news?'

He heard the clicking of a keyboard in the background. 'Right, well, I had the ballistics back about half an hour ago. It was new ammunition for an old rifle. The gun in question was used by the British army in the late eighties–early nineties. There are lots of them around, especially in other parts of the world – a few places like Ukraine and Kuwait. I think they have been sold on under the radar to help resistance fighters, etcetera. A bit of an assumption, I know, but we all love a good conspiracy story. But, however, it does mean that it's a common gun that is easy to use and doesn't need to be handled by anyone overly competent. My brief investigation of the wound confirmed the distance and trajectory of the shot to be consistent with that of the power of this weapon. Sorry, Jack, I think I may have just handed you another haystack with a needle in it.'

Jack let out a soft groan. 'Ok, that's fine. I can work with that, I'll get onto McQuade now. And Aubrie?'

'Yes, Jack?'

'Thank you, for everything.'

He hung up and flicked his way through his recent calls to find his superior's number. She answered after only one ring.

'Jack, you ok?' she sounded concerned, she clearly hadn't expected him to be troubling her tonight.

'Yes, ma'am, I'm fine, just got some info on the gun used on Yanislav's brother.'

He heard her breathe in relief. 'Good. I have a pen, go on.'

Jack explained about the weapon and how little information it actually divulged. McQuade wasn't as discouraged as he was, and Jack wondered inwardly if his lack of enthusiasm may be what was holding the investigation back.

'Ok, well, at least we have enough to get us into local gun clubs to ask around. So it's not a complete loss. All our officers are paired up, especially uniform – don't want anyone making themselves an easy target for our man. Have you passed this on to your new partner?'

'You mean Yanislav? No, not yet, but I will have to

soon, before he beats it out of me. Are there no leads on the bike?' Jack asked, hoping desperately.

'No, nothing yet. I've got Peters going around garages in the city that specialise in bikes, but so far nothing has turned up. We will get there, Jack, just keep plugging away, something will come up. Your team are at the pub tonight; it's Officer Smith's birthday. I tried to give her the day off, but she insisted on coming in and going over witness statements. I believe she is what kids these days refer to as a "swat". They are in the one on the Christmas Steps, perhaps you should go and let your hair down for an hour with them?'

Jack walked back over to the window to peer out. 'I can't. I have some new admirers watching my every move. A pub full of coppers isn't the best place to lead them.'

'Ok, well, keep your head up, Jack, unless someone starts shooting at you. I've got things covered here; just do what you've got to do, and let's see if we can save both our jobs by finding this bastard.'

Jack laughed, he had forgotten it wasn't just his neck on the line. While his was a more literal threat, McQuade was still risking a lot.

'Yes ma'am. I won't let you down.'

He hung up the phone. He hated leaving the conversation on what he thought was probably a lie but it was the only thing he could have said, given the circumstances.

TURN TO CRIMSON

'It's just dark enough now, we can hide and wait here, just wait until the right moment to strike. That's it, keep calm, take deep, slow breaths, it won't be long. Take out your phone and make the call.'

'Hello?' She heard nothing. 'Hello? Who's this?' Still no reply, or at least they were too quiet to be heard above the throng in the pub. 'Hang on, I can't hear you, I'll go outside.'

Officer Smith held her hand over the mouthpiece and handed her bag to her friend, asking her to hold it as she went outside to take the call.

'Sorry, I couldn't hear you, who is this?' She held the smartphone away from her face to look at its screen. She assumed the caller had hung up, but they hadn't – it still said *Call connected*.

She was just about to hang up when it dropped unexpectedly out of her grip. It hit the floor and smashed. She didn't know it but a large dagger had just plunged into her back, cutting between two vertebrae, damaging her spinal cord.

He had held the phone in front of him, he couldn't hear her through the crash helmet anyway. He watched as it flashed up, saying *Connected*. The general noise of people speaking and laughing emanated from it. He waited patiently, waited until he saw her step out of the pub into the dark alleyway. She was standing with her back to him; it was all too perfect, and the plan was going so smoothly.

Laurel Smith looked down to see her white work shirt slowly turn to crimson. Her hands clutched against her body, one hand on her hip because the knife was being hacked into her from that side. She managed to feel a small level of surprise at how warm the damp was in contrast to her cold skin. It was not terrifying but just interesting. Intriguing how unlike any other feeling her body had been through before it was. The darkness came as she passed out. Her body came crashing to the ground just a mere moment after her phone had, both as broken as one another.

The door to the pub opened.
'Shit, this wasn't in the plan.'
The murderer threw the phone he had been using down at the dying body and ran up the old town steps towards the main road. He had cleared one small flight when a scream chased him up the narrow path. He didn't turn to look but kept running up around an opposing building, making a couple more turns before finding his bike. He kicked it into life and, with not even half throttle, was   gone   and   out   of   sight.

ONE OF YOURS

Jack's phone bleeped once again to signify something that he didn't recognise. He picked it up to see that he had a new voicemail. It took him a couple of moments to remember how to retrieve it and then he listened.

'Jack, it's Mrs Keilty, dear. I just had one of my funny turns and I think something is happening. I think he is heading out to kill someone. Anyway, I'll let you get back to work, dear. Bye.'

Jack went to hang up but then realised there was part of the message remaining.

'I know, Jasper, I'll get you some meat now. I need to get that fruit in the pan too if we are going to make jam tonight. Are you going to help your mummy? Yes, you are, what a good boy you are.'

Jack looked at the screen again. There was still six minutes of the message remaining.

As entertaining as it was listening to the private life of the most eccentric person he had ever met, it was time to delete it. Even if he had wanted to act on the information at the beginning of her message, he wouldn't know where to start – short of walking the streets hoping to be in the right place at the right time, anyway.

He found a charger for his phone in a drawer in the

kitchen tangled amongst a variety of other leads and sat back in the living room beneath a blanket. Half a bottle of whisky and several thousand daydreams later and the sun slowly lit the thin cracks in the shutters. He might have slept or stayed up the whole night through; when his brain was in overactive mode, the two states of mind became far less distinct.

'*A new day, one more survived, but where to head next?*' he wondered, rubbing sleep from the corners of his eyes.

There was a knock at the door, he had been waiting for it all night and, in his head, he had a ten pound bet on it being Yanislav. He opened the door and, to his surprise, there was no Polish mafia boss, no neck or head tattoos and not a rollup in sight.

'Taxi for Jack?' a tall black man with a Bluetooth headset on his ear said as he chewed gum loudly.

Jack was confused – delighted, sure, that he was not staring down the barrel of a gun or already being tied to a chair – he couldn't help but feel like he was constantly on the back foot and off-balance.

'Yes, sure, I will … I'll be right with you. Can you just give me a sec?'

The taxi driver nodded and answered his phone in his small ear contraption. 'Yeah, not a problem, I'll be free in about twenty minutes.' He looked at Jack. 'Hurry, mate. Got another job on,' he said, pointing to his ear.

Jack grabbed his phone, debated on the whisky but decided to come back for it another day, and slipped his shoes on. His minders had left at some point during the night and it appeared that Yanislav felt that watching him was no longer a priority because after two minutes in the taxi it became apparent that, for the first time in a while, he was not being followed.

'Where are we going?' Jack finally asked the driver.

'Marriott Hotel. That's right, isn't it?'

Jack thought about that for a moment, he had never actually been in the Marriott Hotel before. 'I don't know.

Who ordered you?'

The man in front of him looked in the mirror suspiciously. 'Well, I assumed you did. It went through the office. It's prepaid, which is unusual. You sure you're meant to be in here?'

It's not just the prepaid part of this that is unusual,' Jack thought.

'Well, I'm Jack and you knocked on my door.'

The taxi driver shrugged his shoulders. 'I haven't got a clue, mate. Just doing as I'm told. Maybe someone there wants to see you.'

Images of all the people Jack couldn't face seeing flashed across his mind. 'That's what I'm afraid of.'

The journey was short and the taxi driver wished him luck ironically as he headed up the steps to the hotel reception. Two bouncers opened the doors for him and nodded him in. What they were actually doing there at that time of the morning was beyond him, but this whole thing had become intriguing enough that he didn't know what to expect anymore.

The receptionist smiled sweetly and greeted him in a soft, European accent.

'Detective O'Connor? You are right on time, if you see Francois there he will take you to your colleague.'

Jack did so diligently, he had suddenly become aware of how dirty and unkempt he was compared to all of the other people milling around the foyer.

A tall, slim, handsome man led Jack through the hotel to the dining room and pointed to where he was to sit.

There, on a small table for two, sat his superior.

'Good morning, Jack, take a seat. I've ordered you a full breakfast including fried bread.'

Jack was stunned into silence but, being so indoctrinated to the police force as he was, he sat without conscious thought.

McQuade looked at him and shook her head. 'You look like shit, Jack.'

'Yes ma'am, I am aware of that.'

She sipped a cup of tea. 'You worked out that I sent you the taxi, did you?'

Jack, still wide eyed with shock replied honestly, 'Not exactly, no.'

His superior rolled her eyes at him. 'Who else knew you were at your house?'

'Well, Yanislav did.'

McQuade laughed. 'And he would send a taxi for you, would he?'

It was true and Jack knew it, he should have worked it out.

'It was the Marriott that threw me, if I'm honest,' he replied, helping himself to the pot of tea.

'Yes, well. There is some sort of conference here, they have asked for police support for this evening so I knew they would have security on the doors; I assumed you would have a tail. And I was able to put it on the business credit card so I thought, why not? Seeing as this is probably going to be our last case. I hope you like black pudding, it cost three quid extra to have that put on and we wouldn't want you wasting tax payers' money, now, would we?' She placed a napkin on her lap and began buttering a slice of toast. 'I spoke to Doctor Sellers this morning, she told me about the gun and how much of a dead end it probably is. Shame, really, but it does tell us one thing – our killer is knowledgeable on police protocol and techniques.'

'Yeah, well, he's been pretty good at giving us nothing at all. It can't be luck, I'm thinking ex-military.'

But then Jack stopped to think, and then he stopped again to feel, and it felt wrong. 'But I just don't get it. No one who murders for pleasure is this meticulous. The pleasure is in the killing, not in the planning.'

McQuade nodded in agreement. 'You're right, Jack, it doesn't fit any profile we have had before, so we might have to think outside of the box on this one.'

Jack picked up a dry bit of toast, he couldn't be bothered with buttering it. 'It feels like it's two people in one – one who plans and gets the details just right, and one who lashes out.'

'Well, you're not going to like what I have to tell you next, Jack. It's why I needed to get you somewhere quiet and alone.' Jack had never seen this face on McQuade before, it was so subdued, almost scared to tell him, in a way. 'There has been another murder, its … it's one of ours, Jack.'

Her head bowed and she couldn't bear to look at him. Jack couldn't handle it, she normally looked at him with such ferocity that his knees would often feel like they would never properly work again.

'It was … it was one of yours, Jack, it was Laurel Smith. She was stabbed twice; the killer was disturbed and ran for it. She was taken to hospital but she didn't make it, she bled out. It was the same weapon and this time she was deliberately chosen, it wasn't random like the other girls. I'm so sorry, Jack, she was with the whole team. I thought they would all be safe.'

The room went quiet, all of the noise drained away as if swallowed up by water. His heartbeat drummed in his ears, his pulse became the only noise he could register. He should have been there, he should have seen this coming, and of course the killer would make it personal. They always did.

McQuade continued speaking but Jack wasn't there to listen, he was back in Clifton, at his house, six years ago. His hands were red again and his wife's cold body offered no embrace, no comfort or reassurance. He had kissed her at least a dozen times as she was removed from the house, each time in the hope that her lips would gently push back against his, giving some sign that he wasn't going to be left alone, left with the guilt of not being there.

'Jack,' McQuade shouted.

Other diners turned to look at the same time as he did;

Jack was far less aware of his superior than the rest of the room.

'Jack, are you listening to me? I said we have a lead, a possible witness. I want you to go first and then I'll send a couple of the team to see them afterwards. Jack, I know this is hard.' McQuade stopped speaking so as to let the waiter place their meals in front of them. 'I know this is hard, but pull yourself together, if not for you or for me, at least for Laurel. Stop drinking, use your head, use Yanislav to help you if you have to, but just get this done. Are you listening to me, Detective?' she asked, cutting into a sausage with hasty frustration.

'Yes, ma'am, sorry, I'll get onto it straight away.' Jack made to stand but was stopped by McQuade's hand moving at lightning speed and grabbing his sleeve.

'No, you won't. You'll eat this food, drink this tea, get your strength up and *then* you can go. And, Jack, when you get home tonight, if you make it, have a shower. Now eat, that's an order.'

WE ARE RIGHTEOUS

'We need more, we need to go back out and try again. The plan was flawed, no need for a plan this time, just act on instinct.'

'She died, she was dead before she hit the ground, and we did it.'

'No, you fucked it up, we didn't see the life leave her, and we didn't feel her die and fade out of existence, did we? You wasted our power, our glorious moment slipped between your fingers and you ran.'

'What was I supposed to do? They could have seen us and they could have stopped us.

'Oh, shut up, we are more powerful than any of them, we could have gutted them all and they can't touch us. No one can touch us now. Get out there, we need this.'

'No, you need this, I can't do it.'

'I am you now, I am the only part of you worth living, to ignore me is to ignore what you have become. Together, we are righteous.'

'I know who should be next.'

'Good boy.'

Mrs Keilty's hands shook, not with fear or anticipation but with a hunger. She needed to continue killing, she needed the blood and the sorrow that could only be seen in the passing of a soul. She needed a bigger hit, it had to be more gruesome, more destructive than before and if she didn't get it, she would die. She couldn't live without this, without satisfying the voice controlling her from the inside.

Her spine ached, this premonition was like nothing she had known before. This demon was so strong, it was almost as real as the cats by her feet, just as tangible as their weight against her legs as they wound themselves in and out. Her heart beat heavily and, with a flutter of tiredness, her eyes were too dry and strained with the emotions pulling on her to cry. She needed to phone Jack, must   phone   Detective   O'Connor.

HARLEY DAVIDSON

Jack answered his phone, he had just arrived at the car park where the witness worked as a security guard.

'Mrs Keilty, I'm just in the middle of something, can I—'

Jack didn't get a chance to fob her off, she spoke directly over the top of him, not realising that he had been speaking at all.

'Detective, you have to find him. He is, he is losing the plot and he is going to kill, going to kill right now. Are you there, can you hear me, dear?'

'Calm down, Mrs Keilty, do you know where he is? Can you give me any information to help me find him?'

The phone went quiet for a second as she thought. 'It's busy, very busy where he is and I think there might be water. No, I don't know about water actually, but it is very busy. A shopping centre maybe. Oh, I don't know, I don't know at all. I just know that the demon is controlling him now and it wants to hurt people.'

Jack could tell that the woman was distraught, it was a new side of her. He had only seen her as calm and playful before. Her carefree attitude was what made her easy to be around, but this was another person all together, which only made the situation even more dire.

'Ok, Mrs Keilty, I have a lead, let me get on with this and I will do my best to find them.'

A man in a hi vis vest headed towards Jack. 'I have to go. Stop worrying and try and stay in your own head for a bit. I'll speak to you later.'

Jack hung up the phone, he knew that it was a little cruel to hang up on her in that condition, but there was nothing he could say to reassure her and even if there had been, his time was better off spent following an actual lead.

The man extended his hand and addressed Jack. 'Are you the copper?' he asked flatly.

'Detective,' Jack corrected him. 'Have you got somewhere we can talk? And sit down, maybe?'

The man led Jack around to the far corner of the carpark. There was a tiny office, comprising of only a couple of computer screens on a desk and a half torn off notebook. The coffee rings on the desk seemed to be the most substantial things in the entire office. On the screens were different parts of the carpark, every few seconds changing the angle or location to reveal another grainy picture.

Jesus, I hope that isn't how we are going to identify our suspect, I can barely make out if that's a car or a wall on that,' Jack thought as he entered the small cabin.

'I hear you have some information for us?' Jack asked, he managed to find a small notepad in his jacket. He hadn't used it in months but he wanted to at least try to look the part, especially after he had already corrected the man on his rank. 'You saw something?'

The man shook his head, his grey ponytail bounced from side to side. Jack had instantly thought that he was an odd-looking man from the outset. He had very little hair on the top half of his head, which had been slicked back regardless of its sparsity, and the long grey strands from the sides and back had been tied together with a black band. He had a handlebar moustache that matched the colour of the rest of his hair perfectly, bar the yellow nicotine stain just above his lip. His forearms had tattoos on them that were so old Jack had difficulty distinguishing what they were of, all except the Harley Davidson one that the man began rubbing.

'No, Detective, I didn't see anything. I heard it.'

Jack's heart dropped, he thought he was onto a genuine lead.

'I had one of your lot down the other day, see, and he said you were looking for a motorbike so he had a look through our CCTV, cos we have one on the main roads, look. He didn't find nothing, anyway. But then yesterday when I heard this bike, well, I thought it might be something that you might want to check out.'

Jack wrote down *heard a bike* in his pad in his least convincing handwriting – it was barely legible, even to himself.

'Ok. But you didn't see what make or colour it was, though? Or who was riding it?'

The man recognised the frustration in Jack's voice and began scratching his arm even harder.

'No, but I know it was a Harley – well, a Harley engine, anyway. A Harley Davidson WR Racer, I'm reckoning. Probably from around nineteen forty-five–forty-six-ish. Very rare model, that.'

Jack looked up from his notepad in surprise.

'You can tell just by hearing it?'

The man nodded, glad he had gotten something right. 'Yeah, recognise the sound easily. I rode one for near on eighteen years. It was a racing bike, really, but I had it on road tyres and everything. Then I was working in a garage one day and an American guy saw it and bought it off me on the spot. Flew it back with him. I joked that the bike was going to see more of the world than I had. Nice guy, he was.'

'So you worked on bikes?' Jack asked, he wanted to check his credentials some more before blindly trusting him.

'Yep, nearly forty years I rode nothing but bikes. Repaired them for work and a hobby. Could strip a Harley and put it back together with my eyes closed, I reckon.'

Jack was convinced. 'And what time did you hear it?'

The man smiled broadly. 'I made a note of it here on me pad. Seven forty-eight.'

Jack's heart had done a complete U-Turn and leapt out of his stomach up in to his throat with excitement.

'That's exactly what I wanted to hear. That's our man. Which way do you think it was heading?'

The ex-biker pointed towards the Bristol hospital.

Jack composed himself and took a moment to think.

'A rare bike is probably easier to find, isn't it? And if it's old it would probably need repairing, wouldn't it?' he wondered inwardly.

'So, this Harley Davidson. Where would you take something like that to be repaired or serviced?'

The old man scratched his head. 'Probably only a couple of places in the city.'

'Can you write them down for me?' Jack asked.

Less than a minute later and Jack was walking down the street, looking up at buildings, trying to find any with CCTV cameras facing the road. He flicked through the contacts on his phone and stopped at his own office. He called it and waited for someone to answer.

'Hello?'

'It's me Jack, who's that?'

The voice on the other end became excited, 'It's me, it's Nitin. I was walking by and heard it ringing.'

'No, that's fine, good timing, actually. I have a list of garages for you, I need you to call them and find out if any of them have dealt with an old Harley Davidson WR Racer recently, then call me back right away.'

Officer Kapoor didn't reply immediately – Jack had caught him off guard.

'Yes, sarge, of course. Did you hear about Smith, sarge?

We are all in a state of shock here.'

'Yes, I heard, and this is our best hope of catching the bastard,' Jack replied with a hint of urgency trickling down the phone with his words.

'Yes, sarge, leave it with me.'

Jack gave him the name of the garages and hung up. He continued walking along the road, his head fixed looking up at the corners of buildings and around shop doorways.

There has to be at least one camera facing the road.'

But why should there be? Their man had not been seen on camera yet, why would it start now?

Because this one was sloppy, it wasn't planned as well as the others, and he had only planned for being seen, not heard, that's why.'

Jack battled internally with the black and white of failure and success, realising he was starting to feel as though he had more than one voice inside of him as well.

He could feel the way his borderline personality disorder was throwing him from one wall to the other. There was no grey area when his mind was stuck in these perpetual motions. Hopping between extremes it was all or nothing and the nothing side often won the battle.

His phone rang in his pocket, it was the office.

'Jesus, I've only walked a couple hundred yards,' he said before answering. 'Nitin?'

'Yes, sarge, it's me. You won't believe this, the first garage on that list you gave me had parts ordered for that engine just under a month ago. The guy on the phone remembered it as he sourced the parts himself and he said they were a shit to get hold of.'

'Bingo. Can you meet me there in twenty minutes? And bring your laptop.' Jack instructed, his arm in the air, already flagging down a taxi.

BOOTS

The taxi arrived at the garage at the same time as Nitin's police car. Both men walked up to the building together.

'It's good to see you, sarge. We heard you had a bit of a bounty on your head, dead or alive.'

Jack laughed. 'I'm as surprised as you are that I'm still alive, believe me.'

They pushed open the doors together and walked into a large show room. Motorbikes flanked them in long, regimented rows, all facing and leaning the same way in perfect symmetry. Chrome mirrors and exhausts shone brightly where they had been waxed and the smell of cleaned leather filled the police officers' nostrils. Even Jack, after his ordeal with Mrs Keilty, felt a kind of draw towards the vehicles, a kind of unreasonable longing. Jack spotted a large bike with a sidecar and felt a pang of humour as he imagined the old lady driving it, wearing her old helmet and goggles.

A man with a black and red polo shirt matching the interior of the show room exactly greeted them and offered to show them around.

'My name's Officer Kapoor and this is Detective O'Connor, I spoke with someone called Nigel earlier. He is expecting us.'

The salesman walked them through the shop, past the parts counter and into a back room. A grubby carpet floor and flaky painted walls exposed where all the money had gone during the last refurb – everywhere but here.

'Two policemen to see you, Nige, have you been a naughty boy?' the first man joked as he headed back out onto the shop floor.

'Come in, come in, can I get you a drink? We have tea, coffee or water, but that's about it, I'm afraid.'

Nigel was clean-shaven and not at all what Jack was expecting to find. He was expecting to be questioning your stereotypical grease monkey who weighed in at the same as that of two motorbikes and had hands the size of alloy wheels. The man in front of them was clearly just your run-of-the-mill office worker, he had a laptop open with an entire page of numbers and not a lot else on the screen.

'No, we're fine, thank you. Just need to ask a few questions about the motorbike that you had parts come in for,' Jack said.

'Ah, yes, the Harley, what a pain in my arse that thing was. Had to get parts from Canada of all places in the end.' He swivelled his office chair around and brought up a new page on the screen. His fingers worked furiously on the keys and he cupped one hand over his mouth to shield a yawn as he scrolled down through the pages.

'Sorry about that, got a newborn at home. Can't stop yawning for five minutes at the moment,' he explained, yawning once more.

'Right, here we are, ordered two months ago, collected last month – the first Tuesday, it says here. Do you want the part numbers and stuff? I have the engine number too, if you want that?'

Jack looked at Kapoor. 'We can trace that, can't we?'

'Probably, but the engine was probably shipped in, might take a few hours but with a few calls I can probably get a registered keeper's address, yeah.'

The man on the computer printed off all of the

information for them. It hadn't been as much as Jack had hoped. The buyer had paid cash and collected himself, leaving almost nothing of a paper trail. But they had that engine number, that was a start.

'Don't suppose you have CCTV footage from then, do you?' Jack asked the man doubtfully.

'What's the date?' the man asked as he himself looked at the calendar. 'Err, yeah we should – just; they get copied over every four weeks so we always have a month on file. It's all digital, though, it's saved to a memory stick, is that ok?'

Kapoor smiled and pulled his laptop out. 'That's perfect.'

It didn't take long for Nigel to locate the memory stick for them and for Officer Kapoor to have the files ready to go on his computer.

He looked down through the list and opened the file with the correct date.

'I wasn't here when the parts were collected so I don't know what time it will be. You might have to go through the whole eight opening hours. If he had paid by card we would have had a receipt for it,' Nigel said to them as he watched over the policeman's shoulder to see what he was doing.

'That's not a problem,' the officer replied and, with a couple of clicks, the footage sped up. 'I'm speeding it up by around sixty times so keep your eyes peeled,' he explained to the two other men.

Just as officer Kapoor had finished speaking, Jack spotted him.

'There, look.'

A large man was on screen, dressed head-to-toe in leather and still wearing the helmet.

Kapoor played it at normal speed and the three men watched as their suspect completed the entire transaction, not once uncovering his face.

'Shit, I thought we had him then. Can we get anything

from this that we didn't already know?' Jack asked his colleague in frustration.

'Actually, sarge, we can, if you can find me a tape measure?' Kapoor looked at the shop worker, who nodded and left the room for several moments.

'If you measure the doorway, sarge, I can get a pretty accurate height measurement of our man.'

Jack took the tape measure from the man and walked out onto the shop floor to measure the doorway. A few of the customers and other workers watched him with uncertain interest.

He returned back to the office to see his colleague playing with a computer program. It had lines up and down the screen with small markers on them.

'It's two hundred and three centimetres,' Jack told the man on the computer.

The mouse ran around the screen, highlighting the top of the doorway to the bottom and marking it, and then doing the same on the man in the picture. Then the policemen typed in an equation and hit the enter key.

'Wow, our man is one hundred and ninety-eight centimetres tall. That's about …' Officer Kapoor tipped his head back and looked at the ceiling as he worked something out, 'six foot six. He's huge.'

Jack stared at the screen. 'And that's accurate, is it?'

Kapoor replied with a nod.

'But the hand span on the victim's neck put him at closer to six foot, six two at the very most. And six foot six with size nine feet, that's impossible. What am I missing here?' The detective paced the room, muttering to himself. 'Think, Jack, think.' He looked back at the screen, and then noticed something. It had just looked like an odd pixelation before, but Jack focused his eyes in hard at the bottom of the suspect's boots.

'Can we zoom in on something a minute? Just there,' he asked the other officer, pointing to the man's heel on the laptop.

He opened a box over the area and brought up a small magnifying curser that enabled the picture to enlarge significantly.

'Oh, shit. Can you find me a picture of the computer game character too?'

Kapoor got out his phone. 'My laptop isn't online in here, obviously, but I can get it up on here, is that ok?'

'Yes, fine, just get me that picture.'

A minute later and Jack had the image in his hand. 'Look' he said, using two fingers to now magnify that picture also. Again, it was focused on the footwear.

Officer Kapoor now saw what Jack saw. The boots had large platforms on the bottoms that not only gave the wearer an extra four inches of height, but also angled in at the front, back and sides.

'No way,' the other officer replied. 'He's had these made to match the game character. That's crazy – fucking clever, but crazy.'

'He is a murderer, crazy is what he does. So, what are we thinking, about six two with size eleven or twelve feet?' Jack asked his colleague.

'Looks like it, sarge, makes more sense than before now, anyway. Hang on. Have you ever seen boots like this?' The police officer turned to the man who worked there who had been quietly watching everything unfold.

'What, riding boots like that? No way, you would struggle just to walk in them, let alone ride,' the man replied.

'I see where you're going,' Jack encouraged Kapoor. 'Do we have anywhere that we know of that would make these to order?'

Officer Kapoor smiled. 'I know a place or two, sarge, I'll get on to it straight after following up the engine. We're closing in on him, sarge, I can feel it.'

'I won't ask how you know anywhere that customises leather boots, but I think you're right,' Jack replied.

Kapoor laughed. 'Comic Con, it's huge over here now.

I went as Frodo Baggins last year. There are specialist shops that make accurate costumes.'

Just then, Jack's phone went again. He was expecting it to either be McQuade or Mrs Keilty, seeing as they were the only two to ever call him these days, but to his surprise it was a Bristol number that he didn't recognise.

He answered, 'Hello?'

The thick, Italian accent of Father Vincenzo Camaldo replied, 'Hello, Detective, I hope I am not calling at an inconvenient time?'

Jack held his hand over the mouthpiece. 'Chase this up, I have some things to attend to. Call me as soon as you get anything.'

'But sarge, we nearly have him—'

Jack didn't listen to the reply but instead walked out of the office, through the showroom and into the carpark.

'Sorry, Father, I'm free now,' he said, removing his hand from around the bottom of the phone.

'Is everything ok, Detective? You sound a bit flustered, I can call back at a more appropriate time, if you wish?' the melodic voice said.

'No, no, it's fine, just having one of those days. I'm surprised to hear from you so soon, though.'

The man on the phone chuckled gently. 'Detective, I only have to work on a Sunday morning, I have plenty of time to be making enquiries. Which is why I am calling you, I have some information on what we discussed. Would you like to meet so I can explain it to you?'

Jack looked around, trying remember exactly where he was. His mind had been racing so much in the last few hours, it had gotten itself lost.

'Ok, shall I come to the cathedral, in, say, half an hour?'

'That would be delightful, I will have the kettle on for your arrival. Coffee, though, I am afraid, I cannot bear tea, it is too bland. Excuse me, I know you English have fought wars over it.'

Jack allowed himself a small laugh, it felt forced but

was still there nonetheless. 'Coffee sounds good to me, I haven't had much sleep anyway. I will be there soon.'

Jack headed towards the town centre, he knew the closest taxi rank was a good mile's walk, but hoped that he would be able to flag one down en route. En route, however, proved to be shorter than expected.

A large black VW van screeched up at the lights where Jack had been waiting to cross. The door slid open forcefully and two men in leather jackets jumped out. They both dipped their heads in the direction of the seats inside and one punched his hand menacingly, drilling the message home to the detective that he was either getting in the easy way, or the by himself way.

BUGGED

The door closed behind Jack and he straightened up his jacket, which was not easy to do as one of the large men pushed himself into the seat next to him.

Yanislav, who was smoking in the front seat, threw his cigarette butt out of the window and turned to face the detective.

'Hello, Jack – I can call you Jack, can't I?' the gang leader asked.

'You could call me Susan if you wanted and you bloody well know it,' Jack thought. But instead of vocalising this, he instead chose to reply with a slight smile and an adjustment of his tie.

'Good. Now, I was wondering if you remembered our last discussion.' Yanislav returned the same smile that Jack had just given him.

'You're enjoying this,' the detective thought but, again, chose his words carefully.

'Vividly so, yes.' He rubbed his jaw for effect.

The man in the front of the car grinned enthusiastically. 'That's good indeed. Because if that is the case, you will remember me telling you how important it was for you to remain important. If you are no longer of use, then we will have to, how you say in England, *cut the fat*. Now, if this is

232

all still fresh in your memory, then I assume that you have some information for me, Jack. Some detective work information, so I can find the bastard who shot my brother. Tell me that this is the case.'

Jack took a look at his surroundings and soon calculated that there was only one way out of it, and that was on the say-so of the man talking to him.

'I have a better description of the killer – a more accurate height and shoe size.'

Jack thought that Yanislav looked like he was chewing his own teeth and wasn't sure if that would be enough to quench his hunger. He would have to give him more.

'And one of my men is tracking down the bike that the killer has been using. The bullet didn't give us anything, so this is our best hope.'

'You have serial number?' the gangster asked him.

'Sort of, it's an imported engine, so we will have to track it differently, it's not like just running a car registration plate.'

The heavy-set man in the front took a few deep breaths. 'And this is the truth? You would not lie to me, Detective O'Connor?'

Jack wasn't sure why, but he found Yanislav Ivanovic even more menacing when he addressed him officially.

'I wouldn't lie to you, Mr Ivanovic, I am a fool but I am not stupid.' It was a nice touch Jack silently rewarded himself for, and it seemed to work.

The gangster rubbed his stubble and eventually nodded.

'I thought you may have gotten bored of me, I haven't had anyone follow me for at least an hour,' Jack said, seeing that Yanislav had relaxed in his seat.

The Polish gang member laughed. 'I have not gotten bored of you, Jack, but some friends of ours have been doing our work for us. There is, how you say, more than one way to skin a cat. You have many people in many places interested in you, Detective, fortunately I am instrumental to some of them, and my price was information on you. They have been watching you closer than you know.'

Jack took a moment to digest what he was being told, until his phone began vibrating loudly, followed by its usual, playful ringtone.

'As if by magic,' Yanislav said, gleefully.

'My phone? My phone has been bugged?' Jack asked the other man, who only smiled, holding a lighter to the end of another cigarette.

'Shit, MI5 have been spying on me. That's why you stopped following me, they just told you where I was and everything I said on my phone calls.'

Yanislav lit another cigarette and blew smoke out of his nose. 'It happened that they were already keeping a close eye on you, Jack, they told me to back off a short distance and leave you to it, and they would give me what I wanted.'

Jack rolled his eyes. 'Fucking Collingwood.' Jack took out his phone and put it on silent. He would only use it when he had to.

'Now, Detective, it is time for you to get out.'

'You couldn't drop me up Clifton, could you, by the cathedral?' Jack knew he was pushing his luck, but he was finding it difficult to remember a time when he wasn't.

To Jack's relief, Yanislav laughed once more. 'You have balls, Jack, big, English balls.' He took a long drag on his cigarette and tapped his driver on the shoulder, indicating him to do as the detective had asked.

FOR YOU, JACK

He didn't know who this kid was, it was Jack who he had been looking for, but perhaps leaving him a little message would suffice.

He watched as the young boy walked a couple of yards from the boat then stopped to take out some headphones, trying to detangle the black, matted mess.

He didn't see the man approaching him, he didn't see the metal knife down by his side, or the black leather appearing, with swift and ruthless execution.

The knife shot forward, his full bodyweight behind it giving it formidable speed. It slipped neatly into the boy's abdomen, only stopping at the widened middle of the blade.

He saw the man now, the headphones leaving his hand so he could investigate, with touch, what was hurting his stomach. A thin trail of blood left the corner of his mouth as it began searching for air.

The man knocked the boy's hands out of the away and shoved the weapon deeper. The young man fell backwards onto a metal bench, blood filling his throat, causing him to cough up more and more blood, spraying his attacker.

He started to whisper.

'I'm sorry, Dad, please stop hurting me. Carla, Carla,

I'm sorry, Carla. Protect Carla.'

The killer knelt down in front of the boy, lifting his blood splattered visor so as to inspect him.

He wanted to watch this one closely, wanted to experience the world that he was creating as closely as he could.

The boy twitched from his feet up through his body and into his face as he stretched out for survival, trying desperately to hold onto what little life was left.

The leather-clad biker watched as his victim's eyes darted around, desperately looking for help, any last-ditch reprieve that could save him.

He gave the knife another push, wanting to see the writhe it could produce, seeing if more pain could be inflicted on the body in front of him. It was almost an experiment, like a small boy tearing wings from a crane-fly just to see how it would react.

Blood dripped through the slats of the bench more and more quickly, sounding like thick rain as they decorated the cobbles beneath.

The attacker pulled the knife free, watching as the skin tore and the body slowly slumped down to one side as the boy drifted away forever.

The man's breathing moved from a steady, calm rhythm to one much heavier, his heart fluttered inside his chest with the excitement, almost reaching a peak of climactic altitude. He couldn't control himself, the pleasure moved him. It moved his hand towards the boy, buried it deep in the wet, scarlet open wound and grabbed at soft flesh. He yanked his entire arm back as he stood up, pulling parts of the young man's intestines out. He let go of the bloody body parts, watched them fall to the ground before turning his head up to the sky.

He rubbed his blood-covered gloved hand over his mouth and sniffed at the red slithers of flesh still clinging to it.

He threw his arms back to puff out his chest and

screamed up at the night sky with relish.

He screamed a long, visceral sound until his throat went sore. He looked down at the fallen boy and smiled.

'For   you,   Jack,   all   for   you.'

SYMBOL OF THE POPE

The van screeched to a halt in the middle of the road and Jack was given the customary push from the vehicle.

'Gentlemen,' he said sarcastically just as the door was slammed in his face and tire smoke filled the air with the scent of burning rubber. Jack ignored the architecture this time, there was not enough space in his mind for a critique right then. His thoughts threatened to burst from their neurological seams and it was all he could do to quell them.

His phone began ringing again and, again, it was Mrs Keilty.

'I'm looking for him, give me a break,' he shouted at his phone. He held the top button for a few seconds and turned it off completely. There was no room to feel guilty for it – after all, he hadn't been able to do much with everything she had told him before. Unless she gave him a name or address, there was little else he could do.

The words of Tanya Red ran through his head, 'It's ok not to be ok, it's ok to be selfish.'

He had spent five years burning himself from the inside out with the pain of finding the person who killed his wife and daughter, why shouldn't he postpone the other investigation for a few minutes? Why shouldn't he put the family he had so desperately let down first for once? He owed everyone else nothing and the two he loved more than life itself everything.

He opened the doors, took a deep breath and entered the large room.

Father Camaldo, who was replacing hymn books in the backs of seats, noticed the detective. He placed all of the remaining books down, clapped his hands together and then opened them warmly to Jack.

Jack didn't know what to do as the older man leaned in and hugged him, so he returned the embrace and let go as soon as was acceptable to do so.

'It is wonderful to see you, Detective.' The priest looked over Jack's shoulder. 'And even better to see that you are able to come unaccompanied, as it were.'

The bearded man's smile was infectious, Jack wasn't sure but he could have sworn that it physically warmed the room.

Jack looked behind himself and then realised what the priest had meant. 'Ah, yes, they got bored of following me around. They reminded me today, though, that they are never far away, unfortunately.'

The old man chuckled. 'They do say that you are never more than eight feet away from a rat in the city.'

Jack returned a laugh. 'That they do, Father, that they do. I wanted to thank you for finding out about this so quickly for me.'

Jack did indeed want to thank the man but, more importantly than that, he wanted to address the subject at hand. The subject that had plagued his life since that disgusting day.

'That is not a problem, Detective, to help is my pleasure.'

'Jack, please call me Jack,' the detective told him as they both took a seat.

Jack wasn't sure why, but it had felt natural to sit on a chair in the very centre of the cathedral, with all of its ceremonial paraphernalia in view in front of them. The stained-glass windows, while not being old like most cathedrals, still gave the sunshine a chance to intrude the room playfully.

'As I said I would, I spoke to a friend of mine who is still very much a part of the Society. His name is Father Davide Lopez. I told him about the investigation and the circumstances of which the Society appeared to have played a part. I told him of your wife and daughter, and I hope you will forgive me, Detective – sorry, I mean Jack – but I googled you. I needed to give him an accurate date of the incident.'

Jack nodded, it was the only right thing to do, but it felt like a wasp sting inside of him, injecting guilt into his soul. The facts of how they had died and how he had not been there to save them was public property. It only took one search on the internet to see the whole of their destruction laid bare. He thanked the priest internally, though, for using the word incident instead of murders.

'So, with this information, I asked him to go through the archives and discover the conclusion of the Society's investigation. It did not take long for him to contact me with the answers to our questions. Or should I say, a surprising lack of answers?

'You see, Father Lopez could not find anything on the investigation. There were no records – except one. It was a single-page document with very little information on it at all. He explained to me that it had a description of a woman – specifically a mother – who had been subjected to demonic abuse before being killed. I asked him if this was definitely the correct case and he assured me that this was the only one from the city of Bristol in more than fifteen years. But there was nothing of your little girl, no information on the pictures that you have seen. It would have been usual protocol for copies to have been taken and maintained in the archive in the Vatican.'

Jack's hand automatically went to his head to tug on

what little hair he had.

The priest paused, Jack recognised it as meaning he had no more to tell him.

'So that's it, is it? Sounds like a cover-up, and a good one, I shouldn't doubt.'

The priest placed a comforting hand onto Jack's shoulder. 'There are instances where, in the Society, information has become … conveniently misplaced, shall we say. In a society that has foundations built upon secrets, it can only be assumed that they run throughout.' The old man took a deep breath and turned away from Jack.

'Father Lopez suggested that there was something that he found that I should not divulge to you. He feared that it may put all three of our lives at risk, but I hope you remember, Detective, that I only search for truth in this life, whatever fate that may bring me.'

Jack looked at the priest who deliberately avoided Jack's eyes for a moment but then relented and faced him again. It was obvious that the old man couldn't help but address Jack as formally as he could. He wondered if it was some form of repentance, a way of treating everyone in a constant form of atonement.

'There was something unusual on this paperwork, something that many people in the Catholic Church would never question. It was the symbol of the Pope himself. Now, while I doubt it was the Pope who left his mark upon the file, it would have been a representative of his Holiness, leading me to believe that they, in turn, believed that this would be sufficient enough to stop anyone probing further.'

Jack was annoyed.

'And this is why I hate religion, a load of self-righteous bastards doing whatever they feel like whenever it pleases them.'

'It might stop anyone else in the Church probing, but luckily I do not feel the burden of god on me, and why is it always symbols with you guys, anyway?'

Father Camaldo looked at the cross hanging on the wall in front of them tellingly.

'That is a good question, Detective. I believe that a symbol or an emblem is a simple way of saying many things without saying a word. This symbol,' he gestured to the cross, 'this particular depiction, the humble cross. While it is one of the simplest images, it holds so much weight, good and, yes, indeed, some bad. Words can only mean what they say, Detective, but symbols can mean many different things to many different people.'

The priest paused for a moment of reflection before continuing.

'While Father Lopez may not be able to research into this any further for you, Detective, as every document witnessed has to be catalogued, stating who and when and for what purpose, he did, however, agree to translate the Aramaic for us. With your permission, I would like to share the pictures with him. Copies only, of course, but yet I understand quite how sensitive this may be for you, Detective.'

'No, that's fine, I just want to get somewhere with this now. I have been letting them down for too long. I'm a detective, for Christ's sake, it's my job.' Jack quickly raised a hand to cup his mouth, realising that he had just used the son of god's name derogatively in church.

The priest let out a full belly laugh. 'Detective, you do not need to worry about offending anyone here. What do you think us priests say when we are angry? We call our Lord every name under the sun and more. Some of us even swear in Latin just to make sure he is getting the message.' He laughed even more. 'It feels good to laugh in such troubled times, does it not?'

The detective managed to cock a half smile. 'It does.' Jack looked pensive. 'I still can't believe that you are so convinced that there is a god. You're just so, well, so normal.'

The priest clapped his hands together and then placed

them onto Jack's shoulders. 'If you consider me normal, Detective, I dare say that says more about you than me. Now, I promised coffee, did I not?'

Jack smiled. 'I could do with something stronger, if I am honest.'

'Detective, you are a man after my own heart.' The priest pulled a hip flask from his pocket. 'Where the English fail with hot drinks, the Scottish more than make up for with malted ones.'

He offered the flask to Jack, who took a large swig and wiped his lips.

'Wow, that's good stuff, Father.'

The priest matched him and growled as the liquid disappeared down his throat.

'Single malt scotch. My third belief. Number one is science, number two is my God and number three is good liquor.'

He handed it back to Jack, who lifted it in the air to toast what the priest had just pronounced and then took another large swig.

Jack didn't speak but handed the silver flask back and turned to face the front of the room, to allow his eyes to become unfocused and his brain to reduce stimulation, willing it to rest. If it had an off switch, now would be a time to use it.

'I have some things to attend to, if you would like you could sit here and rest a while. I doubt there will be much to disturb you. Although, the Lord does work in mysterious ways and you, Detective, never seem to be able to rest.'

Jack smiled and watched the old man walk off in the direction of the small office where Jack had met him before. While he hated the décor, the detective could easily have fallen in love with the silence in there.

The city didn't offer many places of solitude, even when you were alone you were often in the company of the sound of traffic, shouting voices and the odd siren. For someone who worked in the police force, he sure did hate those sirens. The noise of the city was its pace, and it was a running one. Its heart beat rarely slowed, and sometimes Jack found it impossible to keep up. That was why he had agreed to move to Clifton. The strange, village-like area slap bang in the middle of the chaotic city gave him just enough serenity to survive in his own head. Well – the village and the medication, anyway.

He couldn't remember the last time he had taken his medication, and he wasn't sure if that was a good thing or a bad one. Choosing not to dwell on his tablets, he decided to push other anxieties from his mind. He forgot about the gang members who were waiting for an opportune moment to kill him and he couldn't harass his thoughts any longer over the murderer who was still on the loose. His brain going over and over the little evidence was just tiring itself out, after all.

But most of all, he let go of the guilt of his wife and child. The constant self-hatred was destroying him and, deep down, so far down that it was hardly there, he knew his wife would never have blamed him. She would never have wanted him to feel so much pain on top of that of losing the pair of them.

He could hear her voice telling him that everything was ok, that he was going to be ok and that no matter what happened, she loved him and always would. Her voice was the ultimate pain relief, his borderline personality disorder didn't exist when she did.

Jack had once heard of some freedivers who could concentrate solely on their breathing and nothing else. One of them could even slow his heart rate down by controlling his thoughts and focusing on it and it alone. He often thought about how nice it would be to escape the entire world bar one single, all-consuming thought. But that wasn't how his brain was hardwired, its programing was different to most, and keeping it functioning was hard enough without attempting an entire reboot.

Time elapsed and Jack had no idea of how long he had been sat there but he suspected it had been well over an hour. Pulling his phone from his pocket to see the time he remembered that it was still off. Probably not a good thing, considering the circumstances. He left the cathedral and held the on switch down until the small image appeared in the middle of the screen to indicate it was starting up. The sun was surprisingly low in the sky, perhaps he had sat in there for much longer than he had initially thought.

He looked at the small screen to see the time as it loaded, but it vibrated in his hand. It vibrated again right after and then again after that. It vibrated for well over a minute, but it wasn't ringing, it was lots of separate notifications. Most of them were voicemails, but a couple were texts. He opened the texts first.

There were three from Aubrie asking where he was and what the hell he was doing. Each text became more and more aggressive.

Then he opened two from McQuade who had obviously given up on the covert communication. They both told him to call the station urgently.

The last text was from Mrs Keilty. It took him a couple of attempts to read it, she was obviously a novice at it.

Too late. He's dead. Boat.

'What the hell does that mean?'

He opened the voicemail up and listened to the first.

It was Mrs Keilty and she sounded desperate, 'Jack, Jack, answer the phone. He's following someone, a boy I think. He's by some boats – barges, I think. Please, Jack, you have to stop him, dear.'

Jack pulled the phone away from his ear. He had a sick feeling growing in the pit of his stomach, he played the next message.

'Jack, it's McQuade, answer your pissing phone. There was another murder. We've had to move the body, the press were all over it. And there's ...' he heard McQuade hesitate. 'There's something else. It was right outside your boat, Jack. A young lad, about seventeen, eighteen, we think. The body's at the mortuary with Aubrie. Just call me back as soon as you can.'

Jack's hand slowly fell to his side. He didn't need to listen to the rest of the messages. They would only be telling him that the boy's identity had been confirmed and that his name was Daniel, aged eighteen.

FRECKLES

Jack fell to his knees, his entire bodyweight shocking through his knee caps with cracking noises. He didn't feel it, he didn't feel anything, he could hardly breathe. A small candle of hope burned inside of him, hoping that he was wrong about it being the young man he had come to befriend. The young man that he had pitied but learnt to respect. Now another innocent person was dead and it was his fault, it was always his fault. If he hadn't been chasing down these ghosts he could have been there, he could have caught the evil before it had chance to strike, whether it was a demon or not he should have been there.

At some point, the tears had spilled from his eyes and run down his cheeks and started stinging the wounds on his jaw. At what point that happened, Jack didn't know, he had started walking down towards the mortuary without knowing that he was doing so. He was not fuelled by food and water now, not even by the whisky that the priest had given him. No, now he was moving under the influence of hate, pure disdain for the world and the people that inhabited it. Even his borderline personality disorder could not have concocted up such a black and white way of thinking. The world was black and so was everything else, he could no longer see the light, the beautiful stained-glass windows were no longer real. He could have been floating along the miles to where Aubrie was now cutting up his friend. He could have been the first human to fly and still he wouldn't have cared. He didn't notice the half a dozen people that he shoulder barged, or the traffic that nearly collided just to avoid hitting him.

The young man at the desk of the mortuary just pointed down the hall on seeing that it was him who had come bursting through the doors.

Jack took large strides down to the viewing gallery and stopped abruptly a couple of inches from the glass. In front of him lay the naked body of a young man, not yet recognisable because Aubrie was leaning over him, obstructing the face. His heart throbbed and ached in his chest as it rose and fell aggressively. Aubrie noticed him, she pulled down her mask and mouthed Jack's name, and then she stood aside.

And there it was. The fair skin of Daniel, not yet tinged with the grey of decay. Jack pushed his forehead against the glass and screamed at it, screamed at the world, willing it to give this young man – this *boy* – back. He spun around, his arms so tense that the cotton at the seams of his shirt creaked under the strain, threatening to tear. He grabbed hold of an object, not even consciously aware of what it was, and turned and threw it. The large metal bin skimmed up off of a wall and hit the very top corner of the window. The glass smashed instantly into millions of tiny pieces and fell to the ground like water drops. But he wasn't finished, he pulled a picture down from its nail, tossed it aside and punched the spot that it had just occupied. The thin plaster gave way easily under his fist and then suffered a further barrage of blows. Jack's hand had gone right through and found the cinder block wall behind. Jack's body and mind gave up the fight and he dropped, fell back against an untouched patch of wall and he let his own weight drag him down to the floor.

Aubrie ran to him, directly over the broken glass,

brushing the shards out of her way, and climbed up through the smashed window frame.

'Move the body, his father's coming to identify him soon, take him next door to the other room,' she shouted at another person dressed in the same whites who had been helping her with the autopsy.

She knelt beside him, expecting to see him crying, but he wasn't anywhere near it. His face looked harsh and his age was showing with wrinkles around his brow. She reached out and took his hand, which he reluctantly relinquished from its fisted form. She took a look at his cuts surreptitiously as she interlocked her fingers with his. She didn't speak but instead just sat, holding him and stroking his forearm. Eventually, she could see that he was calming down, becoming the Jack that she knew again. He lifted his eyes to meet hers, the effort exhausting him further.

'I'm sorry,' he said, nodding in the direction of the shattered glass.

Aubrie feigned a laugh. 'What, that? It doesn't matter. Apparently open plan working spaces are the new thing, anyway. Come on, let's get you patched up.'

Jack felt weak and it must have been more noticeable than he had hoped because Aubrie was trying her best to support him by placing her arms beneath his.

They walked to her office where she pulled some wipes and tweezers from a drawer. Angling the desk light onto the back of his hand, she pulled small fragments of the wall from his skin. Jack sat obediently, numb through.

'You must have gone through some wood as well, look,' she said, holding up a large splinter to the bulb in the lamp.

Jack didn't answer, he was still too angry and far too embarrassed, and so Aubrie spoke on.

'I take it you knew him, then?' she asked gently. She knew it could easily have sounded like she had made a prejudgement on Jack's relationship with the young man.

'Yeah, he was a friend.' He allowed a small, sarcastic laugh to spurt from his mouth. 'I've only known him about a week, but he was a good kid. He was going to do great things, I could feel it.'

The pathologist cleaned his cuts with a wipe, commented on how impressed she was that he didn't flinch, and wrapped the wounds with a bandage.

'His father will be here soon to identify him,' she said as she stood up. 'I'll go and make sure that he is ready for him.'

As discreet as Aubrie was, Jack found it obvious that she had not just referred to Daniel as a *thing* – a dead body with no person left – like she would normally have done. And he was thankful to her.

He gave himself some more headspace just as he had in the cathedral, only this time he wasn't going to get lost in it. He had a new vigour of determination coursing through his veins. This time was going to be different, he was going to stop this. End it before anyone else suffered because of him. He felt just as responsible as the murderer now, and much more capable than him.

He walked up to the main entrance just as a man and a teenage girl entered. The man was skinny to the point of being gaunt, he had a shaved head with a large black cat tattooed on the side of it. His clothes were a mismatched tracksuit with various stains on it. The girl had the same wild, red hair as Daniel and freckles decorating her face just below her eyes, with tear tracks running over them and down to her mouth.

Jack walked over to them and offered his hand to the man. 'Hello, you must be Daniel's father, I am Detective O'Connor. I'm sorry for your loss.'

Jack played it by the book, he didn't want to get Daniel's memory into trouble by admitting that he knew him, as stupid as that might sound.

'Yeah, that's me. Are you the one that's meant to be stopping this maniac?' the man asked abruptly, looking at

Jack's hand as if it was infected with something.

'Well, yes, I'm heading the case,' Jack replied, again, word for word from the guidelines.

The man snorted. 'Great fucking job you've done, then.'

Aubrie came from around the corner and stood beside Jack.

Just in time before I smacked him one,' Jack thought while still wearing his regretful face.

'If you could come with me, please,' Aubrie said to the father.

He started to walk behind her and turned to bark at his daughter, 'Just stay here and don't fucking run off. I need you to do something for me when we leave.'

Jack looked at the girl who didn't so much as flinch at her father's orders.

'You ok?' he asked flatly. He was not going to put on any pretence with her, she didn't deserve it.

She nodded and wiped her cheek. 'Yeah, I'm ok, it's just hard. Danny was my best friend and now I'm stuck with *him* on my own, and he doesn't even give a shit that he's gone.'

Jack became overwhelmed with sorrow, but he wouldn't let that show, she didn't deserve the weight of that, either.

'You're the detective that Danny was telling me about, aren't you? My name's Carla. He was helping you with a case, wasn't he? He didn't stop talking about you. He said that he wished you were our dad instead of him.' She pointed weakly at the spot that her father had been standing a moment before. 'He really liked you.'

Jack smiled. 'I really liked him, and he was a good kid. I wish … I wish I could have saved him for you. I'm sorry.'

The young girl thought on this for a second and then spoke calmly. 'I think you saved him in more ways than you realise. You don't know what it's like, living at home. We never had any hope of getting out of it, but you gave him hope. In the short time you knew him, you gave him more hope than he had had in his life.'

The resemblance between Daniel and his sister was becoming more and more apparent.

'Is there anything you need, or anything I can do?' Jack asked her hopefully.

Again, the girl deliberated on what he was saying. 'No, I don't think so. Thank you, though, Detective.'

She even said his name with the same respectful note sewn into it that her brother had.

Jack retrieved his wallet from his inside pocket and pulled out a card with his details on it.

'If you think of anything, just call me. I'll catch the killer, I promise you that.'

She smiled as she took the business card from him. 'I know, because Danny said you would.'

Her father came storming back through the door. 'Come on home, we've got to get back on that sodding bus,' he said blankly at his daughter.

'Not even a fucking tear, not even one ounce of remorse for the loss of your own son.' Jack's anger began to boil inside of him once more, it could have been left over from earlier, but he didn't think so. This was a new hatred, one that didn't warrant the destruction of objects and himself like before. This new disdain had a face and it would take a more delicate approach to fix this blight.

The man grabbed his daughter's shoulder and shoved her towards the door.

Aubrie, who had followed a short distance behind, shouted, 'There's no need for that.'

The man turned to give her a look that showed how little he cared.

Jack held Aubrie's arm and shook his head to stop her from pursuing it any further.

'What, you are just going to let him do that to her, are you?' Her eyes trained on Jack with disbelief.

'For now, yes, because if we say or do anything to piss

him off he'll only take it out on her later.' Jack watched as the pathologist did the maths in her head and concluded that he was probably right.

'Don't worry, I will sort something out for her, just as soon as we catch our killer.'

The pair turned to walk back to Aubrie's office when they   heard   a   familiar   voice   calling.

DEMON IN ME

'Detective? Jack, dear?'

They turned to see Mrs Keilty walking in.

'How did she know I was here?' the detective said quietly, more to himself than anyone else.

Aubrie overheard him. 'How did she even *get* here? Does she have a car?'

Jack smiled to himself at the thought of Mrs Keilty parking right outside the doors on her bike.

'Not exactly, no.' He walked towards the older woman and was instantly embraced in a hug, one that was so loving it could kill you.

'What are you doing here?' he asked, prising himself from her arms.

'I need to speak to you, dear, it's important. I had …' she leaned in close so as to speak in a whisper, 'one of my moments.'

Jack gave her the small smile that was all he was able to manage. 'Yes, I know. Unfortunately, I didn't get to him in time, and he was, in fact, a friend of mine.'

Mrs Keilty's face dropped. 'Oh, I'm sorry, dear, that's awful. Are you going to be ok?'

Jack nodded and again managed to give a small, unconvincing grin.

'In that case, I do still need to speak to you, dear. It isn't about that poor young lad, it's about you.'

*

The city was full of shadowy nooks for the down and outs to remain down and out in, they could live off of the bottom of the pile, skimming off the unwanted scum. Three junkies who had just shared a hit, needle and all, didn't even notice the large man in the corner as he sat, knees braced to his chest. He rocked slightly as he uttered words. Telling himself about how they all deserved what they got, how they were not powerful like him. He didn't feel powerful then, as he sat in the dark alone. He felt weak and childlike – except for the voice inside him. The voice that had moved his hands, the voice that had used him to perform evil. Was he evil, or was it just the voice? But he was the voice, the words in his head were his own, surely, otherwise why would they be a part of him? Why would he obey them if it was not his conscious speaking? And this conscious gave him something he had never had before. Its pleasure made him more than he had ever dreamed of being. People had feared him, he was the one with the power as they struggled to live under the weight of his might.

'Listen to yourself, you sound like you think you are a god.'

'A god? Why not? A god gives this world life, and I am taking it away. I am the other side to his coin, I shall be the dark to his light, for without darkness, light cannot exist. God needs me, he should thank me for doing the work he is afraid to do. I am the rapture that must exist to give balance to this disgusting existence. My hands have been given strength beyond that of a mere mortal so I can punish this world as it is fit to be punished.'

He picked up the metal weapon and held it close to his face. The cold metal felt invigorating against his cheek and his tired body found itself becoming alive once again. Alive with intent that life must be purged. He looked at the three mortals across on the other side of the dark, dilapidated building.

'Not worthy of me,' he decided. He placed the large weapon into a leather holdall and walked out into the night, like an owl silently floating between the trees.

*

Jack and Mrs Keilty sat around the desk of the pathologist, who had propped herself on top of a small filing cabinet. Aubrie had got them all a cup of coffee from the vending machine, she cupped hers and blew on it as she and Jack waited to see what the woman's unexpected visit was going to entail.

'So, what is it, Mrs Keilty? Why have you come all the way down here? I could have visited you at home if it was that important,' Jack told her, deciding to leave the muddy brown drink alone.

The woman opposite him took a quick look at the hot drink and visibly turned her nose up at it. She pushed it towards the centre of the desk. 'No thank you, dear, I'm not a fan of coffee.' She turned to Jack. 'I was not sure if you would have been able to come to me, dear, I could see you were in a bit of a state over everything.'

Jack was confused – maybe she was as barmy as he had once thought.

'What do you mean, I don't quite understand?'

'Well, dear, I was having one of my moments—'

Jack interrupted her, 'I thought I said you should try to stay in your own head?'

The old woman agreed with a smile. 'Yes, you did, but, you see, I wasn't trying this time. It was like before – it came to me, I didn't go to it. It was very strong and angry – so much anger – it scared me, dear.'

'I know, I am doing my best to catch him, I really am.' Jack was getting slightly frustrated. What did she think was going to happen? That she could say 'it's happening' and he was just going to run around the city and bump into someone about to commit murder?

'No, I know that,' she protested, 'but I'm not talking about that, I'm on about you, I saw you.'

Jack didn't know what to say. He was surprised at how even Aubrie refused to laugh at the idea, or at least wade in with a scientific approach to the conversation.

'I saw the anger in you, you were so angry – and frightened, too. I saw how the dead boy hurt you so, and what you wanted to do to the person who did it. How did you think I knew you were here? I raced to the police station and asked where all the dead bodies went, they were reluctant to tell me at first, and then I told them I was a friend of yours—'

'Wait,' Jack interjected. 'You saw me in one of your visions? What did you see me doing?'

Mrs Keilty looked scared to speak and she lowered her head as she did so, 'At first I … I just saw what you wanted to do – you wanted to kill someone with your hands and scream and shout at them. Then, when, I was on my way here, I saw glass falling everywhere and your fists hurting. I assumed you punched a window in rage or something. I wanted to stop you from doing anything you would regret, dear, that's why I came.'

Jack looked at Aubrie, her eyes were wider than he had ever seen them. He could tell that she was slowly being converted from a sceptic to a confused scientist.

'Thank you, Mrs Keilty, that was very kind of you, but I'm ok now. I just lost it for a minute, that was all. You're right, I did want to hurt someone, but the person I wanted to hurt most of all was myself for not stopping it from happening.' Jack stopped and looked at the older woman for a moment, trying to work out what it was that she had been able to see. 'Didn't you say it was demons that allow you to see these visions and things?'

The old woman shifted uncomfortably in her chair.

'That's right, yes.'

Jack narrowed his eyes on her. 'Are you saying I have a demon in me, Mrs Keilty?'

She took a deep breath, determined to speak honestly. 'Yes, dear. But, you see, it's not quite as black and white as that. We all have demons within us at some point, it's more to do with what we choose to do with them. I am sorry, dear, I thought you may let it poison you, let it get into your thoughts. I should have known better than that.'

The room fell silent and Jack knew it was because the other two occupants were allowing him some time to think.

Could he really have a demon in him? Of course he could, he punched his way through a wall. Why shouldn't he have one in him? He lived most of his life in the dark patches of his mind, it was only reasonable that he would allow someone else to move in to keep him company. The rages he felt had always seemed like they were a different side to him, like he was just a bystander looking in on a destroyed soul. The hate for himself used to burst out of him and start attacking those who stood closest. It had felt unnatural then, perhaps because it was.

Mrs Keilty decided it was time to wade into Jack's thought stream. 'Demons are powerful things, and they are full of energy. You can use this energy for whatever you decide, dear, the choice is yours, you know?'

FITS THE PROFILE

The bar was crowded, so many people just walking around holding drinks, sipping their lives away, not giving a shit that they meant nothing.

They are a dirty speck that needs to be cleaned – ironically by staining the ground with their blood. So many faces to choose from, which one will look the most beautiful in its last moments? Which one will scream the loudest for me, I wonder? Which one shall I rip the skin from, leaving them just bone? Leaving their beauty as obsolete as it truly is?'

The leather-wearing man sat in a bar in a prime location to view his potential victims, but the particular taste he was craving was not in this one. He would try another, no need to rush, he could take his time making the right choice. His thirst had been quenched with the boy; he had the time to get it just right. It was such a long time since he had planned a murder, such a long time since a computer game had given birth to the idea. The idea had become a reality and was much greater than any gaming experience. Thinking about his naivety at the beginning of this made him embarrassed. He had acted like a stupid boy emulating his favourite superhero from the television. In time, though, he had become the real thing, the man that

259

computer games and films would be based on. The one that books would have their plots orientated around, trying to recreate his brilliance.

He felt a small surge of excitement in the pit of his stomach that caused his fists to clench.

'No, you don't have to rush. Move on to the next bar and find exactly what you are looking for.'

*

Jack walked Mrs Keilty out to her bike and watched her ride away, veering around two cyclists who both thought that she had earned the shake of a fist. As he entered back into Aubrie's office, his phone vibrated in his pocket, he didn't even look at the number but instead answered it in the most detective-like manner he could manage.

'Sarge, it's me,' Officer Kapoor said quickly. 'I've got as far as I can with the engine and the boots. I found a shop that specialises in custom leather and things of that sort, they confirmed that they did in fact make a pair of size eleven boots that match the description that I gave them. Apparently, all they could remember about the guy that bought them was that he paid in cash, he was tall and somewhat overweight. And, get this, he wore a crash helmet the whole time.'

Jack breathed heavily with frustration.

'You have to be kidding me. He wore it in there too? So we don't have anything we didn't already know?'

'No, sarge, and I traced the engine parts and I didn't get very far with that either. Paid for online with, as far as I can see, a fake account and then delivered by an English courier firm to a random address. The couriers were called Delivery UK.'

'Did you get far with them?' Jack asked.

'I tried, sarge. I told them I was looking for something that I ordered and wanted to know if it had arrived. I got so far and then they twigged that I wasn't who I said I was, and they stopped talking. And, of course, they then didn't believe me when I said I was a police officer. They told me to get back to them once I had a warrant. Sorry, sarge, I tried to jump the gun a bit. I've spoken to McQuade and she said that she would try and get us a warrant ASAP.'

Jack closed his eyes tight, he was willing his brain to come up with something that it had overlooked before. There had to be something, he was sure of it.

'No, that's good work, well done. Did the delivery company give you anything else, anything at all?'

Jack heard the other man rustle a piece of paper. 'Only the parcel number, but that's it. It wasn't enough to get any information.'

Aubrie was typing on her computer, when Jack clicked his fingers and pointed for her to move. She gave him a sharp look but did as she was asked, allowing him to sit in her seat.

'Nitin, I have an idea, what was the name of that company again?'

'Delivery UK, why?'

Jack typed into the search bar and brought up the company's website.

'I'm looking to see if it's possible to track the parcel, wait, here we go.'

Jack clicked the small icon of a mail van that opened a smaller, separate box.

'Read out the number to me a minute.'

Officer Kapoor complied and Jack typed it in and, with a hold of his breath, he punched the enter key.

The van travelled back and forth from one side of the browser box to the other before finally loading up a fresh page. It read *Delivered* with an address below.

Jack punched the air. 'Got the bastard! Nitin, get a pen and take this down. Forty-one, Russell Avenue, Kingswood, Bristol.'

He heard him writing it down but was surprised to hear

him go quiet.

'Have you got that?' Jack asked, lacking confidence.

'Yes, sarge. Only I recognise that address but I can't place it. Let me check it now on the database.'

Jack waited as patiently as he was able, punching the stapler on the desk a couple of times to settle his anxiety.

'Sarge?'

'Give me something, anything will do. Just don't tell me it's another dead end.'

'You won't believe this, it's the current address for an emergency contact for a Mr G Peters. That's Officer Graham Peters. It's a mistake, surely?'

The name took a couple of seconds to register – names always did with Jack – but he was surprised at how little of a shock it came to him.

'What? That can't be …' Then Jack paused. 'How stupid have we been? He's the right height, build and, amongst other things, fits the profile perfectly. This can't be that simple, can it?'

'I'm confused, sarge.'

Jack was tempted to rush into things, he wanted to run into the street to search for him, but this was not the time for clumsy hot-headedness. If this really was his man, if the officer on his own team was the man murdering these people, he needed to get it right this time.

'Oh god, sarge. McQuade told me about the shooting, and I just remembered something. Once Officer Peters told me he was off down the range for a few rounds, I thought he meant driving range at the time but now … I think he might have meant shooting range.'

Jack thought about it for a second. It made sense, everything was beginning to fit.

'Just one question, Nitin, which department did he work in before he was ours?'

'Narcotics team, I think, sarge.'

Jack lowered his head.

'Of course he did, he knew exactly where to get his hands on the

*confiscated drugs, he knew exactly how to make some cash in hand so
there would be no paper trail, and he knew exactly how to piss off a
gang of drug dealers at the same time.'*

'And when was the last time you saw him?'

The officer took a moment to think. 'A couple of days
ago, he hasn't been in, sarge, he phoned in sick.'

'You'll need a warrant to track his phone, ask McQuade
for one, but assume you'll get it and carry on regardless. If
you get any shit from it, just blame me. Do it now, won't
you?'

'I'm   on   it,   sarge.'

ONE LAST SMILE

This would be the last bar, his thirst for blood had become exaggerated, no longer calm and selective, he would just have to choose the best of the bunch. The noise was becoming a distraction, the loud music and chatter was clouding everything like a veil of fog.

'Stay focused, keep strong, not long now until blood will pour over you and you will once again feel alive.'

The voices in the man's head had become one, it had become him, and the man that had occupied this mind before was now dormant in an everlasting hibernation.

And then he saw her, and his heart raced.

'That's the one, she is the person you have been waiting for.'

A young woman walked along the bar and then stood on tiptoes to order a drink, gently playing with her hair as she waited. She took a sip through the straw and saw the tall man dressed in leathers looking at her. To his surprise, she smiled and locked gazes with him for a moment longer than was comfortable before turning and giggling. The man looked around the room to see who she was with, which party he would have to try to separate her from, but it was hard to tell. She was of an age where she could be a part of the students all hanging around at the end of the bar, or with the businessmen occupying the tall table with stools, or was she a part of that group of girls? No, definitely not, they wore far too little and walked in uncomfortably high heels, whereas she had black boots and a long coat covering herself up, keeping a sense of dignity that the other women had lost many years ago.

They exchanged another telling look and, instead of joining a group of people, she stood alone at the bar.

'Maybe she is by herself, perhaps she is waiting for someone. In that case, you better make your move soon, now is the time to strike.'

The woman removed the straw from her glass and drank the remainder of her cocktail in one. She pulled a packet of cigarettes from the coat of her pocket and headed for the door, but not before giving the man watching her one last smile.

FUNNY YOU SHOULD SAY THAT

Jack's phone started to ring. 'Nitin, where is he?'

'Sarge, I can't get an accurate trace, I think he has some software on it blocking our system, but I have managed to locate what signal tower the phone last pinged. I'll send through a map but, essentially, it's Park Street and the surrounding areas. Lots of people, lots of bars to choose from. You're going to need men, sarge, lots of them.'

Jack had a feeling of dread. 'Which we can't have because technically we don't know where he is as we don't have a warrant yet, right?'

'Right. I'm going to get together a team here; the second the warrant comes through we have grounds to dispatch. Sorry, Sarge, that's the best I can do.'

Officer Kapoor sounded genuine and Jack knew that he was, and knew that he was already pushing his luck.

'No, that's fine, I will head up Park Street now, see if I get lucky. Keep trying to trace his phone, won't you?'

Jack hung up just as Aubrie re-entered her office.

'Everything ok? Got a lead?' she asked, recognising his haste.

Jack raised an eyebrow. 'You know Peters in my team? Well, he is our murderer. Explains why we have had sod-all evidence to work with – he knew exactly what we would be looking for.'

The pathologist looked confused. 'But we had prints, they should have matched his, he would have been on the database for sure.'

Jack closed his eyes as another bombshell of a realisation landed on him. 'And, as a policeman, he would have had access to the database. He would have just changed them. And he was the one that gave us our first lead with the car, which led us to a dead end. He's played us like a fucking fiddle. He knew everything that was going on in the investigation every step of the way. That's how he was able to murder right under our noses up The Downs.'

'Do you want me to come with you?' Aubrie asked, already unbuttoning her white lab coat.

Jack shook his head. 'No, it's too dangerous. And besides, I don't even know where he is.'

Jack threw his coat on and stormed from the building. He looked at the traffic, it was too heavy to get a taxi so he'd have to run.

Bristol wasn't the flattest of cities and Jack knew he would have to consume some energy just on the off chance that he ran straight into his suspect. He hadn't ever thought much of Officer Peters other than he was lazy and didn't have much wit about him. Now, however, with the fact that he had tricked the entire police department and openly declared war on a very dangerous gang, perhaps it would be prudent to re-evaluate who he was up against.

Jack reached the bottom of Park Street, a half-a-mile-long road on a steep incline, flanked on both sides by dozens of bars.

'Shit, I'll never find him.'

*

The girl was trying to light a cigarette as she stood in the alleyway next to the bar. He watched as she hit her lighter on her leg and shook it with frustration. She looked up and was startled by his presence but, being a confident, young businesswoman, she tried to shake it off.

'You don't have a lighter, do you? I can't get mine working.'

He shook his head. 'I don't smoke,' he said flatly.

She had no idea of the excitement brewing in his veins as he slowly entered the small alleyway. She had no idea that she would be his crowning glory. How she would be the one that he would take the furthest, how she would experience more than anyone else ever had.

'Good for you, they kill you – so I keep getting told by my mother, anyway.' She smiled to him and he returned it, only his was much more gleeful.

'Funny you should say that,' he said as he grabbed her throat and pinned her against the wall. She yelped but it was cut short by the hard brickwork knocking the air out of her lungs.

*

Jack had passed the first few bars looking only through the windows. They had been small and had not yet become overcrowded with party-goers, so he was able to do a quick head count. And none of the heads wore a crash helmet or looked like Officer Peters.

He was marching up the steep incline when he thought he heard a small scream, or whimper, coming from ahead. He stopped still and angled one ear in its direction, hoping to hear something a little clearer. But there was silence.

Up in the direction that he thought he had heard something was a small, dark alleyway. He thought it was most probably drunks finding a dark place to take a piss, but decided it was worth checking out anyway. He jogged up the last forty yards and turned into it.

It was deserted. The noise must have come from somewhere else.

This search was impossible. There were too many bars and above most of them were student accommodations. Some of them had their windows open with music playing loudly accompanied by screeching and laughing voices. There were too many possible victims, too many possible locations to murder in and he needed a shedload of luck, which, up until now, had not been forthcoming.

Jack continued on, his eyes moving from face to face up and down the street, in bars and above them, his mind racing, escaping with frustration.

And then something stuck. At the top of the street he could see a motorbike, parked in a bay on the side of the road. It looked sleek and uncomfortable to ride, but most of all it looked old. He ran up the road, panting as he reached the top. He tried to catch his breath and searched the bike for a badge. He found it on the cap on the fuel tank and read it aloud.

'Harley   Davidson.'

HELP

He had just drawn his large knife out of his bag and held the cold blade to her cheek when he heard footsteps hurrying towards them.

'Shit,' he said, glancing at the entrance to the alley. He placed a hand over her mouth and dragged her behind a bin. 'Say a word and I will gut you. Do you understand?'

His captive nodded and breathed heavily under the weight of his hand on her mouth. Sweat dripped down her forehead as she tried with all her might to stop her heart from exploding with fear.

The large man held a finger to his pursed lips, indicating for her to be quiet as he peered out through a gap in their hiding place.

Detective Jack O'Connor turned the corner in front of them.

His hand clenched the young woman's face even harder at the sight of the policeman.

'How the fuck did he find me?' he asked himself in disbelief. He watched as the policeman looked up and down the dark shadows, squinting as he tried to see in the pitch black. The detective gave up and carried on walking up the road. The man in leather waited for the footsteps to drown away, noting that they had begun running before

finally becoming inaudible.

'Shit, he must have seen the bike.'

The large man stood up, nearly pulling the young woman off of her feet. She didn't struggle but instead held onto the arm around her neck, trying to make it easier for her to just breathe. He pulled her backwards and away from the main road. The footpath was dark and offered a good place to gather himself. He took a moment to look around his surroundings, he didn't want to rush this, he had come too far now.

He brought them into what looked like a small nature reserve, hidden behind the chaos of the city. A couple walked along holding hands in the distance, disappearing over the brow of a hill.

He pulled her tight against him. It looked quiet but he couldn't be sure.

'This way, and if you struggle I'll cut your fucking throat,' he said, making sure his breath fell heavy on her neck.

He pushed her in front of him, up a steep grass embankment where his foot slipped and his ankle turned over in the high boots. His grip relinquished and his captive forced her way from his grip.

'Help!' she screamed as she tried to run. But it was no good, her legs wouldn't work in their usual way.

It took only a couple of yards for him to catch up with her and get his strong, leather-covered arm back around her neck.

'You stupid bitch,' he said, pushing the blade up against her chest, nestling it between her breasts.

*

Jack spun around, he couldn't decide whether to go up or back down the road, and then a sound caught his attention once more. This noise was clearer than before, he recognised a woman's voice screaming for help. It cut through the hubbub of the city like a whistle at a football game. It sounded alien to his surroundings and that instinct inside of him, that part of his human nature that was telling him to flee, rooted him to the spot.

It had only been faint but it had given him a good indication of which direction he needed to head in and, with his lungs finding new capacities and his muscles feeling as though they were those of a teenager, he ran back down the hill and rounded a corner towards the park. He had walked through it a couple of times with his wife and remembered how surprisingly secluded it had been, he had even commented on how it would be a nice place to bring their newborn baby all those years ago. Flashbacks of running his hand over her pregnant swell flourished inside him.

'I can't do that now, control your mind, Jack, concentrate now, you're nearly there, and you can feel it, can't you? Oh, shit, now I'm talking to myself,' he said aloud as he spotted the tall building that he recognised as Cabot Tower. It stood in the middle of the park like beacon, drawing him towards it. He wasn't thinking of where to go, he just let his compulsion guide his feet. The ground was slippery and the path took a longer route than he wanted to. Fighting his way down the small hills, he rounded on the base of the tall tower. A sharp, piercing light flashed off of something metallic, right at the doorway to the monument. His eyes adjusted and there stood   his   suspect.

YOUR FAULT, JACK

'Peters, stop, just stop now, it's over.'

The large man holding the short woman looked around quickly, jerking his captive's small frame between that of his own and the detective.

Jack walked over to them, allowing his lungs to relax a little and giving them a chance to slow his breathing to a more sustainable rate.

'It's over, Graham, it's all over now. Let her go and we can sort this all out. No point adding one more to the list. Armed police will be here soon, just let the girl go.'

The large man looked past Jack at the visible entry points to the park.

'Really, Jack? Because it looks like you're on your own to me. And if she is going to be my last one, why the hell would I let her go now?'

Jack took a couple of steps closer, causing Officer Peters' to instinctively push the blade up to the throat of the girl.

'Back off, Jack, or another one will die because of you. Another innocent's blood on your hands. Just like the boy. I bet you liked that one, did you enjoy how close to home I brought this fight?'

Jack raised his hands in surrender. 'I'm unarmed,

Graham, and you're right, I am on my own. Armed police won't be here until a warrant comes through, and I know that you know how long they can take. Fucking red tape, am I right? So the ball is in your court, what do you want to do?'

The man looked around at his surroundings, he was clearly not prepared for Jack to be asking him for his preference for the course of the subsequent events.

'I could treat you to a show, if you would like?' He pushed the woman down onto her knees and forced her head down to her chest.

'No!' Jack shouted. 'Don't! Just don't do that. Her life won't make your point any more than you already have.'

The young woman whimpered and yelped at being manhandled down to the ground. Jack could hear that she was crying but fighting back the noises that came with it.

The tall man in leather laughed. 'My point? What point would that be, then, Detective?'

Jack tried to take another step closer, he wanted to be in range of a quick attack, a chance of disarming the murderer before he could kill again, but Graham was ready for it and swung the huge blade down, stopping a hair's breadth from her neck.

'Ok, I'm here, I'm not moving.' Jack pointed down at the spot on the ground, indicating the place where he would stand and not advance from.

'I get it, Graham, believe me I do. I hear them too, they call to me and sometimes it's all I can do to shut them up. They promise you things, don't they?' Jack saw a slight glimmer of doubt in the other man's eyes; he carried on. 'They tell you how they can change your life, how they can make you strong. How all you have to do is listen to them and they can give you everything you ever wanted. What was it that you wanted? Let me guess, you wanted to be respected – feared, even. That's it, isn't it? They told you that they could make people scared of you, make *me* scared of you.'

Officer Peters' nostrils flared, Jack could tell that his words were landing like punches on him.

'And you listened, didn't you, Graham? Doing just what they told you to, and in return you got power.'

The man's rage boiled over. 'You liar, they don't speak to you. They chose me, I am special to them. They wouldn't speak to someone as weak and pathetic as you.'

'Oh, they do, Graham, they are speaking to me now, they are telling me to walk over there and smash your face into the ground. They want me to beat your skull with a stone just to see your brains spill out. That's what they are telling me to do, Graham, can't you hear them? They don't care if you kill that girl, all they want is your blood on my hands.'

'Stop lying!' the large man snarled, he didn't want to hear anymore and Jack could see the strength in him waning.

'I'm not lying, they told me about that murder you committed from the rooftop. That single shot to the head. It was perfect, the perfect murder from the perfect assassin; just like the computer game. Was that their idea, as well? To copy the computer game?'

Jack could see Peters' face contorting, like a child being chastised for kicking a cat. 'No, that was your idea, wasn't it? They were happy to play along, happy to allow you to have your fun, but when it came down to the murder, they were disappointed in you, weren't they? They wanted more from you, they wanted the hate, the fire and the torture, isn't that right, Graham?'

The man in black started crying. 'How do you know this?'

'Because they talk to me, too, Graham, you are not special, you are not powerful, they lie to you, Graham, because they want you to do evil.'

The murderer clenched the neck of the woman at his feet hard and she yelped in pain as his tears fell onto her head. He sobbed uncontrollably for a few seconds. Jack was about to take a couple of steps closer when the man's crying took a turn. To the detective's surprise, the man in front of him had started to laugh maniacally.

His head rose with tear tracks that led down to a full smile.

'Bravo, Jack, bravo indeed,' the man said.

He looked calmer than he had a few moments ago, his skin had become taught under his grin and his eyes twinkled.

'How you wish we would speak to you, tell you how you can avenge the murder of your dear wife and sweet child. You wish we would give you strength enough to do something other than drink yourself to death. Your pathetic life does not interest us.'

Jack stood in shock, the voice coming from Officer Peters had changed. It had a similar pitch to that of moments before, but its tone was darker and rougher.

'At last I get to speak to the organ grinder, do I? I wasn't sure if you were going to come out of hiding,' Jack taunted.

The new voice coming from the officer's mouth was raspy and coarse, 'Do not push me, Detective, it is not wise to come between a dog and its dinner.'

Jack's mind raced. Talking a man out of killing a defenceless woman was one thing, but convincing a demon? Now that was not in the handbook.

'Graham, it was very clever. You left only a couple of clues – your handprints and boot print. That was inspired, that really did have us chasing our tails.'

The man in leather laughed manically. 'He's not here anymore, Jack. Graham has left the building.'

Jack shook his head. 'I won't believe that. Graham was the clever one. It was Graham and the drugs, selling the drugs for the money to orchestrate it all, leaving no paper trail and at the same time pissing off someone you were going to kill anyway.' Jack knew he was stalling, he knew he was trying to change the state of play, he just didn't know why or where he was going with it. 'It was all very clever. How long had you been planning it all? Longer than this thing has been inside you, I bet.'

Peters looked angry. 'You know it's your fault, don't you, Detective? You and people just like you. You bullied him and pushed him around, leaving him weak and full of hate. You made him feel worthless, you cracked him, you exposed his soul. You, Detective, gave us the opening we needed to make him this animal. That game was a perfect in for us.' Peters spoke with glee, 'You gave us the opportunity to turn him into a weapon of despair. Every drop of blood should fall on your shoes, Detective.' He tightened the tips of his fingers on the woman's neck with pleasure as he spoke.

'If Graham is guilty, Detective, then so are you.'

The detective turned his nose up at the accusation. 'No, Graham, this is your fault. You made yourself this creature. This was your idea, it was all your idea and now look at you. You're not strong because of your demons, you are weak. You can't even face me and admit it, can you? You are a lost child wanting attention. Well, here you are, Graham. I am here, I am listening, now stop blaming others and own up and tell me what you have done wrong.'

Peters' eyes looked away from the detective.

'That's it,' Jack thought. *'That's my opening, if a demon can get in, then so can I.'*

'I said fucking looking at me, Graham, because I'm watching you. I can see how clever you are. Oh, you had me fooled for a long time, there.' Jack clapped, each blow of his hands seemed to hammer into the other man's psyche. 'You've done it, you've got what you wanted, all except my respect. No, you didn't earn that, you earned my disdain instead. If these demons have made you so strong then show me, show me who you really are.'

Jack was surprised to see Peters starting to cry, but that was it, that was the turning point.

'Aww, are you crying, am I asking too much of you again? Is this why you called upon these so-called demons? To take the blame for you because it's just too hard?' he taunted the murderer.

'Shut up!' Peters spat back. His mouth drooled as it contorted with rage. 'Just shut the fuck up or I will cut her throat.'

Jack shook his head and took a step closer. 'No, you won't, Graham. What's the point? You can't scare me, you can't impress me, and it's all been for nothing.' He took another step closer. 'You've failed, Graham, like you always do.'

'This is your fault, Jack,' Peters said, his hand swinging back and then forward again, jolting in the direction of the young woman's exposed and frail neck.

THE FAIR ASSASSIN

Jack lurched forward but it would be to no effect, and he knew it. He knew he was too far away to stop the blade piercing through the skin and continuing to the arteries. But what Jack didn't know was that he didn't need to stop it.

As he watched, the entire proceeding decreased to a speed that felt like he was watching in slow motion.

He watched as the captive spun around on her knees, missing the blade by the narrowest of margins. She caught Peters' hand with her own and then threw her free arm upward. Her sharply aimed elbow connected perfectly with her capturer's chin, causing his grip on the weapon to loosen and his legs to struggle to stand. If it hadn't been for the robust leather trousers and rigid boots he might have fallen right on top of her. But he didn't, instead he panicked and lunged at her with his hands, looking for her throat. She spun on her knees once more, back the other way, to escape his grip. He righted himself just at the same time as his captive, who had now dropped her long, fawn-coloured coat to the damp floor.

She stood confidently in tall, black heels and tight PVC trousers. Above this she wore a black leather corset on top of more PVC and black gun holsters over her shoulders, both of which held a small pistol. She blew a strand of her straight, black bobbed hair from her mouth and smiled at the large man.

Jack froze with confusion at the same time as Peters did.

'The Fair Assassin,' Peters said, seemingly rooted to the spot momentarily.

The woman spun the weapon that she had repossessed from the large man with great expertise before stopping it dead, pointing it accurately at him. Peters seemed to recover himself and, with new focus, he charged the small woman. He was too slow and the blade of his weapon was too well trained on him. The Fair Assassin rolled underneath him and his large bulk hit the floor with a thud.

Jack looked at the fallen man to see the large, serrated end of the blade sticking out from his midriff – the smooth edge of the weapon was buried deep inside of the bulky flesh.

The young woman stood up and walked over to the detective, pulling her hair from her head. Long, bright-red locks spiralled down past her shoulders and the wig got tossed to the floor.

Jack's mouth silently searched for words before managing only one, 'Tanya?'

The young woman smiled and pranced towards him like a child through a meadow.

'Who did you expect? The Fair Assassin, maybe?' She laughed and threw her arms around the detective. She let go and Jack made his way uncomfortably to the floor, his body was only then reacting to what had just happened.

He looked up at his friend, her green eyes shone back at him like fireflies in a night sky.

His brain helter-skeltered its way through what had just happened, trying desperately to make sense of it all.

She sat down beside him and leaned back on her arms, tossing her hair off of her neck with little throws of her head.

'What … what the hell? I mean, seriously, what the hell are you doing here?' Jack managed to ask her. His mind felt as though it was a racing car engine that had just completed the grand prix and was trying desperately to cool down.

'Jesus Christ, Tan, was there not an easier way to help me find the bastard?'

Tanya laughed. 'You know I have always been one for dramatics. Anyway, I thought it may give an end to all these games he seemed to like playing – you know, a proper ending, a "you lose" type of ending. If I hadn't he might have thought he was still just playing the computer game.'

Jack interlocked his fingers on the top of his head and looked at the other man, now bleeding on the grass and moaning with pain.

'Is he going to die?' he asked Tanya.

'No, I missed any main arteries or veins and all of the main organs. I have probably cut through his small intestines, though, so that'll need some of the tax payers' NHS money spent on it, but other than that and the psychosis he should be fine. He could probably stay there for a good hour or two, if you really wanted him to.'

Jack's breaths steadied and he turned to face her. 'How the hell did you find him? You know you should have just called me, don't you?'

'I tried, your phone was always busy, so I came up with a better plan.' She gestured at her clothing with a hand. 'And as for finding him, I heard about the policewoman and the boy being killed and realised that the rate of the killing was reaching a peak and that his mind was probably reaching a psychotic break.'

Jack looked at her doubtfully.

'I got a degree in psychology, I'll have you know. I got the second-best score in my class. It would have been first but, apparently, they marked me as high as they were allowed considering I completed it in three weeks. Bloody bureaucrats. Anyway, so I asked the doormen at the clubs to look out for anyone acting suspicious. I figured that if you wanted to murder someone at short notice you would go where the people are and, on a Friday night, where else would he go? So, I heard about a guy sitting in a couple of bars staring around at the women, which, in itself, isn't unusual, I know. But I was informed that he didn't buy a single drink. So I took a punt.'

Jack laughed. 'And, what, you just happened to have the costume with you?'

Tanya smiled gleefully. 'No, I was in the club and I borrowed a few items off of the other girls. It's not an exact copy from the computer game, but it's pretty damn close. I quite like it, I think I might make this my new favourite outfit.'

Jack closed his eyes and allowed the madness inside of him to subside and become a bit more bearable.

'Could this nightmare truly be over?'

But then he remembered who was now dead because he was not there to save him and the realisation hit him – Daniel was going to stay that way forever, just as the deaths of his wife and daughter were a part of his every day, and always would be.

Tanya's voice broke the brief silence. 'You didn't believe all that about the demons, did you? I mean, come on, it's typical grandiose delusions.'

Jack had a suspicion that Tanya was worrying about his own mental state more than anything.

'It's complicated. In the last week I have been presented with overwhelming evidence that may even be enough to convince you. But, really, no – I don't believe that a demon committed those crimes. But I do believe that whatever was in him,' he pointed at the man on the floor, who stirred and contorted in pain, 'I have inside me. It scares me, Tan, and I don't know what to do about it.'

Jack's phone rang, saving him from what he felt had

already turned into an embarrassing conversation. He leaned back on the grass and answered.

'Sarge, I have the warrant and fifty men waiting to flood Park Street. Just give us the nod.'

'Tell them to stand down,' Jack told Officer Kapoor. 'I've got Peters here with me. All I need is an ambulance and yourself to go with him to hospital. We are right at the base of Cabot Tower.'

Jack heard McQuade in the background of the call, 'Tell him I will be there as well. I want to see this with my own eyes.'

Jack smiled. 'Why don't you invite McQuade along as well?' he said to Kapoor before hanging up.

Tanya stood up and brushed loose grass from her tight-fitting outfit, examining her appearance.

'You don't need me to stay, do you? I wouldn't want to steal your thunder.'

He opened his eyes and looked up at her as she stood over him.

She tied her hair back and picked up her coat. 'After all, who is going to believe that The Fair Assassin actually existed?'

'Yeah, probably for the best,' Jack agreed. He sat up to watch her walk from the park.

He knew she was right, no one would believe the ramblings of a serial killer, even if they had been true. He looked again at the man struggling to stay conscious on the floor. His madness mirrored that of Jack's – the hate that he could see in the fallen man lived inside of him. Only in him it hid, it stayed in stasis, in forgotten corners, waiting to   be   woken.

IS THIS EVIDENCE?

Officer Kapoor and McQuade arrived with two paramedics. Jack kept his version of events to a minimum. Far less lies to remember that way while typing up his report.

He had spotted the suspect on Park Street, then chased him to this point, where they struggled over the weapon and Peters somehow managed to stab himself. It was easy – mainly because it was more believable than the truth and left no dirty patches that needed to be washed away with complicated evidence. The only words that that the bleeding man had managed to utter were 'Fair Assassin', which, if nothing else, made Jack's story become all the more believable.

The paramedics and officers began securing the murderer and processing him. Kapoor read the man his rights and was already filling in paperwork. For someone who had worked alongside this man, even called him a friend, Jack was impressed at his professionalism.

'Jack, can I have a quick word?' McQuade asked, calling him aside. 'I had a chap from the IT department have a look at my phone earlier. He said that he knew you, had met you, something to do with an older woman. Was that anything to do with this case, by any chance?'

Jack gave her a blank look. 'Not that I can remember. It was probably personal stuff I needed help with. Us boys like to chat about relationships too, ma'am.'

McQuade looked unconvinced but didn't press him for anything more on the matter. 'That wasn't what I wanted to speak to you about, anyway. It turns out I was right about my phone being bugged. The IT guy, I forget his name, found that my mobile was being tracked and that the landlines in my office and yours had actually been bugged. He found these in the mouth piece.'

She held out a hand to show him the two small computer chips. 'They have a long-range antenna built it and can be picked up through analogue and digital receptors. Apparently, they are made in China but most secret services use them as a standard device.'

Jack took one of the devices from her and held it up to the light.

'Clever little gadget. Can we keep them?'

McQuade laughed. 'That was the first thing that I asked, but, apparently, you have to have the right frequency decoder or something or other, I didn't really understand the waffle. But what I want to know is, who the hell has been bugging us and why? You don't have any ideas, do you?'

Jack chewed the inside of his cheek in thought, he pretended to be considering her question but instead he was wondering whether or not it would be prudent to keep his visit from Casper Collingwood a secret.

'I should imagine it's just routine in a big case like this one for MI5 to keep tabs on us. Big brother and all that.'

Again, McQuade didn't seem impressed with the answer, or fooled by it, but she recognised a brick wall when faced with one.

'Is this evidence?' Officer Kapoor shouted over to them, waving a black wig around like a strange, unenthusiastic cheerleader.

'No, that was already here, probably a party of hens

coming through on their way to town.' Jack walked over to the other officer and took the fake hair from him. 'It's alright, I'll stick it in the bin on my way home.'

Kapoor looked shocked. 'You're not walking, are you, sarge? We have a patrol car, me or McQuade can drop you home.'

Jack shook his head. 'No, I need the fresh air to think. I'll be in first thing to write up the report. And don't let McQuade hear you offer her up as a taxi driver, she'll have your knackers for paperweights.'

Both officers turned to see McQuade heading towards the ambulance with the paramedics and the laden gurney.

'I think she may be going with the ambulance anyway. Probably wants a chance at throttling Peters herself.'

Jack's mind wandered around inside his own head, for some reason Peters' arrest felt like danger for him. He then remembered the drug lord Yanislav Ivanovic, and how unimpressed he would be not to have his hands on the man who murdered his brother.

'Nitin, could you research something for me? Could you find all the villages near some mountains called the Urals or something? I think they may be in Russia. And then see if there are any major criminals from them currently missing?'

The other officer looked confused. 'Sure, sarge, but why?'

'Something our friend Yanislav mentioned about bears.'

UNDER ARREST

One week had passed but the tang of regret, guilt and grief stayed present. Jack knew that at some point it would fade until it was only a shadow of pain, but for those shadows to appear he would need some bright days. Peters had been charged and Jack's time in court wasn't for another few weeks.

Those finer details of putting people away always seemed to drag out. Jack couldn't see how his defence was going to get anywhere. Every statement that Graham Peters made appeared to be more insane than the last, giving the courts no choice but to place him within a secure unit in a hospital for the criminally insane while awaiting trial.

Jack didn't like the fact that he would probably be kept in better accommodation there than the wages he had previously been on would allow, but the fact that his liberties had been stripped would have to be enough.

The crematorium was only half full. Daniel's father and sister sat at the front with a couple of other relatives around them. Three young boys wearing hats from the pizza place that Daniel had worked at spoke in hushed tones near the back. They had gotten some un-agreeable looks in regards to their headwear, but even Jack knew that Daniel would have found it a nice touch.

'It's just a shame they didn't have the foresight to pull the coffin in a cart using the mopeds.'

'That's him there, is it? The one with the tattoos that should be sobbing?' Tanya whispered into Jack's ear. They sat at the very back so as to be inconspicuous, but in a room built to occupy fifty or so that only held a dozen, there was precious little to blend in with.

'That's the one, yeah. You sure you're ok doing this?' Jack replied.

Tanya gave him a gentle kiss on the cheek and then wiped away the bright-red lipstick mark that had been left.

'Of course, I don't mind. I'll wait for you in the car.'

Jack made to stand to accompany her, but Tanya pushed him down in to his seat.

'Stay. Grieve. It'll help.'

It wasn't grieving that was the problem, it was the fact that it had been his own fault and that was currently tearing him apart. Somewhere inside of him there was a voice speaking. It sounded like the young lad who lay in a wooden box in front of him and it was telling him that he forgave him. The voice was far too quiet though and Jack ignored it. Even if the dead could forgive, he couldn't allow himself to. He would never absolve himself of the responsibility of this crime, and the half dozen others that weighed on him.

Twenty minutes later, Jack returned to the car and drove them both in silence to the wake, a couple of miles down the road.

Mr Brook, Daniel's father, had clearly not bothered to spend any money on the event. It was in the back room of a pub, which had advertised out the front that there was a free function room available to use. The buffet table had a couple of platters full only of food that went straight from freezer to oven – except for the three large pizzas that the boys in the hats had brought with them.

Daniel's sister made a beeline for Jack and Tanya the moment they entered the dark room.

'Detective, it's great to see you,' she said, giving Jack an identical smile to the one that Daniel had enjoyed expressing so much.

'Please, call me Jack. This is my friend Tanya.'

Tanya took the hand of the young girl and gripped it tightly while offering her a warm smile.

'It's nice to meet you,' the girl answered, being the picture of politeness in what was clearly a difficult time for her.

'How are you holding up?' Jack asked, diverting his gaze to her father and back.

She gave a half-hearted smile. 'Yeah, not as good as my old man. The landlord has put one hundred and fifty quid behind the bar and Dad's determined to drink most of it himself.'

Jack watched as her gaunt father downed a pint of lager to the cheer of similar-looking men around him.

Jack looked back at the girl in front of him. Something was different. She was wearing dark glasses that Jack had assumed were to hide her eyes – no doubt sore from crying. But, as big as they were, they didn't completely obscure the swelling on her forehead. A fleshy lump that was covered in foundation, a clear attempt at masking its true colour.

'Let me see your eyes a minute?' he asked her.

She took a step back before reluctantly dropping her head, defeated. She removed the white frames, tucked her hair behind her ear and lifted her face. She had hidden it well, but the black eye was clearly visible. The fact that the gap between her left eyelids was less than half that of the other was a clear indication of a brutal attack.

'When did he do that?' Jack asked. He didn't need to name names, they both knew who he was speaking about.

She looked guilty for showing Jack her injury and placed the glasses back on. 'Yesterday. I told him that

Danny would have wanted music and, well, let's just say that Dad thought I was trying to waste his money.'

Something inside of Jack shifted and stirred, like a wild animal being gently prodded from a deep sleep. He could quite easily walk over to the man and cut him open, just as the killer had done to his son. But no, that wouldn't solve anything, and what he had planned would make life better for everyone else involved.

'I'm going to go and give my condolences to your dad. Is that ok with you, Jack?' Tanya asked with a telling note in her voice.

Jack thought as hard as he could about consequences and concluded that doing something and getting it wrong would be better than doing nothing at all. He nodded to Tanya and turned back to the young girl.

'I'm going to try and make things a bit better for you, I hope that's ok,' Jack told her.

Her face dropped and she turned to look at Tanya, now closing on her father.

She turned back to Jack and pleaded, 'Please don't say anything to him. It'll only make it worse and he'll take it out on me.'

Jack held both of her forearms and pulled her closer to look directly into her eyes. 'You have to trust me, Carla, you don't need him and you never did. You have to trust me.'

Her panic evaporated quickly and she agreed, 'I do trust you. Danny did, so I do.'

Jack smiled. 'Good. Because in a moment, your dad is going to try and hit my friend and I am going to arrest him. Then you are going to go with her somewhere safe and I'll meet you there. Does that sound ok?'

Carla's eyes widened – the bruised one only by a fraction – as she realised what Jack was saying. There was a mixture of fear and trepidation in them but again she nodded her head to agree.

Jack had given Tanya a loose script to work from to

wind up the fist-happy man, but he only half expected her to stick to it. Within a minute, the drunk was in Tanya's face, pushing his forehead down onto hers. He towered above her and it only succeeded to annoy him more that Tanya did not look at all scared.

Tanya shoved the large man in the chest hard enough to send him into a table full of drinks. They cascaded to the floor. The smashing of glass always added to a hostile atmosphere. The man sprang back at her and swung a haphazard fist, which, to Jack's surprise, connected with Tanya's face.

Carla's hands shot to her mouth in horror and Jack's legs launched in to action. He ran across the room and forced a handcuff around the man's left wrist. He struggled and hit the floor, Jack's weight landing on his back, knocking the wind out of him.

'Mr Brook, you are under arrest.' The second cuff clicked into place and Jack continued to read the man his rights as he pulled him aggressively to his feet and escorted him from the building.

Jack was relieved that Mr Brook's friends had not joined in with the action. Perhaps they weren't drunk enough, stupid enough or actually friendly enough with Mr Brook to try to help him.

Carla and Tanya followed them out of the building, joined by one or two of the more curious guests. Jack hated doing it there, he had not wanted to ruin the day for Carla, but it was crucial to have witnesses and it had been going on more than long enough in his book.

Jack threw the man into a police car that he had managed to commandeer – he felt that might give a better effect to the whole preceding and let everyone know exactly where Mr Brook would be going.

Jack slammed the door and walked over to where Tanya was standing with her arm around Carla.

'You going to be ok?' he asked the young girl.

She smiled. 'I think so, although I'm not sure I have

anywhere to go.'

'It'll be ok, I've sorted something out for you. It had to be this way, I'm afraid. It was only a matter of time before he hurt you seriously. Speaking of which …' He looked at Tanya. 'You let him hit you?'

Tanya dabbed her split lip with her finger and examined the blood. 'Well, I thought the charges would stick better. You should have heard what he was saying, Jack, what a vile man. You better throw the book at him. If he gets out, I'll deal with him my way.'

'He won't be getting out soon, I promise,' Jack replied, but instead of addressing it to Tanya, he looked at the young girl.

Seeing that she looked nervous, Tanya pulled her in close for a hug. 'Come on, we can put the top down on the car and beep the horn at some fit lads.'

Tanya pointed her car keys at a bright-orange convertible Audi A8 and pressed them. The indicators flashed to life and so did Carla's eyes.

'That's your car?' she asked and both girls walked towards the vehicle.

Jack laughed at how quickly the situation had been remedied and how quickly he had become invisible. The car had stood out like a sore thumb in these surroundings. It didn't belong, and neither did that girl. The wheels spun and the sports car was gone.

'Wave goodbye to your daughter, Mr Brook,' Jack said, knocking on the window.

The man in the car spat at the window and swore loudly.

'Charming.'

Jack walked Mr Brook into the police station and handed him over to the duty officer.

He explained briefly what had happened and ordered the other officer to get some witnesses statements from the wake and to gather some stonewall evidence against him. Jack knew that when he said that he wanted stonewall evidence it was usually taken as code for 'we are not letting this bastard go'.

Jack had just turned the handle of the door to his office when a familiarly formidable voice called him.

'Detective, I said two weeks off minimum.' It was McQuade and, as harsh as she could make her words sound, the friendly tone of her voice betrayed them. 'Although it's good to see you.'

'Thank you, ma'am, it's good to see you too,' he replied and, for the first time, he actually meant it.

'Don't thank me just yet, I was going to call you in anyway, but I heard that you were bringing someone in. GBH at a funeral, wasn't it? I don't know how but you're like a magnet for trouble.'

'It was at the wake, not the funeral, but, yeah, I do seem to have a knack for being in the wrong place at the wrong time,' Jack said, giving McQuade the hint that he probably wasn't going to like what she was going to ask next of him.

'Yes and what a gift that is. We have a high-profile informant in one of our interview rooms and he has refused to speak to anyone but you. And do you know what is funny? Officer Kapoor said that this might happen and, when it did, to give you this envelope. Now, how do you think that he had the foresight to predict that then? Psychic, maybe?' She widened her eyes wildly at him.

'I couldn't say, ma'am. He is a very good detective, though.' Jack felt as though their relationship had returned to its usual, natural condition. It was more of a game than anything, one that both of them hated to lose.

'I thought you may say something along those lines.' She slammed the envelope into his chest. 'Room three. Go on, get to it, and then your two weeks off starts over again, and if you come back in early again it will start again, only that time it will be without pay. I was going to ask if I was being understood but I won't bother.'

GOOD FRIEND

Yanislav sat in the small room alone, his fists clenched, resting on the table. He didn't even look up as Jack took up the seat opposite him, placing the envelope on the table.

Eventually, the silence was broken by the gang member's voice. 'I told you that the killer must be brought to me. No exceptions. So, Detective, may I ask why it has transpired that the killer was not brought to me and was instead taken to and treated at the Bristol hospital? Why he was under armed guard and why the is tax payers' money being wasted at such a great expense when I could have sorted the problem for no cost?'

The veins in the man's hands were prominent and the tight, white skin of the palms had patches of pink where the blood flowed fast and warm. The tension from his rigid body filled the room, it tried to blanket Jack, attempting to infect him with fear.

Jack took a steady breath in through his nose and tore the top off of the envelope. This enraged Yanislav even further.

His fists slammed down on the table, echoing off the walls.

'This is disrespectful, Detective, if there is one thing

that I cannot abide, it is disrespect. I hope by now you are aware of how far my reach goes and how much power I am able to invoke.'

Jack slid the paperwork from its enclosure, ignoring the threats and reading the contents slowly.

'I can make you disappear, Detective. Even with all of your loyal officers and fan base I can make sure that nobody finds you, ever. Are you listening to me, Detective O'Connor? I will kill you. Your life has become surplus to requirements and in the next few days I will be removing you from this country. Piece by piece. You do understand that I was here for an apology? I may have even let you live. But now, I will make sure that you scream for forgiveness. I am in a police station threatening a police officer with his life, and there is nothing you can do to stop me.' Yanislav smiled gleefully. 'It would appear, Detective, that this meeting can be ended early.'

Finally, Jack replied, 'I don't think so.'

The gang member snarled but listened to Jack carefully.

'You are right, of course. I do now know how far your reach can go and that you are, in fact, in bed with MI5.' Jack knew that turn of phrase would annoy Yanislav and, if he were honest, it was meant to. 'It's just a figure of speech. I also know that there is precious little I can do to stop you, Mr Ivanovic, because you have some very powerful allies out there. But the thing is, I don't need to stop a Mr Ivanovic, do I?'

The man got to his feet, looking confused. 'What is this nonsense?'

Jack placed a piece of paper down gently on the desk. 'No, the man that I need to stop is called,' he pretended to look at the writing on the document for effect, 'Mr Alkaev – Luka Alkaev, to be exact. You see, right here, he came to this country as an illegal immigrant, on the run from the Russian Politsiya – that means police, just in case you don't speak Russian. He is wanted for …' Jack let out a long, low whistle as he pulled out another piece of paper. This one was full of notes from margin to margin. It had *ARREST WARRANT* written in block capitals at the top.

'Just about everything I could think of that would get a man extradited. Money laundering, theft, murder, conspiracy to murder, and so on, and so on.'

Yanislav's face turned purple as his body fought back the rage building up inside of him.

'Are you ok, Mr Ivanovic? I only ask because, you know what, this Luka Alkaev looks a lot like you, only much less angry.' Jack placed another document on the table. This time it was an enlarged picture of the identity details and face from a passport.

The gangster stayed rooted to the spot. Jack knew that he was trying calculate his options so, instead, Jack laid out the equations for him.

'Now, I have left copies of these details with a good friend of mine from outside of the law. I have left orders with said friend to give these over to the Russian authorities, along with all the details of your current operations here in Bristol, if anything were to happen to me. This includes your home address and all of your places of work. So, if anything were to happen to me, let's say, if I were to meet an untimely death, even if it isn't your fault, you will have Russian Special Forces knocking on your door before you can down a shot of vodka. And, just for good measures, I have ordered my friend, my oh-so-very-good friend, to let slip to some of your business associates who it is that has been tipping off MI5. I feel that there may be a handful of people out there that may decide that you are bad for business. You see, Mr Alkaev, once you are on the books, even with our trusted secret service, all of your information gets logged, but they do have a way of making it disappear.'

Jack waited to see what would happen next. He knew there was still a good chance that the gang member would think he was bluffing and try to kill him then and there. He tried to look relaxed and in control but, in reality, Jack was wondering if he could get to the door before the man could get his hands around his throat.

Yanislav returned to his usual colour and rubbed his nose in thought.

'Well played, Detective. I look forward to some more fun and games in the future. I assume that these copies are for me?'

Jack gestured for the man to help himself. He picked up the papers and reluctantly left the room, allowing Jack's muscles to relax and his lungs exhale with great relief.

Jack didn't bother doing his report for Mr Brook right away. He was doing him a favour – letting him try out the size of a cell for twenty-four hours so it would be less of a shock when he got to his new permanent residence.

HE HAS DIED

The drive home was as tricky and irritating as ever it had been and, after swearing at 'god damn rush-hour traffic' a dozen times, Jack finally made it to his old house in Clifton. He parked behind the garish orange car that Tanya had been driving earlier, jogged up the steps and entered through the door.

He found Tanya and Carla in the living room, playing tennis on a games console. Jack recognised the console as one of the ones from the YouTube clips where people accidentally hit each other, or something made of glass got smashed. He watched as the young girl jumped high in the air and performed a textbook smash, causing the tiny, on-screen tennis ball to go whizzing by the opponent at the other end of the animated court.

'Ok, that's enough computer games for me,' Jack joked.

At first, he thought that they hadn't noticed that him arriving but, from their lack of surprise, it was apparent that they knew he was there, the game had just been far too enthralling for them to pause.

'Tanya bought it for me on our way here, and the television. Isn't she awesome?' Carla said in excitement before sitting down on the sofa and huffing the hair from her face.

Jack smiled at Tanya. 'Yeah, she's pretty awesome alright.'

'Awesome at killing, too, not that you would believe it,' he said to himself as an afterthought. Tanya performed a mock curtsy and then offered one of the controllers over and held the other like a professional tennis player awaiting a serve, her back bent as she danced from side to side.

She taunted Jack, 'Come on, old man, just one match?'

The detective couldn't help but laugh. 'Maybe later, I need to talk with Carla first.'

'Oh, ok then, spoil sport. Shall I leave you to it?' Tanya asked gesturing towards the door.

Jack shook his head. 'No, it's ok, you stay.'

Carla interrupted. 'Is this about what's going to happen to me? I guess I'll be going into foster care or something like that until I'm eighteen, right? And then I'll try to get into university. So it's not all bad.'

Tanya sat beside her and Jack pulled over a foot stool and sat in front of her.

'Well, that is a plan, I suppose, but I had something a little different in mind.'

The girl's only response was the furrowing of her eyebrows.

Jack continued, he didn't want to punish her any longer by not telling her.

'I was thinking that you could live here. For as long as you want. What do you think?'

The girl's face lit up with delight. 'With you?' she asked hopefully.

'No, not with me. I don't think that would be appropriate. And besides, this place has too many difficult memories for me. But I'll check in on you, all the time, and I'm sure Tanya will too, if you would like that?'

Tanya nodded to say that she wouldn't mind being a part of it.

'I … I won't be able to afford the bills and things. Not until I get a job, anyway.' Carla was clearly overwhelmed.

Jack shook his head. 'Don't be silly, I'll sort all of that out. I only live down in the centre so I'll be a phone call away. Just treat this as your own house but without any of the hassle of the boring stuff. And then, when you go to university, you can either stay here to save money or you can move out. I think I owe it to Daniel to make sure that you are looked after. I'm just trying to make things right – well, as right as they can be. You're not quite sixteen yet so you will be given an advocate through social services, but I can't see how it would be a problem. And as soon as it's your birthday you can pretty much decide what you want. So, what do you say?'

'About her going to university,' Tanya said, filling Jack with a sense of dread. She really was too unpredictable for the health of his nerves. 'Our young Carla turns sixteen in a month and, legally, she could get a place there now if she wanted to.'

The young girl turned to face Tanya. 'Don't I have to finish my GCSEs first? And even then, I might have to go to college first and get my A Levels before they offer me a place.'

The redhead sat up straight with authority. 'That is how it usually works but, seeing as I am on the committee board and about to give them a whopping donation for some new science labs that they have been trying to fund for about five years, I'm pretty sure I can get them to bend the rules somewhat.'

Jack could see Tanya's intention and he liked it, but he wasn't sure if that was the best way.

'Do you really think that she'll be ready for that, considering what she has just been through?' he asked Tanya with a hint of 'backup a little' implied.

She tossed her red hair and sat back in the chair. 'It's just an idea.'

Carla agreed to stay at the Clifton residence after Jack had spent more than ten minutes explaining why she should not feel guilty at the expense, and that he really didn't want to live there. He even used the excuse of squatters trying to take over any residence left unattended for more than a week. It couldn't bring Daniel back but, at the very least, Jack knew that the lad would have loved to have seen his sister happy and safe. And that's what she was – she was safe from the torture that only a father could inflict.

Jack insisted that the girls continue playing while he boiled the kettle. The kitchen was pretty much how he remembered it – all their old utensils and electricals had been returned by the previous tenants and all lay in boxes in the corner. He just had time to wonder if there would be any teabags or coffee laying around when the loud thud of the door knocker sounded.

Jack approached the door cautiously, met by Tanya in the hallway, who was obviously also in high-alert mode.

'It's a priest,' Carla shouted from the living room.

She had obviously looked out of the living room window, which worried Jack, but to be fair, he hadn't told her not to.

The detective opened the door a little way and was relieved to see Father Camaldo standing with his usual, warm smile.

Jack opened the door wider. 'Come in, Father.'

The detective showed the priest through to the kitchen, away from the two girls who had once more begun playing virtual tennis.

'I would offer you a coffee, Father, but I'm not sure I have any,' Jack said, closing the door to the room to block out any noise.

'Thank you, Detective, but I am not here on pleasure. In fact, the complete opposite.'

Jack looked at the man, he seemed defeated, almost as broken-hearted as he himself had been a week previous.

'Go on,' the detective urged.

'Do you remember Father Lopez?'

Jack nodded at this. 'The priest we are going to send

the pictures to, to decipher the language in them. I'm sorry I haven't brought them over yet, I had other things that I needed to put right first.'

Father Vincenzo Camaldo looked empty now. 'I am afraid he will no longer be helping us. I am afraid, Detective, that he has died.'

The pit of Jack's stomach felt its usual surge as a wave of guilt sloshed inside.

Father Camaldo looked directly at Jack now. 'I have been told that it was a heart attack, but I do not believe this. I think he may have been murdered.'

Jack didn't avert his gaze from the other man. Instead, he met it and as best he could without using words, expressed how sorry he was.

'So what are we going to do now, Jack?' Tanya's voice broke the silence. She had opened the door without either man noticing and was leant against the frame.

Jack took a deep breath and thought for a moment before his mind was made up.

'I'm a detective, aren't I? Let's find the truth.'

THE END

EPILOGUE

10 days previous

The slim figure pulled the hood of her running jacket up over her head. She crept quietly around the corner of a big, steel container, making sure that her footsteps were gentle and silent, the gravel trying to betray her with every step as she narrowed in on the storage container.

She peered around the last metal edge, only to see that there was no one there.

She was turning on her heels to leave when there was a quick movement and something slammed against the steel wall in front of her, blocking the exit.

Her heart jumped as well as her body, she fell back against another container and then froze, panic confusing her limbs.

'Doctor Aubrie Sellers, a bit late for a stroll, isn't it? Don't you know there is a killer on the loose?'

Tanya Red held a police baton that she had used to bang against the metal wall, creating the desired effect. She pushed it slowly, retracting the telescopic arm down to its shortest length.

Aubrie righted herself and stood tall. 'What do you

want? How do you know who I am?'

The other woman laughed. 'I know who everyone is. Everyone worth knowing, anyway, and you just about make that list, I suppose. As for what I want … well, I want the same as you. Jack O'Connor.'

Aubrie pulled her hood back. 'You're Tanya Red, aren't you? I've heard about you.'

Tanya smiled. 'Of course you have.'

'I heard that you're a murderer and I heard that you stalk Jack.'

Tanya's smile faded. She flicked out the police baton again, it grew in an instant and she pointed it directly at the pathologist.

'You obviously haven't heard the truth about me, otherwise you would have tried to run by now. So you're either brave, stupid or misinformed. Which one is it?'

Aubrie walked closer to Tanya, keeping eye contact as best she could.

'Well I'm not running, and I know I'm not stupid. But as for misinformed, I think that might be you. I don't want Jack, I just care about him. I'm a friend, a *real* friend.'

Her words, laced with accusation, irritated the other woman.

'I'm calling bullshit on that one. Look at you, creeping around at night, trying to catch him out. Who's the stalker now, I wonder? You don't care about him, you just want to *help him*,' Tanya said with a pathetic tone and a childish pout. It was clear she thought Aubrie's intentions were immature.

'So what? He's struggling, he needs help,' Aubrie said in response.

Tanya laughed. 'Typical little girl attitude – see someone broken and "oh, it must be my duty to fix them."' Tanya's mouth contorted as she became angry. 'You don't understand him, you never will. The pain is a part of him now.'

'But it doesn't have to be,' the taller woman argued.

Tanya didn't shout back; instead, her face turned to one of stark realisation. 'Yes, yes it does. He *is* the pain now, the pain is him. He can't live without it, it's all that keeps him going. You need to stop trying to change him. If you love him, you need to love all of him. Even his demons.'

Aubrie laughed ironically. 'And what? You love all of him, do you? You don't just love the fact that he doesn't see you for what you are? A psychopath? You can't love him, you can't love anything – you don't have the capacity. He deserves to be happy, not to be brought down to your level at every opportunity.'

'And if I am a psychopath, if I really don't care, why am I the only one trying to help him find Jessica and Felicity's killer? Why am I the only person trying to bring him closure? Sometimes the only thing that can help is getting what you want. And Jack wants revenge. He needs to know that his life stands for something. What are you doing besides batting those long eyelashes and trying to get him in bed? For someone so clever you are rather stupid. He's not broken, he's hurting. You are right on one thing, though, he does deserve to be happy. But that's just something you can't give him.'

Aubrie made to leave, but Tanya slammed the tip of the baton in her way again.

'Stop trying to change him, let him be who he is.'

Aubrie looked into Tanya's eyes and was dismayed to see tears. 'I can't do that. You're right, I do love him and I will do all I can to help him move on.'

She shoved the metal rod out of the way and started to walk away again.

'It won't work,' Tanya shouted after her, her voice quavering with emotion.

Aubrie turned to face her, she wanted her to know that she was serious. 'I have to try. You do what you think is right, and I'll do what I have to.' She paused, examining the young woman in front of her. 'Maybe we both love him. Perhaps he needs both of us.'

Tanya gave a small, comforted laugh. 'The light.' She pointed at Aubrie. 'And the dark.' She put her finger on her own chest.

ABOUT THE AUTHOR

Cameron is happily engaged and a father of two, Shepton Mallet resident, who loves to relax, walking around the local landmarks, cycling to Sheptons Colett Park, and drinking copious amounts of tea in the local cafes, when he's writing.

Being diagnosed with Borderline Personality Disorder, inspired Cameron to explore how this condition can trigger deep feelings which emerge as creative writing and storytelling.

He decided that by writing a novel where the main character has similar personality traits to his own, he could deal in a more holistic way with his varying emotions and use these emotions effectively to raise awareness of this disorder.